Casualty Of Duty

A novel by

David W. Drexler

Casualty of Duty

First published November 2005 by Exposure Publishing
An imprint of Meadow Books.
35 Stonefield Way, Burgess Hill, West Sussex, RH15 8DW, UK

Printed simultaneously in the United States of America
And the United Kingdom.

All the characters in this book are fictitious, and any resemblance to actual persons living or dead is purely coincidental.

British Library Cataloguing-In-Publication Data
A Record of This Publication is available from the British Library

Drexler, David W.
Casualty of Duty by David W. Drexler. – 1st edition

ISBN: 190536377X

Contents

Chapter 1 The Court Martial

The clerk of the court walked briskly to the front of the room, turned to us, came to attention and announced "All rise." The judge, General Wayne Caulkins, and my five jurors marched in. General Caulkins waited until all five were at their chairs, standing at attention, before stating "This General Court Martial is now convened. The clerk will state the authority under which this court is convened and the charges of the accused."

"The General Court Martial of Captain Gary D. Hallstead has been convened by order of the President of the United States under his authority as Commander-In-Chief of the armed forces of the United States of America pursuant to Article 32 of the Unified Code of Military Justice." The clerk continued.

"The list of charges entered on Department of Defense Form 458, reads as follows. That Captain Gary D. Hallstead committed acts of sedition, conspiracy, and Treason.

Specifically that Captain Hallstead did knowingly and willfully engage in a conspiracy, to illegally alter the election of the President of the United States by specifically providing false voter counts in the state of Texas. That he did knowingly and willfully engage in an act of sedition, the purpose being to over throw the government of the United States of America through the changing of the Presidential election results of 1996. That he did knowingly and willfully engage in an act of Treason with High Crimes and Misdemeanors in which he became a domestic enemy of the United States of America by violating his oath of duty, to wit; to protect and defend the Constitution of the United States of America against all enemies both foreign and domestic, by providing aid and comfort to the enemy through the conspiracy to overthrow the government of the United States of America."

Captain Hallstead sat motionless listening to the charges of sedition, conspiracy and treason. The only charge that evoked any emotion was the charge of Treason. *My God*, he thought, *treason*! *How in the world did it come to this? I was only doing my duty. I wasn't trying to over throw my government; I was trying to save it.*

The judge and his jury, oh I mean my jury sat down. The presiding judge picks the jury in a military trial. He also appoints an investigating officer, the prosecuting attorney and even my defense counsel. With a stacked deck like this, most civilians would view this trial as a done deal already.

General Caulkins called out my name, but looked at my defense counsel when he asked for a plea on all charges. My lawyer, Second Lieutenant Christopher Faber, grabbed my right arm gently in a signal for me to rise. We stood at attention as he responded to the General, "Not Guilty sir, on all charges."

Not guilty on all charges, I thought, *well at least on sedition and treason. Conspiracy? I guess I was guilty of conspiracy.* I could tell from the beginning, Faber was not convinced of my innocence even after hearing my whole story. It became more evident by the tone of his voice when he halfheartedly gave my not guilty plea to the judge. *A defense attorney who doesn't believe his client, wonderful*, I thought. *They not only give me a lawyer just out of law school with relatively no military justice experience, but one who doesn't show any enthusiasm in defending me.*

The judge turned to the prosecutor's table, where Major Billings, the head of the prosecution team sat, and asked him to proceed with his opening statement.

Major Billings would, in military trial protocol, tell the jury how he will prove my guilt beyond a shadow of a doubt. He inter-twined the investigating officer's report with his own hyperbola to paint a picture of a loose cannon at the Department of Defense. A man, he said so obsessed with his own view of the world, that he violated his Constitutional Oath of Office by plotting to over throw the election of the President of the United States.

I sat there feeling angry at Major Billings's choice of words. When I put aside his words and thought about what he was really accusing me of, I had to admit, my actions could be considered pretty bad if you didn't know the whole story. The constant pounding of Major Billing's fist on the desk, as he made his points of each accusation, reminded me of a judge's gavel just before handing out a sentence on each count. I could hear it, loud and strong, guilty of conspiracy, guilty of sedition, guilty of treason.

I had often heard people say these past few weeks, how could he have done this? Looking back, I still don't know how it could have been prevented. I guess I should have seen it coming. I mean I was only doing my job. If anyone were in my shoes they would agree it was justified? With all the sloppy election balloting and fraud in the last election, reform was necessary, wasn't it? Stop it Gary. You keep rationalizing what you did. You know it was wrong. I now felt the guilt pouring over me. I had caused a murder; violated my wife's trust; and violated my oath as an officer in the Army.

Capt. Gary Hallstead, a military computer expert, was going over the events that brought him to his trial. He was pondering what effect this was going to have on the country. His only problem was whether they would see this as a criminal act by him or an act of patriotism, as he did. He only prayed for forgiveness from his wife and children. He thought *my country has a right to do with me what they will. I only hope the members of this trial will only want to get at the truth.*

I remember the first time I sat at a tribunal similar to this court. It was much the same except the judge and jury were United States Senators.

***

It was January of 1993 when I last sat before the Senate Committee on Government Affairs.

I was a nervous Captain who had spent six years designing computer systems for the Defense Department, sitting in front of United States Senators who were firing tough questions at me. No one had prepared me for this. I was used to Generals and my project mangers yelling about target dates and computer system flaws, but I was not used to Senators who could interrogate with the best of them.

After all we were talking about changing the United States election system. Yes, it was only a pilot, affecting a hand full of Senate elections in states that had agreed to be the guinea pigs for election reform. None of this would be necessary except for the fact that just over a year ago we had an election for President won by the narrowest of margins. With the loser screaming about voter fraud and irregularities, everybody knew something had to be done. Hell, even the Supreme Court got involved. I kept thinking *I'm not a politician; I'm a computer guy assigned to do a project, just like a dozen projects I've done before.* I should have felt flattered that I was picked to head up the project, but I was more worried about the potential fall out if something went wrong. Mainly because of the questions the Senators were asking. I was impressed with the level of detail they had about computer systems. I tried to forget it was probably their aides that had come up with the more detailed questions. True or not it was the Senators asking them, not their aides, and I had to respond accordingly.

The computer system they were requesting would have a profound affect on how elections would be conducted in the country, now and in the future. It was serious business.

At the time I was apolitical. I wasn't interested in politics, I despised it. When some of my team at DOD caught wind of this possible project, the comments were mixed. Dale Schoolcraft was excited, hoping he would get a chance to work on it. Dale was one of my best programmer/analysts and saw this project as a challenge to his programming skills. Larry Davis saw it different. Larry, my expert on network systems, loved politics. It was like a hobby to him; he was very knowledgeable on the subject and made me feel unpatriotic at times not knowing what was going on politically. But Larry was also a cynic when hearing about another government program. He thought it was just a way for those in power to devise another method, to somehow stay in power. I was going to be the project manager on this project which was a fact at least in my mind. My goal was to complete this project, on time, error free, without any political overtones.

I did allow myself a personal thought. *This project could be my ticket to promotion. I had the normal amount of ambition like anyone else does, without being cut throat about it. I had been fortunate so far in my career, doing the things I liked to do, like computer programming and system design.*

I convinced myself I was finally being recognized for my talents by my boss, Colonel Edgerton. That's why I'm here and not him. I didn't want to be mean in thinking about the Colonel, but he was getting a little past his prime. He was giving me a chance to show off my expertise and a chance to maybe take over his job after his retirement. The truth was, Colonel Edgerton was past his prime. He hadn't kept up the latest computer technology and was marking time until he had his thirty years in. He and I both knew he wouldn't be able to handle the Senator's questions. I felt sorry for him; he is an honorable man whose time has past. I respect him though for realizing his limitations and giving me this chance.

Working for the Department of Defense was a dream of mine ever since graduating from the Academy. I had always been interested in computers and was lucky to get Major Cole as an instructor. The Major must have seen something in me that he liked. He had the Department of Defense invite me over for an interview even before I graduated.

I must admit when I started at DOD I was hoping for some exciting and important assignments, but when I was assigned my first project, reality set in. They still did payroll, inventory, and accounting systems at the DOD, not exactly the most interesting work in the computer profession. That's where I was stuck for five years; I made the most of it. I was a good employee, nose to the grindstone and never complained about anything. I figured this was the best way to work into more important assignments later on.

I started out doing a lot of programming, writing code, testing and implementing small projects. Most of the new people in computer systems jobs started out the same way. I was worried though, because the fact is I am a very good programmer and it might tend to keep me from advancing to design work. Every computer programmer's dream career path was to advance into design and ultimately into a project managers position.

I was receiving good performance reports and ever increasing responsibilities. Finally, what I thought was my big break came. I was assigned to do a pilot project linking some of our record's centers. I was teamed up with Larry Davis, an experienced programmer at the DOD. Larry, like me, was a stickler for perfection. We were successful in setting up a network that linked five of our records centers. These centers were developed to hold regional records of all our service personnel.

They were clearinghouses for active duty as well as retirees' records. The main purpose was payroll; however, all the medical files were also kept there.

I thought it funny we were piloting five centers; when there was only seven total. Why go through all the trouble of doing five when it was just as easy to do them all?

We centralized the centers at DOD. It cost a small fortune for the added disk space. But hey, this was the Federal Government, money was not an object. The project had the biggest budget of any computer system handled so far at the DOD. Most of that being the cost of civilian programmers brought in to help us with the project.

The outside world, that's what we in the military call anyone not in the military, was paying top wages to people in the computer field. It was hard to compete with them in getting top computer people. I must admit we were a little jealous of them and even resentful. You can't blame us. Here we were working side by side with civilian computer people making over twice the pay as the military people. I know the saying; you'll never get rich in the military, but that didn't ease the resentment we had.

Larry and I, being the professionals we are, managed to put that resentment aside and worked hard to complete our assignments on time. It was exciting completing this project. It had been implemented successfully. After a month of cleaning up some loose ends, Larry and I were looking for another project.

I was going through my K-219, time worked report. This report was getting tougher and tougher to fill out. It is the form we used to assign our work time for the week. I was getting embarrassed putting in 7.5 hours every day for maintenance and enhancements to a system that was completed some time ago. Truth was we were done two weeks ago and there wasn't a lot of critical work left to be done by me, let alone having a full staff still assigned to the project.

Now with the new election project about to start, my staff and I were busy cleaning up leftover mundane tasks and looking forward to the new project.

I sat back to ponder what tasks I had accomplished for the week that would add up to 40 hours of work when I thought, *time for a smoke and the latest rumors. With the election project, we should all have something new to talk about on the smoking patio.*

The *smoking patio* was a place the DOD had designated where smoking was permitted. Those of us still chained to that addiction had a place where we could go and indulge in the filthy habit. Having provided this refuge, the DOD didn't take into account the law of unintended consequences. It became not only a place to suck in the nicotine, but it was the hub of the rumor mill.

Larry, Dale and I were main stays on the patio. We all started smoking early in life. We thought about quitting when the building went smoke free, but when the DOD gave us this patio, all thoughts of quitting went out window.

Dale and I talked about sports, computers, and everyday life. Dale's conversations were interesting, as he was always on the edge of cutting technology in the computer business and loved to share it. But I actually looked forward to seeing Larry there; he was always on the cutting edge of the rumor mill.

As I opened the heavy glass door to the patio I saw Larry's eyes light up. He obviously had another hot rumor and was waiting for me to come out so he could pass it on. After all what good is a hot rumor if you can't tell someone about it?

"Guess what I just heard?" he asked. He didn't wait until I asked. "I got this from a very reliable source, up top."

"Okay, what?" I said.

Larry was smiling from ear to ear.

"We, or more you, are going to have a new boss. The Colonel has turned in his papers."

"Colonel Edgerton is retiring?" I asked.

"Yup, I got it straight from General Thomas's secretary, Major Keenan." Larry said proudly, showing off his connections.

Dale asked "What do you think this will do to the new project. We're still going to be the team right?"

I tried to comfort Dale, knowing losing the election project would break his heart. "I don't think the new boss will change the team. They may take a more active role than Colonel Edgerton was going to, but I think we will still have the project."

Larry spoke up "That's not all. I think I know who it is, and I think he's a civilian."

"Now how in the world do you know that?" I asked.

"Well when I was out here this morning, about 5:30, there was a man out here smoking, talking on a cell phone. When he saw me, he finished with his phone call. He either was done or didn't want me to hear anything"

"Your so dramatic Larry, get on with it." I instructed Larry.

"There was just the two of us so I walked over, just trying to be friendly, and said I haven't seen you out here before, are you new?" Larry paused to take a drag on his cigarette.

"He looked at me and said, not for long. He put out his cigarette and left. What do you make of that?"

I asked "So how does that translate into the fact he is our new boss?"

Larry was now more contrite. "Well I suppose it doesn't. I just had feeling."

Dale asked "What does he look like?"

Larry looked to the sky and replied "He's a small man, like five foot six. Thin, you know kind of wiry looking, with cold eyes." Larry smiled, he knew he was about to be harassed by all of us for his description of the mystery man.

It was time to get back to work, I threw away my butt and headed toward the patio door, the others followed me. At least Larry didn't have time to bore us with his usual political discussions.

When I returned to my office I was startled by a man standing inside my office door. He was wearing an Army uniform. Being in the military, when you see a uniform, your eyes automatically focus towards the shoulders looking for rank. He was a Lt. Colonel.

"Captain, I am instructed to have you report to E-112 at 14 hundred today, it concerns your next assignment."

Then he turned and left, as quickly as he appeared.

E-112, I thought, *that's E level!* The Department of Defense building was divided into five sides. That's why they call it the Pentagon. Each side has five floors, we call them levels. My office was on the ground floor, level A. Level E was where the really big shooters were, five floors up. Rumor was, nothing but Generals had their offices there. *Did I hear him right? He did say E level didn't he? Yes he did, E-112, I remember it exactly as he said it.* I reached into my top drawer and pulled out my building directory. At least I should try and find out his name and title. The last page had E-Level at the top as the heading. Starting at the bottom, I scrolled up. 200's, 100's, here it is 112. The office number was here but there was no name associated to it, just Special Operations. I knew this guy was different but what kind of person on E-Level would have an office without their name on it? *I wondered what in the world this was going to be about. If this was the new boss, I hope he wasn't going to take the project away. E-Level, the new boss couldn't be on E-Level could he? Colonel Edgerton was always on C level; he never made it to E Level. But it's possible the new boss would be an E-Level guy; what with the importance of this election project.*

I had two hours to kill. It was lunchtime but I wasn't about to eat. My stomach was as nervous as the rest of me. It was 13:30 when I decided to leave my office for the trip up to E level. You had to go to a special elevator and not only show your ID, but state your name and where you were going. The guard then checked a list. If you were on it, he pushed the up button to bring the elevator down. I entered the elevator, pointed my finger to press the E floor button. I couldn't find it. The only buttons were up and down. There were obviously no stops allowed on this elevator except A and E levels. The elevator stopped, the door opened. I saw a sign straight ahead on the wall that had the office numbers with arrows showing which way to turn. As I exited the elevator, a guard appeared, he seemed to appear from thin air, and once again checked my ID, asked where I was going and what time my appointment was. After he had checked his list, he motioned me to turn right and proceed.

E-110, E111, E112, and here it is. I was surprised the door looked just like my office. I guess I expected something special. I hesitated at the door, wondering if I should knock, or just go in. I decided to show I was confident and aggressive by opening the door and walking in. To my surprise there sat a Captain, same rank as me, at a desk that looked like something a receptionist would have. He said "Captain, please have a seat." There were 2 chairs and a small table. That was it. No magazines, books, or anything else. As I sat down I could hear the Captain say, on the phone, "Sir, Captain Hallstead is here. Yes sir." It sounded like I was supposed to in, but I decided to wait until told to do so.

It wasn't a second later, the Captain behind the desk stood and said "Captain please follow me." We proceeded out the door and down the hall. We came to a door that was labeled, Private E112. The Captain knocked, lightly, on the door and immediately opened it. He was standing there, halfway in the door way, looking back at me. He nodded for me to enter and I walked in. The Captain left, closing the door behind him.

I stood all alone in a very small room, no desk or any furniture at all. It was smaller than the receptionist room I was just in. I looked around and noticed there was another door, straight ahead and to my left. It seemed I was standing there for hours when actually it was only a few seconds, when the door opened. Here, in the door way stood a man in a civilian's suit. He motioned me to come in. The room I entered was long and narrow, with a conference table and chairs, that's all I noticed about the room. Then I was struck with the uniformed men sitting at the table. There was a four star General and a one star General. There were four civilians in suits. Eight of us total. I was told by my mystery civilian in the suit to sit down and relax. That was a shock. That was first time he ever showed any civility toward me. He opened the meeting, which showed me this guy has some power, with the introductions. Not the normal introductions you would expect, they were short and to the point.

My mystery man in the suit said "Gentlemen this is Captain Gary Hallstead. He is one of our top project analysts. Captain Hallstead, from your left is Mr. Volick, Mr. Shiner from the Senate Committee on Government Affairs. Next are Mr. Moyer and Ms. Trackerson from the same committee in the House, and General Boyer and General Gunder from the Department of Defense.

Captain, this meeting is concerning your next assignment. I'm going to give you a brief synopsis and the House and Senate representatives here will give you more details. In fact, in our terminology, they will be your clients on the project. I don't have to remind you Captain we are not to question things from a political nature, only carry out the instructions of the Congress. The House and Senate, based on our latest information, will be voting sometime later to authorize the pilot program, about which you have testified at hearings. The details have been worked out in the Government Affairs Committees and will be sent to the full House and Senate. We are told it will pass in both houses. We will need to be ready to implement this pilot as soon as possible. The project will computerize, nationally, Senate and House elections in a controlled environment. Five states will be used, with five Senate races, and five House races in each of the states. You will put aside anything you currently have and staff up for this right away. Understand?"

"Yes sir", I replied. I tried not to have a puzzled look on my face. If he knew I testified at the hearings, he must know I already knew all about the project and was assigned to be the manager.

The mystery man continued. "You can see with the people at this meeting, you will receive anything you need to accomplish your project. There is only one other thing I want to mention. This project is so important, sensitive, and impacting on the country, we will need top secret security. That is why it is being assigned to the DOD and not being bid out to a civilian company. Get together with your clients and set up a schedule of design meetings while they are here. They have assured me they are available from now until implementation. Oh yes, I will want you to set up a standard meeting with myself and you, every Monday and Wednesday at 3 o'clock in the afternoon, until further notice. I will expect a detailed update at these meetings."

I thought to myself, *oh great; I report to a man that has not even told me his name. At least I think he's my new boss, he really hasn't said that. Do I just come out now and ask his name and if he's my boss? Will that sound stupid in front of all these people? I had to do something, he looked like he was about to leave.*

I got up and walked toward him and said in almost a whisper, "Sir." I got his attention. He waited as I walked over to him. Still in a whisper, I leaned over and asked. "I am embarrassed to say sir; I never did get your name."

He looked at me, smiled for an instant, and said "sorry, I'm Carl Minster. Is that it?"

"Yes sir. Well just one more thing I assume then I am reporting directly to you."

"That's correct Captain, you will report directly to me."

"Yes sir, thank you sir I'll go over and set up the meetings with the clients right now."

After talking to the clients over an hour, I returned to my office. I needed to block off the conference room schedule for my client meetings. The clients said they felt more secure coming here to DOD for any meetings. I also set up my calendar for the twice a week meetings with Carl Minster.

I couldn't help but think about Larry's description of the man on the patio. It sure fit Minster to a tee, but I would have to add to Larry's description. Minster was abrupt and to the point, the no nonsense type. Add that to his physical characteristics and you have another Napoleon. *Well,* I *thought, serious projects require serious men. As long as the rest of the team didn't have to interact with him it will be okay.* I always wanted my teams to have fun doing their work while keeping a sense of professionalism about themselves.

My next task was to layout what kind of people I will need on this project. First and foremost I'll need a top notch programmer, someone with experience in network engineering. Although I could do that type of coding, I was the manager, and besides, I could always jump in if needed. Larry Davis would be my man. Larry and I had worked together for years. Larry was the best network engineer I had ever seen. *Let's see, Dale and Sue would be my mainframe people. They were not only great programmers, but used to working under pressure and putting in long hours. I'll need some people at the state's sites. I'll talk to Larry first about who he recommends. As far as the mainframe tasks I'll see who Dale suggests. Now I'll want to set up a meeting with the database group and tech support. They will need some lead time for equipment and communication lines. I'll work on the preliminary design and then get the group together tomorrow.*

***

Everyone arrived at my office on time for the 9:00 am meeting I called. I explained the general project and of course how important it was. I didn't need to really explain the importance; everyone figured that out for themselves after hearing what the project entailed. I was able to tell them the states involved. These were big states; California, Texas, Pennsylvania, Florida, and New York.

Larry joked: "why not Rhode Island, Vermont, and the Dakotas?"

Dale chimed in; "You need one more, how about Wyoming."

I was glad to see the group was loose and relaxed, given the importance of the project.

"Larry", I said. "Come up a list of people you'll need on the networking end, here and at the sites we are piloting. Dale, please handle the state level for any mainframe work needed on their end. My understanding is Congress is going to allocate the funds necessary to install the same voting machines in all the precincts of the 5 states. These machines will be networked to the state and nationally to us. We will be responsible for every vote in those states. So we will need a big database. I have already set up a meeting with the database group to obtain the space necessary to hold that much information. Every vote will be able to be validated."

Dale asked "what kind of data are we going to be carrying in the system besides the vote numbers?"

I replied "Good question. Here is where it gets a little tricky. We need to have every name of the person that voted; but not how they voted. Locally, the election workers are going to have to set up a bar code on their registration rolls. Voters will be given new registration cards with a bar code. They will check in with this bar code. When they go to their machine to vote, the machine will ask them to insert their card. That is the bar code we need to capture. The machine will not record how they voted, just that they voted. Of course any duplicates will cause an error." I felt it necessary to tell my team any information needed to get the job done. Everything I learned from the clients, I would relate to my group. That's how we have successfully worked on past projects and I saw no need to change.

We had a good jump on the project. Even with a good jump, I knew there would be long days and nights ahead. I built a project time line based on my experience, building into it time for illness, family emergencies, and yes the inevitable design changes. The target date had already been set for us. *Typical*, I thought, *just like every project I've worked on. We don't get to layout the project and tell the clients when it will be done. They tell us the deadline and we work a plan backwards to meet the date.*

Every Monday and Wednesday I made my way up the E-level elevator to report to Carl Minster. I was no longer intimidated by the guard or even the fact I had access to the highest level of the Department of Defense. But one thing I still didn't feel comfortable about; I didn't call him Carl yet, it was still Mr. Minster. Before meeting with Mr. Minster I had scheduled update meetings with my staff and the clients, any changes made by the client that was going to possibly cause a delay, were recorded on to a change order form. I was going to make certain my butt was covered. I was not afraid to make them sign every change order. I would take these change orders to my staff and asked for estimates on how long it would take to make the change. Armed with these, I went to my meeting with Mr. Minster, confident in knowing if the project was off track he would know why.

After the third change order, the changes were really getting to be Mickey Mouse cosmetic enhancements, and a possible hindrance to the target date. At my last meeting with Mr. Minster, he finally showed some emotion. He was obviously ticked off at the clients. He tossed the change order down.

Minster looked at me angrily, and said "this is going to stop now!"

I felt relived and relaxed with Mr. Minster for the first time since the project started. I was so relaxed I called him Carl for the first time.

"Carl, you understand its not that these changes can't be done or even that they aren't better than what we designed. It's just that what we have works and is on target."

Carl agreed "I understand Captain. I will talk to them and put a stop to anything that's not critical to the project." He didn't even flinch at me calling him Carl.

"Alright Captain", Carl continued, "Let's skip the details, what's the bottom line? Where are we?" My staff meetings were loose and fun generally. But when it came for the updates on tasks and targets my staff knew it was time to be serious. They had assured me we were on schedule. That meant we were only 2 weeks away from a unit test. I relayed the upcoming schedule to Carl.

"Carl, we are 2 weeks from unit testing in house. If all goes well, we are 4 more weeks to running a parallel test in the field." I could see a slight grin come across his face. He was pleased.

Carl said, "Good, keep me up to date Captain. That's all." I knew that was my cue to leave.

It seemed like only hours since I meant with Minster, but here it was Wednesday and time to give Carl another update.

I made my way down to the smoking patio to get some courage before my next regular meeting with Minster. I never stopped and asked Larry or Dale to come along. I thought it would be like I was commanding them to come and smoke with me. I thought that would not be appropriate behavior as their boss.

Once you entered the smoking patio, all rank was neutralized. We were all a brotherhood of smokers, outcasts from the society of non-smokers. We were there with a common bond. Larry and Dale soon appeared, a smile always appeared on each of our faces whenever anyone entered the smoking patio. That meant we weren't alone. Dale and my only concern was not if, but when Larry would start in on one of his political rants.

Larry joined Dale and me. "Hey you know what. I was thinking if this election project goes well, I'm thinking they might roll it out for the Presidential election."

Oh God, I thought, *we haven't even finished this project yet and Larry has us doing this for the Presidential election.*

Larry continued. "You know the election is shaping up to be pretty interesting. If President Anderson is running again for re-election he won't be guaranteed a win. He's got some trouble with the economy and the immigration situation. You mark my words this problem with illegal immigrants is going to get big. I'll even bet you…"

"Larry it's time to get back to work." I had to stop Larry or we would be out here for hours listening to his political diatribe.

You know the saying, time flies when you're having fun, *that* is so true, but we actually were having fun. The system was coming together nicely. I called Carl's office and notified him we were about to run our unit test in house. I was so confident in the system I asked him to observe our trial run. I even asked Carl if I should invite the clients from the Senate and House and any of the Generals that were at our original meeting.

To my surprise Carl said "I'll be there, but let's leave out everyone else until I see the results." It was clear he didn't have as much faith in the system as I did.

The unit test went as planned. It was a thoroughly complete test with lots of data. It included all possible errors as well as unique situations. I was as proud of this test as new father looking to hand out cigars. Even Carl was impressed. He walked around shaking the staff's hands and telling them what a good job they had done. My staff was expecting him. I had told them that Carl was coming. I didn't tell them anything about Carl except that he was our boss. After Carl shook the last hand he turned to me and motioned me to a more private corner of the room.

Carl said, "This looks almost ready to roll out. I want you to get the parallel going ASAP. Do you have time to run 2 parallels?"

"Two parallels?" I asked. "Why 2?"

Carl said "if the parallel goes as well as this test, then I want the clients and my management to see it. I don't want them to see any problems. It only makes them uncomfortable to see any problems. You must understand these are not computer people. If they see one problem, no matter how small, they will start to have doubts. For the most part our clients are politicians. If they have any doubts about our computer system dealing with elections, it will never see the light of day."

"I understand sir", I said. "We will be ready in 3 weeks for the first parallel."

We were on schedule for the parallel, but I was worried about the voting machines. Four of the states were up and running. There seemed to be a hold up in Texas. The machines were installed in Texas but had not had their own testing done yet.

I notified Carl of the hold up and within an hour, Carl returned my call and said "Captain tell your man in Texas the machines should be ready in the morning." I had learned that when Carl said something, you could bank on it.

The next morning, even before I could call Larry about Texas, he was at my office door.

Larry told me, "I got a call from Burt in Texas. He says the machines are tested and ready to go."

Somehow I wasn't surprised. Like I knew, when Carl tells you something you can bank on it, he seems to have a great deal of power. I checked with the rest of the staff before calling Carl. I told him the parallel would begin in 3 days.

He seemed pleased.

Chapter 2 Office Politics

The simulation of our project ran smoothly and without problems. Carl Minster was satisfied enough to give us the go ahead to show the clients. Getting ready to run the system test was no small undertaking, in fact it was a massive undertaking with 5 large states, millions of votes, and a complex network.

Most of the time was invested in checking, and validating our voter test base. Dale, our mainframe computer expert, had put together a clever mini system to make sure very vote was counted and validated back to the voter registration system. It took 4 days, but we were able to prove the results of the mock election to our satisfaction.

We felt so assured of our procedures; we scheduled the next system test for the clients once we reset all the machines and data files. The second test ran as well as the first one. Why shouldn't it. It was exactly like the original. The team knew it was more of a dog and pony show for management and the clients, and less about the system which had already been proven. After the system test was run for the clients, it was all smiles and handshakes. The clients and generals and our management, mainly Carl Minster, were pleased with the results. Every one seemed happy except me. I suddenly realized the next time we would run the system it would be for real. Its one thing to run tests that really didn't mean anything, quite another when it's done for real.

The next time our system runs, 5 United States Senators, and 165 members of the House will be chosen. We will also be using the new voting machines, and every vote will be counted and validated with our system. I was nervous to say the least.

I wasn't so much nervous about our system; it had been tested thoroughly and came through with flying colors. I was nervous about what unknown glitch might appear that we might not have accounted for. I was a bit concerned with the states we were piloting, New York,

Florida, Texas, California, and Pennsylvania were large states with millions of voters. I would have been more comfortable with smaller states. What I didn't know was that these five states were picked because the political parties wanted to roll out the system for the next Presidential campaign, if all went well.

The Party Chairmen had negotiated New York and Pennsylvania for the Democrats, Florida and California for the Republicans with Texas being the controversial state from the 1992 Presidential Election. Texas was controversial in 1992 because it was the deciding state in electing the Democrat, Dan Anderson President. The election in Texas was so close that recount after recount was requested by both sides. Charges of fraud and mishandling the ballots were flying from both parties. If it wasn't so serious a matter, electing a President, the whole thing was becoming a comedy act. Finally the Supreme Court stepped in and decided to stop the counting of ballots for the tenth time and accept the results. I still don't understand who brought the Supreme Court into the mix or why they did it. I guess you have to be a lawyer to understand it.

Finally the day of reckoning for our system had arrived. The Congressional Elections were about to get underway. Our team was ready and we were confident in our system. It would be a long night and even longer day as we prepared to monitor the results. Dale, Larry and I were each taking six hour shifts and scheduled our time so we would all be together the day after the election. We needed to be together to go over the final results of the vote as well as the system internals that was used to validate the results.

You can't believe the relief I felt when the elections were finally concluded and the preliminary results were showing everything was satisfactory. I was excited to present these successes to both parties. I knew it would be something special to both political parties to have a system they could both agree on. It would be especially satisfying after the 1992 election fiasco.

I was not one to get too excited about elections and politics. I had become jaded to politician's promises and campaign rhetoric. They all seemed to be the same once they were elected, the promises evaporated and the campaign differences between candidates just disappeared. The 1992 election caught the nation's interest and had every one riveted to the television night after night, as the Texas election workers recounted ballots. At first the interest was one of anticipation as the nation waited to see if we had a President or not. As days turned into weeks, the people's anticipation turned into one of distain. Both political parties were sending teams of lawyers into Texas to oversee the recounting of ballots. The ballots, punch card ballots, were now becoming the focus of attention as each side argued whether a particular punched ballot was sufficiently punched through to be counted as a good vote.

The Supreme Court was ultimately handed the case and decided 5 to 4 to end the counting, proclaiming in affect President Anderson to be the winner. I didn't have an opinion one way or the other. I was just glad, like most of the country, the election was over. But amongst the two political parties it was a decision that would create a great deal of animosity and it didn't go away.

I can see now the importance of our computer system. We had to not only develop a system that would mechanically assure a fair election, but also alleviate the fears and suspicions of the major political parties. By accomplishing the latter goal, we were in affect helping to heal our country.

Our system had performed as expected; the team and I were pleased with the results. We held a small celebration in the office and patted each other on the back. I held back a little on my exuberance until I heard more from either the clients or my boss, Carl Minster. It had been my experience on other projects; the boss would always make an appearance to the team and offer congratulations on a successful implementation. As I looked around the room for any sign of Carl I was approached by my secretary, Tina, holding a piece of paper. I knew it had be a message of some sort due the color of the paper. She held out the folded message and said "Mr. Minster called and wants you to come to his office right away."

I acknowledged the receipt of the message by nodding to Tina and immediately made my way to the E-Level elevator. My thoughts of why Carl wanted to see me alone were running more to the negative than the positive. *Maybe things had not gone as smoothly as I thought?*

I was ushered into Carl's office as soon as I arrived. He was obviously waiting to see me. I was really taken aback when Carl asked me to prepare to give testimony to the Senate Election Reform

Committee in one week on our system and the results of this last election. That was all Carl had to say, nothing about the teams effort or good job, nothing. I couldn't help but to continue to think of Carl Minster as a strange man. But I do respect his no nonsense, direct style.

I am not comfortable speaking in front of large groups of people. It didn't matter who they were. Powerful or just regular people, friends or strangers; I just didn't like it. It wasn't that I didn't know the subject. I knew this computer system and our results from the election inside out. Besides, I thought, *why isn't Carl doing the testifying to the committee? Generally, it's the accepted practice for the most senior management person to give testimony to Congressional Committees. Oh well, I guess I should just be quiet and prepare to give the testimony. One, thing though, they are going to hear it my way and not some sanitized version. Carl didn't say anything about the style of my report. I'll tell them where I thought the system was excellent and where it might need improvement.*

***

The Chairman of the Committee opened the meeting with, "Captain Hallstead, welcome to the Committee Hearings on Election reform. We have been told, you as the Project Manager, would be the best person to give us the results of the Department of Defense's computerized election system, used in this Nations last Congressional election. I understand you have an opening statement and when you finish, we will allow time for Committee members to ask questions."

I began, "Thank you Senator. Yes, I have an opening statement that will give the Committee an overview of the results of the election and the performance of our computer system. I will be happy to stay as long as needed to answer questions from the Committee."

I proceeded to give my report on the results of the election as it was impacted by our computer system. I had to be careful not to get too technical. I needed to avoid the use of too much computer jargon. I knew my audience of United States Senators were intelligent people, but the use of too much computer terminology would tend to lose any one not familiar with it. I took a deep breath and began my testimony, giving a generic overview of the procedures, but a detailed account of any elections anomalies that occurred.

I told the Senators how we had setup a network in each county of the five states, feeding results real-time to that states Secretary of Election's office as well as the election headquarters at our site in Virginia. The actual voting machines in each precinct were developed by a private company, Election Recording Inc. Our system was electronically tied into each of these machines, to gather and verify the votes. The numbers were recorded by precincts, current voter rolls, and instant registration counts with the goal of validating the number of voters. With thousands of precincts involved the chances of something going wrong was significant.

We had a total of 125 questionable ballots. My God that was really insignificant, but 125 was 125 too many when it comes to guaranteeing every vote would be counted and verified. We scrambled as soon as we were notified of the complaints from the local election officials. Turns out 102 of the questions were due to the fact these people were registered twice in their respective precincts. This actually brought out what was a local problem and was quickly resolved.

The remaining 23 were people who attempted to vote more than once. It was a situation where they completed their vote and touched the complete button on the screen. They then decided to change their vote, asked for a new ballot, and were given one. The problem was again local because the election worker inadvertently put the first ballot in a pile of ballots to be reviewed as a problem. There wasn't really a problem and those ballots should have gone to the possible duplicate pile to be validated. This was remarkable! Basically the system had worked flawlessly. It even discovered local procedural problems that would be easily solved for the next time. The local election workers were actually grateful for pointing out these problems. They had taken notes on how to prevent potential errors in the future, whether they used our computer system or not.

I had told the committee everything, the good parts as well as the problem areas. I was proud of the way my team had handled and fixed these problem areas. It was getting late in the day and the questions kept coming. I didn't mind the time as much as I did being asked the same question ten different ways. To be honest, I think some of the Senators were only speaking to be recorded in the minutes of the hearing.

When my testimony was over, I waited outside the committee room. Carl had told me to wait because he felt an important vote was about to take place, some of which my testimony would be a deciding factor. The kind of questions I was asked led me to believe they might just actually want to move this system forward. I never dreamed they would actually consider using this system for a Presidential election. I noticed Carl was allowed to stay in the room. *Boy, this guy must be somebody* I thought. All I could hear was a murmur of voices. I couldn't make out anything specific. Then it was quiet and I heard footsteps coming toward the door where I was waiting. People were filing out. I didn't recognize anyone right away. Then I saw Carl moving toward the door and his eyes were locked on me.

Carl walked right up to me and said "It was 15-0 to setup the system for the '96 Presidential election. Get your team together tomorrow and start looking at what its going to take to get this done."

I replied, "It takes more than this vote to get all the approvals to be a done deal, doesn't it?"

Carl looked slyly at me and said, "Trust me it's going to be a routine matter in the full Senate, and the House is going to follow shortly."

"Yes sir, I'll get on it right away." I thought to myself, *why did I even question Carl, he's always right.* As I walked out of the Senate building, I thought, in the typical smugness of a computer system designer after a system first works; *if it worked once, it will work again. I trusted my superiors; I trusted my government; I trusted everyone was doing the right thing.*

***

My team was excited at the news. They were really pumped up by the prospects of being involved in such a notable undertaking. I was snapping out orders to everyone feeling like I knew exactly what had to be done. It was all mechanical to me. I was generally apolitical; I didn't allow myself, as a military man to get involved in politics. I did, once in while, prefer who my Commander in Chief was, but I kept that to myself. Most of my team realized and respected that. With all of us, civilian and military, working for the Department of Defense, most kept their political opinions to themselves. Well, everybody but Larry. Larry Davis was definitely an outspoken man, who gave you his opinion whether you asked him or not. I had hoped Larry would be more excited about the project than the election to keep his thoughts to himself.

Larry had been in the service, Navy I think, and had a lot of political opinions about the government. He wasn't shy in talking about which candidate would serve the military better, especially during a Presidential race. I usually let him rattle on, going in one ear and out the other, until he realized I wasn't really listening to him. When he realized I was not listening, he knew I didn't want to hear any more of it, he stopped talking and went about his business. I think he knew I put up with his political opinions more than anyone else would because of his value to the team. Larry was a sharp programmer and saved my projects more than once.

Dale and the rest of the group never talked about politics at all. I couldn't even guess how they felt about the candidates or issues. Larry made up for all the rest.

I finished barking out orders and everyone was leaving immediately to start their task lists. Everyone, that is except Larry. He got up and walked over to my desk where I was standing. I thought, *okay here it comes. Larry's going to have some comment on the election.*

Larry got a little smile on his lips and said, "So boss, do you think Anderson will run again?" He was trying to get a response out of me.

I said seriously, "I don't know Larry. If he is running again, so what. We have a system to build, that's all I know right now and frankly that's all I care about right now."

Larry, being the detailed man he was, knew that was true and that was all he was going to get out of me. He replied, "You got me there. We'll just have to wait and see."

I knew he was dying to go out to the smoking patio to continue the conversation but he must of thought, now is not the time and he left to get back to work.

***

Larry Davis appeared at my office door, trying to catch his breath. He wasn't sick. He looked like he had something important to tell me. I was a little concerned, waiting for him to tell me because I thought it was something to do with the project. But no, Larry wanted to tell me that

President Anderson had announced his intention to seek a second term. This was not exactly news and wasn't that important to me. It really didn't matter to me who was running for President; I had a project to do. It was true the project concerned the election. But all I was concerned about is that the project was done right and shouldn't have any impact on who was elected.

I looked up from my desk and asked Larry, "What was so important about this news? How is this so important I had to know about it right away Larry? Never mind, hold it until we go out to the smoking patio."

We made our way out to the patio, with my real goal to just have a cigarette.

Larry wanted to give me his political philosophy and how he thought President Anderson wouldn't run again because his poll numbers were very bad. I didn't want to get into another conversation about politics with Larry. I had always tried to discourage that sort of thing, especially at the office. I just stood there smoking my cigarette and thought; *I'll listen to Larry ramble on a little while this time. I needed a break anyway; I had been working pretty hard.*

Once out on the smoking patio, I opened the conversation just to be polite. "Larry, so you think President Anderson really doesn't have a chance?" I immediately regretted it. *Why in the world did I give him an opening?*

Larry was surprised at my question because he knew I usually discouraged such talk about politics. Grasping at my opening, he grabbed a smoke, lit up, took a deep breath, and then said to me; "Well, you know he's not doing well in the polls. True, President Anderson is very popular amongst Democrats and has a fair amount of support from Independents. However, you know he's very liberal. He's in trouble this time if the Republicans pick the right candidate. He doesn't have any support in the military."

I couldn't help it, I had to interrupt, "Larry, don't talk about the military and the President that way. He's our Commander-in-Chief and we all took an oath..."

Larry snapped back, "You took an oath, not me. I've been out of the service 20 years."

I said, "Ok, but be careful how you talk about my Commander-in-Chief. Like it or not I have to carry out his orders because I did take an oath. Anyway, how do you come by this stuff about the military not being behind him?" Larry got a smug look over his face; I've seen that look before. It's when Larry knows something you don't and wants you to hang on his next word.

Larry said, "I've got friends all over, even in the Democratic National Committee. I'm telling you this guy will do or say anything to get re-elected. He's a poll watcher. Whichever way the polls go, that's the way he will govern. I'm telling you this as a military man because I firmly believe he will even get us into a war to get re-elected."

Now that really got my interest. I might have to pay more attention to this election if somebody's going to put our troops at risk simply to win an election.

Larry had won. He finally got me interested enough in politics to pay attention to what the candidates were doing and saying. As time went on, Larry and I started to go out to the smoking patio everyday at the same time. We even started to take our lunches out with us and sit on the benches the DOD so thoughtfully provided. We both had always brought our own lunches to work.

Now we would have lunch together and talk politics every time we met. Larry loved it and I needed a lesson in Civics anyway. With Larry's friends in the thick of political campaigns in both parties, it was actually pretty exciting to be getting the inside scoop.

Larry would always bring the morning paper with him and point out the stories that were planted by the campaigns. He would then explain to me, using his sources, what the real purpose of the story was. They were usually designed to sway public opinion one way or the other, depending on who submitted them.

The Democratic Party had their man already. The question I soon became curious about was who the Republicans were going to have as their candidate.

Larry, realizing he had hooked me into the world of political discussion, wouldn't give me a direct answer. He had decided I needed more background before moving the discussion forward.

It all seemed innocent enough, learning about politics while designing an election system. It was a great lesson in Civics or so I thought. It would turn out to be more a lesson in survival.

Chapter 3 Presidential Candidates

Over the next few weeks, between Larry, his contacts, and reading the newspapers, I watched American politics unfold. As it turned out, it wasn't a pretty sight. Following the two parties was a real eye opener for someone like me who had a naive view of my government leaders.

Larry explained November was a little early for President Anderson to make his reelection announcement. The usual time was in December, just before Christmas, to give people a sense of security and alleviate any uncertainty when the government may have a change at the helm. But Larry figured it was done because of Anderson's poor poll numbers and needed the extra campaign time.

I was still curious who the Republican candidate would be and didn't stop asking Larry about it.

Larry finally gave in and gave me his educated and connected opinion. "Captain I can tell you who I think is on the short list, but you could still get some surprises. You just don't know the size of these guy's egos. They all think they are the one to run the country. The most lightly candidate I have to believe is Senator Bill Barnes. He's my man. I think he'll get the nomination; he has a lot support in the Party. At least he is the only one acting like he is going to run. I really can't think of anyone else who… Wait a minute there is…"

"Who? Who else are you thinking about?" I asked.

"Well, there is Kline. Ray Kline. But nobody takes him serious."

"Why not?" I asked.

"He is, too be honest, an extremist. Forget about him."

"So you think this Barnes is the guy?" I asked.

Larry said "Yes. I don't see anybody else, but you never know in politics."

Shortly after Larry and my discussion on the Republican Presidential candidate, came the shock of all shocks to not only us, but to the Republican Party.

Ray Kline, famous for his conservative writings and most recently his TV appearances as the conservative every liberal loves to hate, announced he was forming an exploratory committee for the purpose of seeking the Republican nomination for President.

Kline had always been identified as the conservative's favorite front man; he espoused and defended the conservative position on all the issues for the past seven years. He especially had been critical of the Anderson administration on the immigration and China trade issues. Kline's America First rhetoric was never taken seriously by anyone except the people that counted, that being the conservative wing of the Republican Party. The average American voter was who Kline would pin his hopes on. Now even the mainstream press was getting nervous as Ray was striking a cord with the general public. Ray's tirade against China and Mexico was thought of as so much hot air, but that was before he might become a candidate for President of the United States.

The next time Larry and I got together, I said, half laughing, "I'll bet this Kline thing really throws a monkey wrench into everything."

Larry was not happy. Larry was such a party guy, all he could see was the chance this would end up making Republicans look stupid.

"I don't think its funny Gary. Kline could make us all look like right-wing idiots. Have you ever really listened to him on that talk show he has? He's a buffoon."

"Larry, look I'm not saying I like him. But, you have to admit this race sure is a lot more interesting now. I don't know exactly how he stands on the issues, but he sure is fun to listen to. I saw his announcement about forming that committee thing and he was pretty exciting. Besides, your guy, Senator Barnes, hasn't announced yet so Kline is the only one I have to go by on the Republican side."

Larry said, "We'll see. I bet Kline doesn't end up running. And if he does I can't see him winning any primaries. He just likes to hear himself talk. I'll take him more serious if he actually has the guts to run."

It didn't take long; on November 15th, 1995, Ray Kline announced he was entering the Republican primaries as a candidate for President of the United States. I thought *that sure got everyone's attention. At least the race was going to be exciting. Up to now it had been dull and boring. Anderson was running a rose garden campaign, looking Presidential every chance he got, and nobody else had stepped forward on the Republican side.*

Larry cautioned me not to get too excited at the prospects of having a Kline campaign. He told me wait until Barnes announces and you will soon see Kline fade into the background.

I learned a lot from Larry about politics. He continued to instruct me on the ins and outs of the political world.

At our patio meetings he talked about the fact there are always two groups of people in a political party, the leadership, and the plain old volunteers who do the entire grunt work. They are two different groups of people with two different ideas on what a campaign needs to do to be successful.

The masses of regular Republicans was not as worried about the turn of events as the Republican leadership was. They realized the picking of the right candidate was the most important issue now. They knew for all the events turning their way; President Anderson was a formidable candidate and a great campaigner. The Republican candidate must be a person that needed one quality above all; that is he must be liked by the voters. That simple quality was better than a thousand good poll numbers. People are not stupid. The American people have to genuinely like a candidate or that candidate is going nowhere. This is something that these plain old volunteers had a good handle on.

Being volunteers meant just that. They had regular jobs and led regular lives. They are the Americans that suffer in economic down turns. They are the ones who have to convince their friends and neighbors to vote for their guy. The leadership was more worried about winning state primaries at this point in time. They wanted a candidate who could quickly accumulate enough delegates to shut out any opposition, and then they could concentrate on the general election. The leadership thought that having a great legislator, knowledgeable in Washington ways were qualities that will get you elected. The truth is you must be liked by the voters. Even I knew that.

There was no doubt about who was going to run for President on the Republican side. The question was whether the regulars in the Republican Party were ready to accept him. It wasn't that they wanted Ray Kline; they needed someone capable of beating Anderson.

Senator William Barnes, known as Bill Barnes, had made no pretense about wanting to be President. The Senator had run in the primaries in 1976 and again in 1988. He lost both times to candidates he felt were inferior to himself. He was easily elected back into the Senate. He was from a Midwestern state where only Republicans had a chance of being elected to any office. What most people outside of the inner party didn't know was that Bill Barnes was in for the long haul. He wanted the Presidency as bad as anyone ever did.

He collected favors from the party during past campaigns and saved them for such a day as now. Bill Barnes was not a man to go quietly off into the sunset. He was popular amongst his Senate friends, only because of his leadership and parliamentary skills in getting the party's agenda done.

As a person he could be very moody and even depressed when things didn't go his way. When he could not win his parties primary elections for President in the past, he didn't sulk long and turned out to be a tireless campaigner for the party's nominee. Bill Barnes had spent a total 24 years in the Senate and was a respected legislator. But that's all he had in his presidential portfolio. He had a sharp tongue and his humor was biting. These traits had not served him well in his previous runs for President.

In the Presidential debates of the past, Bill Barnes had expressed some pretty negative thoughts about his opponents. It had not gone over well with the Republican electorate or the American people. In other words, he was not liked by the voters. But he had one thing going for him. All those years of legislating, trading votes, and making campaign appearances for fellow Republicans, did buy him loyalty from the party, and Barnes knew how to use it. He also knew this race was first for the parties nomination, and he was about to call in all those favors from party members, who were also delegates.

December was the traditional kick off month for candidates to declare their intentions to run for the nomination. Seems like every election it came earlier and earlier. I guess it has to be early enough to raise money for the short, but grueling, and expensive primary season ahead. Just like clock work Senator Barnes announced an event at his home in Nebraska. Everyone knew what the event was going to be, Bill Barnes for President.

This was going to be a first for me, listening to another politician's announcement speech. Larry had done his job. He's even got me listening to political speeches. I was a little ashamed. Here it was one of the few nights I could spend time with my family and I was going to fretter it away listening to some boring guy talk about who knows what.

I had hoped my wife, Sally, would understand. She was the picture of a home body. Anytime the family could be together she wanted us to do things as a family, and I could understand that. My hours on the test election project were hard on Sally. She was a good wife though and never openly complained. I kept telling myself there will be time enough to spend together when these projects slow down. But, here's another project, this one bigger than ever, meaning more nights, weekends, and holidays at the office.

I've to explain to Sally on numerous occasions how important this project was, not only for the DOD, but also for the country, trying to not give her any information I was not allowed to. I told her; think of it as an overseas stint I was on. After all the years as a military wife, surely she could understand that logic. I still felt guilty.

I turned on the television and hesitated, what was that channel C-Span was on? I had never watched C-Span before. I thought it was for people who had nothing else to do like retirees and political junkies. I looked around the family room for the TV guide. I had a pile of unread newspapers by my favorite chair. Sally began piling them up over the past few months. I knew I would never get to read them, but I insisted Sally keep them where I could find them. As I fumbled through the stack, I got excited like a little kid. Here it is! The TV guide. You would think I found gold. I flipped to the end. I remembered the channel lineup was at the end of the guide; let's see I think it is C-Span channel 52. I sat down in my chair and tuned into channel 52. Here it is. I read the crawler at the bottom of the screen. *Senator William (Bill) Barnes announces his Presidential candidacy at his hometown Leesburg, Nebraska at 7:00 P.M.*

My watch said 6:55 P.M. Only 5 minutes to go. Sally walked into the family room with our children, Josh and Liz.

"You're home early tonight", she said with a tone of sarcasm. She didn't normally act like that. I figured she saw me looking intently at the TV expecting me to watch a show. She brought our two children in with her, clutching them at her side, almost in a protective mode. I sensed she was not happy at me coming home for the first time in quite awhile and now settling to watch television.

"Are you watching something?" she asked, knowing full well I was.

"Larry said I should catch this guy's speech. He has a good chance of becoming our next President." I said it that way hoping Sally would see that this was not some comedy show, but something that really mattered.

"Can we watch it with you?"

I thought, *this was going to be boring for not only the kids but to Sally also.* I tried to put the best spin I could on my answer. I knew she was only saying that to be together as a family. "Sure, sit down. But I don't think the kids are going to like it. It's supposed to start in 5 minutes. Can you get the kids some coloring books or something? I really think this won't be interesting to them."

Sally said nothing but went over to the book, and crayon box to find them.

Barnes's speech was no surprise. It was long, almost an hour and boring. He talked about his 24 years in the Senate. I think he went through every piece of legislation he ever passed in the Senate. He talked all about the past. He did not mention his two failed attempts at the nomination. He kept talking about his great relationships with past Senators, Presidents and world leaders.

I kept waiting to hear two things. Why I should vote for him to be my candidate, and what he was going to do about the nation's concerns and problems. I heard none of that in his speech. Barnes was not even a good speaker. It was bad enough he didn't say anything, but he did it in a monotonous tone that would put anyone to sleep. When it came to the end of his speech, Bill spoke almost matter of fact in his announcement to run for the nomination of his party. The band played, balloons were dropped, and that was it. This really shocked me. This is the guy Larry said could be our next President? Larry's political judgment just fell to a new low for me.

Next day at the office I couldn't wait to jump Larry about this wasted hour spent watching Barnes's speech. Larry, just grinned, sat down and was about to give me another political lesson.

"You have to understand something", Larry started out. I was always intrigued when he said that. "Bill Barnes thinks he is owed this nomination by the party. He thinks after all the years he's served the party that this time around, it's his turn. He's 70 years old and this will be his last hurrah and he is not expecting any opposition from within the party. I watched his speech too, Barnes speaks that way. My only fear is that he is over confident. But with Anderson's troubles, he knows he's ahead in the polls in spite of his dull and boring nature."

"But Larry", I interjected. "He didn't say anything. I mean what does he stand for? You talked about this trade problem with China, and the immigration trouble earlier. I want to know where Barnes stands on these things. I'm not going to support a guy just because he might be better than another guy." Listen to me the expert now. Larry didn't know how to answer me. He saw I was getting a bit agitated.

Larry said, "Let's just see what he says down the road. I'm sure he'll have to speak to these issues sooner or later."

Looking at my watch gave me the shot of reality I needed. We had to get back to work.

"Larry, we need to keep these conversations short and only at lunchtime, ok?"

Larry just nodded and left. He knew I was serious about returning to work.

I couldn't help but return to the question, what if some else ran? I'm an independent guy. I can make my own decisions. After all, I was in charge of the most important project the government has ever done in the election arena. I should be able to sort out all this political stuff.

There are more important issues to me in this race than just what Larry tells me, my family for one. What about the future of my kids? You tend to think of yourself and your wife until the kids come along. Then, they become the first thing you think of when dealing with the future, their education, job prospects, war, and opportunity for a good life. My job as a parent was to raise my children to be good citizens, and make sure they have all the opportunity needed to be successful in life. I guess that's where it matters who I vote for. Larry did me one favor. He made me realize voting is more important than I had considered before. Presidential candidates are chosen in primaries; therefore it is important to follow this process.

Feeling smug and confident in my rationalization, I was anxiously awaiting any further announcements. The Republican Party's nomination was wide open as far as I was concerned. Barnes may think he is owed the position, but with his announcement speech, I think there is room for others. We will see.

***

Needing a little more self assurance on the issues, I sought out Larry to ask him if we could have a drink after work, I had some questions on the issues. Larry jumped at the chance, thinking it an opportunity to smooth over Barnes's announcement speech.

Larry started out with a rehash of the 1992 election. He said "President Anderson had won his first election, in some people's minds, in a questionable manner, especially Republicans. After all, it isn't every election that is decided by the Supreme Court, a majority of which were appointed by Democrats. It came down to one state, Texas. The President had won Texas by only 824 votes out of over 9 million. Oh how I remember that fiasco. You had claims of fraud and cheating from both sides. State courts, legislators, and Federal courts all were getting into it.

The two candidates had hired well known, expensive attorneys, and before the election night had ended; were already setting up defense fund accounts to pay for a challenge. It was beginning to look like the American people wouldn't know who their President was going to be for some time."

I had remembered it was everywhere: television, radio, newspapers, and water cooler talk for weeks. But I wasn't that concerned. Frankly, I didn't know enough to be interested. I figured the right people would step up and sort it all out. Really, except for the Commander-in-Chief role, most lifers in the military were only concerned with what pay increase Congress would authorize. I remember the Republicans were bitter about the outcome of that election. I guess I would be too. It was like losing a basketball game on a questionable call from the referee in the last few seconds of play.

Larry continued with history. "Texas was close due to the increase in Hispanic immigrants. He said the whole Southwest part of the country was at risk for the Republicans because of this. It has to do with the Electoral College."

I had to admit my ignorance of the Electoral College to Larry. "Larry, I've heard of the Electoral College but I'm not quite sure how it works. Could you go over that for me?"

Larry explained the way the Electoral College worked, twice.

He patiently went over the fact that each State was assigned a number of electors. He then hit me with something I never knew about the census the government took every ten years. I could tell Larry was a bit frustrated in the fact that I didn't know why the census was originally mandated in the Constitution. He was speaking to me in a tone much like an elementary teacher would.

"You see Captain; there are 435 Congressmen in the House of Representatives. After the census is conducted, every ten years, the total population count is divided by the 435 congressional seats available. That number is then divided into the population of each State. The result is the number of Representatives each State is entitled to. Each State then adds two to that number, one for each of their Senators, and the total becomes that State's electoral vote. The total number of Representatives, 435, plus the total number of Senators, 100, equals 535. They gave 3 electoral votes to the District of Columbia some time ago, to come up with a total of 538 total electoral votes possible. When a candidate wins the popular vote from a State, they get all the electoral votes for that State. The Constitution says a candidate must have a majority of electoral votes to be elected. So, half plus 1 of 538 is 270. See? That's how Presidential elections are really won."

"I see. That's fascinating Larry. I understand now why candidates don't just go to the large States to get the popular vote. They need a mathematical formula to get those 270." Once Larry brought the math into it, 270 electoral votes to get elected, I was much more interested. I now saw it as a math problem, how to put the right states together by their electoral vote, and come up with the 270 to win.

Larry continued telling me the Democratic National Committee was not comfortable with Anderson's last election either. Texas had a large number of electoral votes that could just as well go back to the Republicans and give them the election next time. They held a meeting to come up with a strategy, like any political party would, to help shore up Anderson's electoral count for this election.

Larry learned what their strategy was, through his sources.

"The Democrats had decided, with Anderson's blessing, that they need more Hispanic votes in the Southwest to insure re-election, especially Texas."

Even I figured that out. But how were they going to accomplish it? Maybe a new Vice President was going to be chosen. After all Anderson never mentioned the Vice President by name in his announcement for re-election. In the back of my mind, I had this gnawing feeling about Larry and his so-called friends in high places. I was becoming really curious how a regular guy like Larry would have such contacts in the inner workings of a major political party.

Larry said "Vice President William Tierney had already done his duty in the last election. He was primarily picked the first time to help deliver Pennsylvania, which he accomplished in '92. The only time you ever hear from him was at election time. They seemed to bring him out of the closet, wind him up, and send him to Pennsylvania a dozen times. It is an important state, with its 27 electoral votes. It also has been in contention the last few Presidential Elections, but had went Democratic the last two elections."

The demographics, according to Larry, were definitely leaning for President Anderson and Vice President Tierney when it came to Pennsylvania. With Vice President Tierney's popularity there, it was all but conceded by the Republicans. The problem for Anderson will be that there are no Senators, Governors, or even Representatives in the Southwest states that could or would help him as vice presidential candidates.

Larry said "Here's where it gets interesting. The Anderson campaign, the Democratic National Committee (DNC), and the President himself, has agreed they will need a plan to bring the Hispanic voters over to the Anderson camp in bigger numbers. They are devising a Hispanic Strategy. The Democrats had long courted the Hispanic people through the OHD (Organization of Hispanic Descendants). The President and the DNC will join forces with the OHD in order to execute their Hispanic Strategy. The Hispanic Strategy will be comprised of many different elements.

One, using the Justice Department, the President would send U.S. Marshals to Texas to investigate voter registration practices in primarily

Hispanic areas. Two, he will send Democrat operatives and Civil Rights attorneys to Hispanic neighborhoods. There, they will endeavor to find and register as many people as possible. Three, he will continue to meet with Mexico's President Hernandez and the OHD, to find ways to encourage families to join their relatives, already in the United States. This last strategy has been quietly used over the past two years. It was used as a loophole in an executive order President Anderson issued to open immigration borders in the Southwest to Mexican citizens who had established families in the United States. The loophole, and how it is being used, has been discovered only recently by a group of conservatives. They are publicizing this problem in their conservative magazines. However, they haven't been able to get a major newspaper, or noteworthy politician to take up this story. It was considered too controversial and sensitive for anyone to stick their neck out for."

Larry was riveting with his inside knowledge; I wondered how he obtained such sensitive information.

Larry went to say. "Needless to say, this infuriated the Republicans. The President using the Justice Department, Mexico, OHD, and others to open immigration is seen as election vote buying and is rallying non-Hispanic Republicans nationwide. It seemed a fever of anti-immigration was not the intended consequence of the Democrats. As conservative commentators pounded home this story to their listening and reader faithful, a sense of outrage was swelling. Anderson is not helped in the polls by all this; he is suffering a notable drop in support amongst Independent voters."

I couldn't argue with Larry's analysis, I just didn't know how much of his information he got from his friends, was creditable. One thing I knew was that if I was going to play the electoral vote game with Larry, I needed more information.

It became obvious to me just what a political neophyte I was. The fact was, whether Larry had all these friends with insider information or not, I was lacking in basic political understanding. It was fascinating, listening and learning from Larry. I decided to start doing a lot more research on my own, so I could at least sound intelligent when talking to Larry.

Larry went on with his Civics lesson. He explained that the rising unemployment was a concern to the Democrat strategists. The unemployment rate was a key indicator to any campaign of trouble ahead. We had just come off four years of good economic times. It looked like a correction cycle was developing. Larry had preached to me good and bad economic times were always cycling and recycling. Sometimes they could be influenced and corrected by actions of a government and sometimes not. This depended on the previous administration and what actions they did or did not take. It generally took 12 to 18 months for any government action on the economy to take affect. Sometimes the economy had to wring out the bad factors, such as inflation, in order to recover, and it could a brutal time for anyone in power.

The administration in power at election time would reap the benefits of a good economy or take the blame for a bad one. Larry enlightened me with the two words that defined politics at election time; timing and perception. He said candidates are judged not by who they are, but who they are perceived to be. Timing is equated to issues. If the issues of the day are issues you are identified as being strong in, then you will succeed. That is why trying to force issues to your strengths can be dangerous and may even backfire.

That's what was beginning to happen on the economic front. President Anderson's opening up trade with China was not a big issue three years ago. After all, everybody was getting goods cheap. The consumer always looks for the cheapest price. Quality is a factor, but if the quality is viewed as acceptable, then the cheaper price item will always win out. In three short years, we were being inundated with goods from China.

Immigration, along with President Anderson's opening up trade with China, was beginning to back fire on the Democrat's campaign strategy. The Republicans were happy with the backlash and did nothing to calm the situation. The Republicans had majorities in the House and Senate, but were only giving lip service to the immigration and China issues. They saw this as a political win for them. They fully expected to benefit from this at the polls in November. They were comfortable in the thought that the white Democrats living in the Southwest, afraid of the invasion from Mexico, would break ranks and either vote Republican, or stay home and not vote at all.

This made me angry. For both political parties to play around with America's security and economy for their own gain was appalling to me.

I was still pretty naïve, however, and thought maybe this is necessary for the country in the big picture. Maybe it's for the good of the country and the majority of Americans. Who was I to question the United States government? They all can't be that way. Maybe they could.

The issue of China's massive imports, started three years ago by the Anderson administration, was coming home to roast, showing up in the unemployment figures. Stories emerged on conservative talk radio and TV about China and Mexico taking jobs from America. A constant barrage of talking points was being hammered over and over by the conservatives. Republicans now had a two-prong attack on Anderson. They were both pointing to the real third rail of American politics, that being JOBS. Social Security was long thought to be the so called third rail of American politics, an issue no politician in his right mind would attempt to change. But according to the polls Larry and I were watching, jobs seemed to be the overriding issue of this election.

Larry had told me about a friend who worked at Anderson's campaign headquarters. Seems this guy, although a low level college intern, had access to their meeting notes. This kid, I call everyone a kid under 30, was the son of one of Larry's old Navy buddies. He had told Larry, just a week ago, that the campaign was having a lot of meetings about the recent polls. There was a lot of shouting at these meetings and they weren't shouts of joy. Larry and I could only speculate that the Democrats were not happy with the immigration policies of their leader.

Larry was smiling like a Cheshire cat. I knew Larry was a Republican and was chomping at the bit to get on with the election. He was confident they would win if the election was held today. I anticipated his next statement. I told him, "Hold on Larry, you don't know who the Republican candidate is yet. He could be as bad as Anderson, even worse."

Larry said "nobody could be that bad."

"Not even Kline? I said.

Larry didn't say anything. I knew that rubbed him the wrong way.

"Look Captain, just wait until Barnes gives his speech on immigration, you will be pleasantly surprised."

Chapter 4 Who is My Candidate?

Not surprisingly, "None of The Above" was leading the latest Presidential poll. It seemed the whole country was thinking the same as me. The economy was slowing. There was a constant spewing of bad news by the major television new shows. I kept thinking somebody has to step up and lead the nation. I don't care if it was Barnes, Kline or Anderson. One of them had to have some solution. There really wasn't much of a choice; you had President Anderson who was sitting on a status quo platform. "Stay the course", he kept saying. *Yeah and the course is going to take us into a national recession.* I thought.

What about Senator Barnes and his plan? His speeches were all about agreeing with President Anderson on the China trade issue. He kept saying we need free, but fair trade. Barnes was one of the chief architects of the "China Free Trade" legislation. How was Barnes going to criticize Anderson on an issue he was responsible for enacting? Barnes seemed to be playing to the farmers from his home state, Nebraska, almost like he was running for the Senate again, not the Presidency. Trade to China was good for the farmers. They were able to sell their crops overseas and with agricultural supports and with the Export-Import Bank, they did not have to worry about getting paid. In the meantime for every million dollars in crop sales, China was importing a billion dollars worth of goods to the United States. OK. Maybe I didn't understand what did they call it on TV? Oh yeah, macro- economics, the big picture. All I know is that the economy was getting worse and nobody seemed to have a clue how to fix it.

What about the other big issue in the news, immigration. I knew from Larry and his contacts how the Democrats were using the Hispanic strategy. But what did Barnes think? I'll wait until lunch and nail Larry with that one. His boy, Barnes, is going to need some defending.

Lunchtime came at the smoking patio, and Larry didn't show. If he was busy working I didn't want to take him away from something important. I continued to eat and finished my lunch. It was one of the small things I looked forward to everyday. Sally would pack me a lunch everyday without fail. The project was keeping me at the office until 9:00 and sometimes 10:00 at night. I didn't get home until midnight most nights. Sally, being the thoughtful domestic homemaker she was, would always have leftover supper in the fridge for me. Every morning I could count on finding my lunch in the fridge, right where I had found my supper the night before. She was such a good wife and a good person that I sometimes wondered why I was so fortunate in having her as my wife.

Frankly, I married her, primarily due to her being such a good person. She was one of those women somc would call a Stepford Wife. Not in my eyes. She was kind, generous, and someone you trust. She spent her whole day raising our children, cleaning, cooking, and handling all of the bills. I don't know how she found time for her church activities. She was active in choir, Ladies Guild, and the Love Fund for the needy. I suppose that helped her in the evenings when I was at work. She even dragged the kids to all her meetings. She said it was a better influence than getting a baby sitter and watching television all night. There were times I felt I needed to attend church more, if only for her sake.

I didn't see Larry at lunch the rest of the week. Except at staff meetings, he was conspicuously absent at our lunch time sessions. A project as important as ours, the Presidential Election, had to be kept first in our priorities. The staff was reporting every detailed task and nothing but successful results were occurring. That kept all the higher-ups happy, especially Minster. Frankly, Minster was the only person I wanted to please. He was my boss and had a personality that was to say the least unique. I understood that, but he still scared the hell out of me. There was something about him, I couldn't say exactly what yet, but something that made me not only uncomfortable, but nervous.

Settling down to another of Sally's lunches, I saw Larry coming onto the patio.

"How's it going Larry?"

"Fine", Larry said. He sat down and opened his lunch on the bench. It was like he never missed a session.

"Can we watch Barnes after lunch? He's on C-Span again, speaking to the Organization of Hispanic Descendants." I knew this was Larry's way of saying; see, I told you he would address the immigration issue. He knew I didn't have a television in the office, but that we could get C-Span live through the internet. I was just as anxious as Larry to see what Barnes had to say, but I played it down.

"Sure, if that's what you want to see."

After lunch we went into my office and closed the door. I had Larry find the live feed from C-Span on the internet.

Barnes was introduced by the President of the Organization of Hispanic Descendants, Felix Ortega, to lukewarm applause. I could tell the lack of enthusiasm was pleasing to Larry. Barnes then launched into a history of people of Hispanic descent, and their contributions to America. I think this was an effort to gain a little support from the crowd; otherwise, this could get awkward real fast. After what seemed like his naming of every person of Hispanic descent that helped develop our country, Barnes moved into his main topic, immigration. He continued in a historical mode touting the benefits immigration had brought to America. How the Irish and Chinese had built the railroads, and the hard working farmers and machinists from Germany. The great melting pot of America that started and grew the businesses in the east, and the pioneers that crossed the vast deserts and settled the west, all helped build America. How, without immigration, we would not be enjoying the fruits of their labors today. I was getting bored.

I thought, *Ok, what about today, Senator? What about curbing the illegal ones? They are putting such a strain on local government's infrastructure. How about all the jobs they are taking?*

My attention returned as Barnes continued, "We need immigrants. We need people who want to assimilate into America to feel welcome. We have too many situations where families are kept apart by rules that are too strict. It is absolutely immoral to keep families separated. We need a way to bring families together but in a controlled manner. I understand how difficult it is for some of the families longing to be united. Just like the Germans of East Berlin longing to be with their loved ones; many will risk breaking the law to obtain freedom. While I can't condone these actions, I understand their motivation. I know we all share those family values that has made America great. The Hispanic people have always been known as a hard working people. Let's be honest.

Some complain about losing jobs to immigrants. We here know that most jobs taken by immigrants are those jobs that would go wanting anyway. The truth of the matter is most people doing the complaining wouldn't do those jobs anyway." The crowd was now receptive. Barnes was receiving large amounts of applause at these lines.

I looked at Larry in disbelieve.

Larry read my face and said, "I don't like it either Gary. But the Republicans have to fight for the Southwest. They need California and Texas. If they lose any more minority votes there, they are going to lose for sure."

I clicked off the television signal on my computer. Shock and disgust filled my head. Larry quietly left without a comment.

I didn't know it at the time, but it became known later that the Republicans were just as upset with that speech as I was. Barnes's speech came out of left field, literally. The party had wanted Barnes to walk a fine line between encouraging and condemning immigration. They wanted to keep a large voting block in the Southwest at least neutral. This would ensure them a chance to get just enough votes from both the Hispanic and non-Hispanic groups to win California and Texas.

***

The Republican Party was in a quandary. They had felt the election was theirs to lose. The China trade and immigration issues were leading the polls by the American people. The people were quite concerned about their effects on jobs.

The party was now beginning to doubt the candidate to run on these issues was Bill Barnes. They decided to search for another candidate, but very quietly, almost secretly. The search would have to include criteria not only of someone more issue sensitive, but someone who was liked by the voters. A big state with a large number of electoral votes was definitely needed. If they were going to possibly lose Texas, they needed a state of comparable size in electoral votes. At least the 32, they were going lose.

The only person and state that fit that requirement was New York. It not only had 33 electoral votes, but it also had a popular Republican

Governor. A bonus was the fact the state normally went Democrat in Presidential elections, but Republican Governor Powell won it with over 60 percent in both of his runs for that office. A switch in New York from Democratic to Republican would give the Republicans a big boost in winning the Presidency.

The biggest problem facing these party king makers was how to persuade Jay Powell to run. They knew Powell had his sights set on running for the Senate. Since he was limited to two terms as Governor, this last year Powell had let it be known to the party, he was definitely interested in the Senate seat being vacated by Michael Sanchez. He did this early enough to discourage having a primary fight.

Michael Sanchez was a Republican, but not considered so by New Yorkers. The people of New York saw Sanchez more as an Independent person, neither Liberal nor Conservative. He was a popular four-term Senator who brought home the bacon to New York. Sanchez was not afraid to take on anyone, Democrat or Republican Presidents, when it came to serving his state. It helped Powell tremendously that Sanchez gave his word he would endorse him when the time came. Not only would an endorsement help, but the fact that Sanchez carried New York City's heavily Hispanic vote couldn't hurt either.

Gov. Powell was a not a favorite of the Conservatives either in New York or nationally. This was due to the fact that he had well known liberal stands on social issues such as abortion, gay marriage etc. These did not sit well with the conservative wing of the Republican Party. He was, however, from a big state the Republicans would need to win and more importantly he had taken a stand against the China trade policy of the Anderson administration.

Powell could not be pinned down on his views about immigration. He had said little, if anything at all, on the topic. The party felt this was not a detriment because of the Sanchez endorsement. He could walk the fine line needed on that topic.

The Republican National Committee chair, along with other trusted members, such as Senate heavy weight Senator Damon Larson met with Gov. Powell privately. Whatever they did, they were able to persuade Powell to run.

Gov. Powell's people called the media and asked them to attend Powell's announcement of his intention to seek the Republican Party's nomination for President. It would be held at Ellis Island, in his home state of New York. It would culminate with a photo opportunity at the Statue of Liberty. How interesting, I thought, another Republican pandering to the issue of immigration. I wondered to myself how long it would be before all the candidates, President Anderson, Senator Barnes, and Gov. Powell, were giving the exact same stump speeches on immigration.

It was reported out of Senator Barnes's camp that the Senator welcomed the competition and they would have a good discussion of the issues. What else was he going to say, that the party was about to screw him again? Senator Barnes wasn't concerned. He knew he still held a number of loyal delegates especially when it came to the at-large delegates. All the party's elected officials, the House, and Senate members were automatically at-large delegates in their states. These were the people who owed Barnes big time. Barnes had given them money and campaign support over the years, and felt they owed him their loyalty.

The Democrats were mulling over the affect their stand on immigration had on those non-Hispanic voters in the immigration troubled states. They were comfortable with Barnes. Even as Barnes was trying to appeal to the Hispanic people, they knew full well they would not be deserted by the core groups their party represented. But Ray Kline, that was a different story. The Democrat's nervousness soon abated. They rationalized that even if Kline were to become the candidate, they would more than likely receive stronger support from the Hispanic community. It would be nice for them also if the Republicans were to have a contentious and divisive primary. The only caveat was that Barnes and Kline would split the vote and allow Powell to win. The Democrats were more afraid of Powell, as a moderate, than Barnes or Kline.

The Republican Party's worry was more of a practical one. They knew that primaries are often won by the more ideological wing of the party. The ideological wing of any party has an intensity that cannot be matched by any pragmatic campaign strategy. Barnes and Powell could split the vote and Kline would have a solid base of supporters who could get out the vote for him. I bet the lights were burning late at the RNC that night.

Then again, a case could be made that Kline was too conservative and would in all likelihood shoot himself in the foot. On one hand, the RNC figured Kline had the fire and emotion and could stir up the troops, but on the other hand he had said and written many controversial things. For now, the party would not say anything negative about Kline. They didn't want to alienate the conservatives. They needed them. Not only that, they didn't need to say anything. The mainstream press will do it for them. The thinking was, the party can disavow Kline's more controversial remarks without losing a lot of the conservatives.

Kline, at first blush, had all the qualities you would want in a primary race. In general you want someone who is a good speaker, has decent physical looks, has a strong core of supporters, and is genuinely liked by the voters. Kline had all these qualities and one more thing. He had the pulse of the American people when it came to the issues of the day. Speculation was that Kline announced he had launched an exploratory committee to only have an influence on the party's platform. That was the line leaked to the press by the RNC. It was an attempt to say Kline was not a serious candidate. The RNC had hoped this would put a damper on Kline supporters so they wouldn't send him money. Without money, the mother's milk of politics, no candidate can be taken seriously.

Barnes was trying to be Anderson and Powell was walking the tight rope on immigration trying to be all things to all people.

Kline had decided to make his announcement an opportunity to obtain free publicity and make a veiled appeal for funds; rather than a photo opportunity. Trying to pick a home state was a bit difficult for Kline. He had been in Washington D.C. so long; working for various departments of government, he had a hard time convincing anyone he was a native of a particular state. Although Kline was actually from Baltimore Maryland, he decided to give his announcement address from Washington D.C. He figured he might be seen as a fraud if he claimed to be from Maryland, so why not just look Presidential and make the announcement from the heart of the seat of the United States Government.

Kline was quite interesting in his announcement speech. He not only talked about issues, but actually told the people how his campaign was going to operate. I thought *this is odd. I never heard the other candidates talk about campaign strategy. Maybe it was his way of letting people know he was serious about the race.*

He told the viewers he had secured initial financing from friends and family, he hired election law attorneys, and was sending out fund raising letters. His fund raising list was purchased from Robert Wigent, the most successful conservative fundraiser of all time. Getting Robert Wigent, I was told later, was a very big thing. Wigent was well known in political circles as man who could really raise the money. Kline also told us his attorneys were busy obtaining ballot position either through petition drives or law suits if necessary. Taking a slap at the RNC and the rest of the Republican establishment, he told us this would be needed to counter the party trying to prevent him from getting on all the states' ballots.

Maybe I did have a candidatc I could support after all.

Larry was involved with setting up our ballot machine software all week. He had to travel a lot with these tasks. I spent my lunchtime reading up on Kline through the internet. He was definitely different. He had written a lot of articles through the years. A paper trail I know that I would not want. I could see that some of these articles could come back to haunt him.

My curiosity was peeked with Kline's America First theme, which ran through all of his writings. Doing a search on immigration, gave me tons of material Kline had written on the subject. He had foreseen the oncoming problem with Mexico years before. How it would be not only a problem, but more of an invasion of the United States. How it would be used to traffic drugs, and even terrorists into our country. At the time, Kline appeared to another Senator McCarthy, but was more correct than people like to admit.

His opinions on trade with China were just as prolific. Kline had warned the United States government that opening up uncontrolled trade with China would result in dire consequences with our economy. I thought, *this guy's got it right. He's the only one who knows what's going on. Why the big concern over him as President?* I searched for Kline's web page next. I was excited to see he had one already. Reading everything I could find, I must admit I was becoming a fan of Ray Kline.

Kline's website had a page with campaign chairs and volunteers. It made me feel Kline might not be as forthcoming as I was led to believe. He had to have known he was going to run all along to set up all these chairman and volunteers so quickly. But, with his politics of America

First, his warning over the years of immigration problems, and his stand on exporting jobs to China he had caught my attention.

The first polls out on the internet since Kline announced showed him running behind Barnes and Powell. What was interesting was that the poll breakdown showed Kline had developed a following not only among conservative Republicans, but now he was connecting to moderate and conservative Democrats as well as Independents. Still, third is third. But, with Barnes at 32%, Powell 27%, Kline 20% and undecided at 21%, the race was far from being a done deal. Kline's comment on this poll was that he had a lot more of the undecided vote than people might think. He had developed a true Populist message and it was resonating.

***

Senator Damon Larson, the chief negotiator at the Gov. Powell for President Movement, was still worried about the Kline candidacy.

Larson was pondering the possibilities of a Kline candidacy when he got the call from Ralph Sampson, the Chairman of the Republican National Committee.

Sampson requested Larson's help in persuading Powell to get into the race. His thinking, however, was more the terrible poll numbers Barnes was receiving. Sampson was not concerned about Kline, likening him to a temporary blimp on the radar screen. Sampson stressed to Senator Larson the need to have an alternative to Senator Barnes.

Senator Larson agreed, but cautioned Sampson to not dismiss Kline out of hand. Larson had a keen sense of politics when it came to judging the mood of the voters. The voters were not happy with President Anderson and definitely did not want a clone of him as their next President.

Larson asked Sampson to keep tabs on Kline's poll numbers and inform him immediately of any surge towards Kline. Larson didn't want to seem panicked to Sampson and assured him that the Party's candidate would eventually be either Senator Barnes or Gov. Powell, but keep an eye on Kline none the less.

Chapter 5 Surprise in the Primary

Looks like President Anderson will let the Republicans beat each other up. Anderson's a smart man and will continue to look Presidential as long as the Republicans look anything but. Anderson continued to have photo opportunities in the rose garden, signing feel good legislation. Who could be against school lunch subsidies? Or how about day care centers? Warm and fuzzy, this was the image being put out by the Anderson's campaign. A lot of these bills seemed to come to the President's desk just as the Republican primary season was starting. I wondered out loud, *if the Congress was controlled by the Republicans, why would they be giving the incumbent President all these good news stories?*

When I saw Barnes at the bill signing, my question was answered. Barnes, being the leader of the Senate, could control when legislation was brought up for a vote. He is trying to get as much good press as the President is. It looked to me that Barnes was more afraid of Powell, a fellow moderate, than the conservative Kline. It's probably why Barnes seems to be positioning himself closer to President Anderson.

The early primaries favored Barnes. The Republicans had combined Iowa, New Hampshire, and South Carolina into the first test of the candidates. Iowa was a farm state that fit well into Barnes's farm state strategy. New Hampshire was close to New York and an Eastern state, but was nothing like New York demographically. The people of New Hampshire were very independent. Although not a farm state, Barnes had good support amongst the Congressman and Senators from that state.

South Carolina could take the initial wind out of Barnes's sails. It had a good number of conservatives and was being severely affected by China imports of textile goods. Kline was campaigning hard in South Carolina. Kline was appealing to the textile workers. He was hoping to overcome Barnes's Republican advantage by getting these normally Democratic voters to cross over. With President Anderson having no party opposition, Kline was trying to appeal to Democrats in states with high unemployment like South Carolina.

This is exactly what happened. Barnes carried Iowa and New Hampshire convincingly as Kline swept through South Carolina. This must have sent a bad message to the Barnes' campaign. Maybe Kline was a force to be dealt with. Gov. Powell was not as concerned. He saw his strength coming later in the Eastern and Midwestern states. In the next group of primary states, you had Florida and Georgia, where Kline was working hard. Colorado and Minnesota were next, states that were friendly to Powell. Rhode Island was a slam dunk for Powell. Another state that day was Barnes's home state of Nebraska.

It seemed to take forever to get to the primaries. I was anxiously awaiting them. I had started a sheet with the states and their number of delegates, columns of totals after each set of primaries, with the candidate's names at the top. I put together spreadsheets for everything. It was naturally what a computer person would do, making it easier to follow the race. Rhode Island and Nebraska came in as expected.

Barnes surprised everyone by taking Florida, Minnesota and Colorado. Florida was projected to be close by the pundits. Minnesota and Colorado were supposed to be strong for Powell. All the pundits were being proven wrong. Barnes was running away with these early states. I didn't know much about politics, but one thing I did know is momentum. Whether it's sports or politics, momentum is the precursor to a bandwagon effect. The other interesting result was Kline winning Georgia.

I was getting disappointed by the day. I had hoped these primaries would be a diversion from the project. It was something to look forward to week after week, like watching a close football game quarter after quarter.

Our election project was coming in ahead of time. The setup of all the computers was going well in the five states, and they were all tying together nicely here at the Department of Defense. We were going to be ready for the big show Election Day. Larry was busy traveling to all five states, making sure each state was ready with their voter lists and registrations. I was definitely missing Larry and our lunchtime political chats. I wasn't waiting for Larry any more; I was seeking out information on my own. I was going to be ready for Larry when he returned again. I was no longer going to be politically naïve.

My wife Sally sure wasn't interested in politics, not at all. Fact Sally saw all politicians as something less than honorable. Her role models were the pastor and members of our church. "At least", she said, "They were helping people and not taking money for it." I guess she had a point, simple as it was, but somebody's going to get elected President and to the Congress. These people will affect our lives whether we like it or not. I might as well be informed and have a choice in who that's going to be. I'll wait for the next set of states and see who does well and who doesn't.

The media's political opinion talking heads, as well as the major political experts were predicating big wins for Gov. Powell in New York, Wisconsin, and Michigan. In addition, there were two southern states that same week, North Carolina and Alabama. Nobody said a thing about these states, I wondered why. If they were right about Powell's ability to win some big states, then we might just have a race after all.

I anxiously watched as the returns were reported. Gov. Powell had won his home state of New York, barely beating Barnes. By barely beating Barnes in his home state, Powell had to be nervous about his chances elsewhere. Barnes carried Wisconsin handily. Barnes just had too many loyal delegates, especially the Republican House and Senate members who stuck by him. All the political experts were now singing Powell's political death knell. He was essentially through as a candidate having won only one of the big states available this week. Powell's campaign staff knew the race would move to the South and West, where their man was not strong. Powell's strategy was to carry enough big Midwestern states that would total enough delegates to make him competitive. Even I could see Powell had no chance to get enough delegates to stay in the race. Besides it was getting close to filing for the Senate in New York and he didn't want to go into that race looking like a loser. Rumor was if Powell didn't win New Jersey, he was pulling his staff and money to get ready for the Senate race.

The upsets that happened that week were big, but still not as big as Kline's win in Michigan! Everyone was looking toward Barnes and Powell to be fighting it out for Michigan. What they missed was Kline's crossover appeal to the Democrats. In addition, mid week, Kline picked up a majority of the delegates in North Carolina and Alabama. Ray Kline had not campaigned much in the Midwest. He counted on a South and Southwestern strategy, but he did spend a lot of time in Michigan because of their blue collar conservative workers, hoping they would cross over. They did. Michigan was a Democrat stronghold, but it was also home to the moderate wing of the Republican Party. Barnes had counted on this moderate wing to win the state for him. The media had been reporting Kline was not a serious candidate because of his appeal to the more conservative Democrats in Michigan. They all reported that Kline was just trying to move Barnes into a more conservative position on the issues. All that stopped when, out of the blue, Ray Kline carried Michigan. The political professionals would have to rethink their opinion of Ray Kline.

***

At the Barnes campaign headquarters all the talk was focused on Kline's win in Michigan. Barnes's team was disappointed their man was not able to carry the state. What they were impressed with was the fact that Kline had beat Barnes and Powell. Michigan was a state that traditionally provided a win for the more moderate wing of the Republican Party. Many argued Barnes and Powell had split the moderate Republican vote, allowing Kline to reap the benefit.

Barnes's chief pollster, Joe Valley, had a different take after analyzing the returns in detail.

"You know Kline didn't win by Powell and us splitting the moderate vote. He won with the cross over Democrats. Take a look at these exit polls we did. See, close to half of all Kline's votes came from crossover voters. The Senator asked me to bring these exit interviews over to him as soon as I got them. I'm going now."

Joe went to the Senators office at the back of the headquarters. The door was open and Barnes could be seen reading the newspaper. Joe went right in.

"Senator, I have those exit polls from the Michigan race here."

"Great Joe, sit down and let's go over them. How bad is it?"

"Well the good news is that we beat Powell soundly."

"And the bad news?" asked Barnes.

"I don't think you could call it bad news Senator. Kline won with a significant Democrat cross over vote. If he wasn't there we would have won the state."

"But Joe, he was there. And I do call it bad news. It doesn't bode well for us when your opponent is attracting Democrat voters. Kline has a number of states coming up in which he will do well. I think this thing might tighten up."

"True Senator, but I have to point out the state's he's strong in are small and regional. Looking at the big picture I think we will have the nomination locked up with California."

"I am looking at the big picture, Joe. Not the nomination, hell I know we have that. It's the general election that bothers me. With Kline out of the picture where do you think those cross over Democrat voters are going to go? They are going right back home to Anderson. Joe I know you're the pollster and not the campaign manager, but I value your opinion. What do you think the polls would show if the general election tickets were Anderson/Tierney and Barnes/Kline?"

"Kline! You're not seriously considering Ray Kline for your running mate are you?"

"I asked you a question Joe."

Joe paused to think over his answer. Should he give the Senator his personal opinion, or his professional advice as a pollster? "Senator to be honest as much as I personally don't like it, a Barnes/Kline ticket, under the current climate in the country, would be a winner."

"That's what I think too Joe. Thanks, that's all."

***

As the campaign moved South and West, Gov. Powell knew he was out of it and seriously scaled back his campaign schedule. Ray Kline was doing well in the South but the Southern states didn't have as many delegate votes as the Midwest and the Northeast. Michigan was a unique state with its crossover laws and large number of Conservative Democrats, there would be no other Midwest possibilities like it for

Kline. Ray Kline was picking up steam and more importantly delegates in the South and Southwest, while Barnes was steadily adding to his total in Middle America.

The nomination looked like it was in the hands of the California voters. They would be voting in June with their ten percent of the delegate votes. It had boiled down to Senator Barnes and Ray Kline.

The closer Ray Kline inched to Senator Barnes; the more Kline cranked up the rhetoric. He seemed almost out of control as he called for a thousand mile wall across the Southwest manned by guards armed to shoot potential border violators. He continued his campaign against trade with China by announcing he would stop all importing of goods made in China unless large tariffs were imposed. Tough talk yes. But Kline carried Arizona, New Mexico and Nevada. Kline had his hopes pinned on the backlash of white, blue-collar Democrats in those states, generated because of immigration problems. You could say Kline was playing on the fears and prejudice of people, whatever the reason, it was working for Kline. Combine those victories in the Southwest with the Southern states he was doing well in, plus Idaho in the Northwest, and he was now a serious contender.

All eyes were now on Texas. Texas was one of those states that nationally had been won by both the Democrats and Republicans over the last four elections. It was a true swing state. The Democrats had started their Hispanic strategy last year and were working hard to deliver Texas for President Anderson again in the General Election, but this time by an unquestionable margin. No more Supreme Court decisions needed thank you.

The Republican primary was going to be trickier. While Texas was not affected by the economy as much as the rest of the nation, it was a border state of Mexico and the talk of immigration was hot. It seemed ripe for the picking by Kline. Barnes was campaigning in the large cities, hoping to draw the suburbanites to his rallies. The large city rallies were chosen by Barnes staff in hopes to garner some ethnic votes to his side. Kline stuck to his suburban and rural strategy, getting conservative Republicans and Democrats to join his America First crusade.

The night of the Texas primary I was glued to my computer screen. I had my spreadsheet out looking for all the possibilities a win by Kline would bring. I thought, *What if? What if Kline wins Texas? Boy oh boy, that would put Kline close enough to Barnes to bring the election down to California.* The returns were coming in fast and furious. Barnes won the larger cities of Texas, where most of the population was, but Kline had managed to win a large portion of the suburbs and a great deal of the rural counties that had a small Hispanic population. These gave Kline just enough of a percentage to win the at large delegates as well as a majority of county delegates. "*Yes"!* I screamed. *We now have a real race,* I said to myself. I was chomping at the bit waiting for the California primary election.

Just before the Republican primary in California the Republican National Committee chairman, Ralph Sampson, in conjunction with the Barnes campaign staff, was starting to leak excerpts from Kline's books. Written years ago, these books contained some paragraphs that could be interpreted as not very favorable to minorities, even racist by some.

Sampson saw the potential for Kline to win the nomination and as a loyal Republican didn't want the party to suffer for years to come like Barry Goldwater's candidacy did in 1964. It was a sign they were desperate to stop Kline. When I did that same research on Kline, I admit I was also bothered by some of his writings, but what the hell; we needed someone to shake things up. I confess I was now leaning to Kline myself. I was caught up with the game more than looking at the man's content of his character. It didn't occur to me, at the time of these primaries, but electing a President is serious business not just a football game.

June came quickly and I was looking forward to the California primary. Since President Anderson had no opposition, it was possible to see many cross over voters from the Democrats to the Republican race. I figured it could have a big impact. The unknown factor was what type of voter would cross over and for what purpose? If Kline could get a large amount of conservative Democrats to turn out, he might have a chance to beat Barnes. I had learned my lesson watching returns from other states; you didn't know where the votes were coming from when they were reported. The bigger cities tended to favor Barnes while the rural and suburban cities voted for Kline in heavier numbers.

California's primary numbers were starting to roll in shortly after 9:00 PM. Most of the television stations were predicting a win for

Barnes, according to their exit polling. My wife, Sally, had put the kids to bed at 8:00 PM and joined me in the family room. Hearing the reporter's pronouncement of a Barnes victory was her excuse for nodding off to sleep. I should have awakened her and ushered her off to bed, but I still held out hope that Kline would pull an upset. It was close to midnight when the final verdict was clear; Barnes had won with 47% of the vote, Kline managed 39%, and Powell 14%. It was over. Since California was a winner take all state, Barnes was assured of winning all the delegates, and therefore the nomination. I shook Sally, quite vigorously, and told her it was time to go to bed. She must have had some interest because her first reaction was "Who won?" I told her Barnes had won California and locked up the nomination, her only response was "Oh, that's good, Right?" It was too late to get into an argument with her about my feelings for Barnes and Kline, so I replied, "Well, it's good for Barnes."

***

Two months later, the primary elections finished, it was time for the Party's Conventions to start. August 10th 1996, the Republican convention was convening in Atlanta, Georgia.

I had managed to put the whole Presidential Election out of my mind for two whole months, concentrating on the election project as my first priority.

Even Larry didn't bother me much about it, realizing we had a project to complete regardless of who the candidates were. Our project was going smooth, the best any project I had ever worked on. So smooth, I kept waiting for something to go wrong. The last meeting with my staff to go over our status of the project gave me such confidence that I was looking forward to watching the Republican Convention this week.

Gov. Powell officially released his delegates and gave his endorsement to Barnes right after the California election, but Kline still held his delegates and has said very little about whether he would release them or not.

The first night of the Convention coverage, was all about what Kline and his delegates would do. In the Barnes camp the report was they were trying to figure out a way not to alienate the Kline supporters and possibly get Kline to endorse Barnes, however talk was actively pointing to a possible 3rd party run by Kline's delegates at the convention.

The Kline delegates were mad their candidate had lost. They were basically regular people, not professional politicians, who were wedded to a man and a cause. Angry conservatives who were already talking about the possibility of not only walking out of the convention, but starting a third party for Kline.

The media was having a field day with some of the more outspoken Kline delegates. This kind of controversy was right up their alley. Television reporters on the floor of the convention were interviewing every Kline delegate they could find. The wackier the story, the better the media loved it. And there were enough wacky ones there to pick from. You had people advocating the Southwest states succeeding from the Union. Others were trying to explain to the *New York Times* reporter why income taxes were illegal. NBC even found one, as serious as he could be, explaining that the 2nd Amendment allowed him to own a tank! There were sane and rational Kline delegates there, but the media wouldn't seek them out for interviews. They wouldn't make good television. It was like the circus had come to town. To be fair I did see that there were some reporters and television crews concentrating on the more practical and political aspects of Kline's success and how it might affect Barnes's campaign for President.

Would Kline's delegates walk out? Would they form a 3rd party? The more moderate Republican National Committee members were more concerned at the moment with who Barnes would select to be his running mate. They thought about Gov. Powell. Could Powell deliver New York was the big question. If so they would have a good shot of winning in November. They thought maybe picking a conservative would help smooth over the Kline delegates. No, they eventually concluded there wasn't anything that would satisfy the Kline people unless it was Kline himself who was chosen to be the Vice Presidential running mate with Senator Barnes. The elders of the party had to admit to themselves, the real problem was they had nobody to pick from that would help them win a state they needed. They needed somebody from Texas, California, or Michigan, but there was nobody.

***

Ralph Sampson, the Republican National Committee chairman, was beside himself. He was worried the convention was turning into the Ray Kline show. Sampson called a meeting of his most trusted committeemen to find a solution. He began sternly, "We're looking like idiots with this Kline thing. We've got to find somebody now and leak it so that becomes the story, not Kline. I don't care if it's a dog catcher from Wyoming. We've got to get this done and done *NOW*!"

Pete Williamson, a committeeman from Ohio, spoke up, "I don't see we have much of a choice. We need Powell. I know he will not quiet the Kline people, but he has a shot at delivering New York for us."

Sampson shot back, "You go and tell that mob we're picking Powell and see what happens."

Williamson shot back, "You got a better idea? I'm all ears."

Sampson polled the rest of the party chiefs there. Nobody could think of another possibility. Sampson concluded with "I guess Powell is our only choice. If there's no objection I'm going over to see Powell and run it by him."

"You want anybody to come with you?" asked Williamson. "It might show Powell there's a movement developing behind our suggestion".

"No. I'll go alone. Jay and I go way back. I think he'll listen to me. I guess there really is nobody else for Vice President."

Ralph Sampson made his way over to Gov. Powell's suite, confident he and the group had made the right decision on a Vice-Presidential candidate. *They wanted, no needed Gov. Powell*, he thought to himself, he was trying to come up with the right approach, the right words to say to Powell. Sampson knew this would be a hard sell to Powell. The Governor had a clear shot at being elected Senator from New York and what he was going to be asked to do would certainly put that into jeopardy.

Sampson had found the right words and approach. He would play hardball. If Powell refused to accept the nomination, Sampson was prepared to blackmail him into taking it. If he didn't agree to take the VP slot, there would be no money or support from the National Senate Election Committee, which Sampson held the purse strings on, coming

Powell's way. Powell felt betrayed after hearing Sampson's proposal. He had been offered Sampson's support for the Senate race after Powell dropped out of the Presidential race and gave his support and delegates to Barnes. Powell had no choice. With no money or support coming from the National Party, he knew his race for the Senate was all but finished.

After confirming Gov. Powell would accept the position, Sampson headed over to talk to Senator Barnes.

What Sampson didn't know was that Barnes had been working on his own choice for his running mate. He had his campaign staff busy conducting their own polls, showing the strongest team would be a Barnes-Kline ticket. Not very happy with having to choose Kline, none the less Barnes had given this quite a bit of consideration. The advantages he was thinking about were conservative money and lots of enthusiastic campaign workers. He concluded he would be able to handle most of Kline's loyal followers but not all of them. However, he thought he would still be the Presidential candidate, not Kline. Barnes thought he could control Kline if he controlled the Vice President's functions. Any speech, appearance, or interview by the Vice President would have to be cleared through the President's office. Barnes and his staff felt with this type of control over Kline, plus getting Kline to sign such an agreement, they would be able to use Kline and his supporters for their own purpose.

Sampson called the Barnes' suite and was invited up. To his shock, Barnes came out with it no sooner than Ralph had stepped into the room. Barnes's choice would be Ray Kline for Vice President. A Barnes/Kline ticket would be a winner in Barnes's mind.

Sampson pleaded and begged with Barnes, but to no avail. Barnes was sure this would be the way to win. He tried to assure Sampson he would have total control over Kline and would not offer him the position unless Kline agreed to his terms. Sampson left very concerned and upset.

Sampson quickly made his way over to see Senator Larson. Damon Larson was one of the most experienced political operatives in the Senate. He was also the most knowledgeable man the Republicans had on national election tactics. Sampson explained to Larson what had just transpired.

"Damon, what are we going to do? The man's a loose cannon waiting to go off."

Larson replied, "Now he's our loose cannon. Like it or not. If Barnes's set on him, I don't see we have much of a choice. The campaign is going to be tough. I guess the only thing we can do is find a way to help Barnes control Kline."

Sampson could only sigh and say, "God help us."

***

Barnes called Ray Kline and asked him to meet him in his suite at the hotel. Barnes had his most trusted aides with him for moral support, and he was ready to layout the law to Kline. Should he accept Barnes offer to be his running mate.

Barnes had a controlling nature that his campaign staff and even friends knew not to get in the way of. They were fully prepared to let him do all the talking. Kline and his campaign manager were ushered into a room that obviously was once a bedroom and now converted into a small office. There was just enough room for Barnes, Kline, and their staff to sit.

Barnes opened the conversation, "Ray, I know we have had our differences in the past. I realize some things were said in the heat of battle over the last few months, but I have put those things behind me and I hope you can do the same."

Barnes didn't wait for an acknowledgment by Kline. Kline just nodded in agreement. He was going to wait and see where Barnes was going with this meeting before he agreed to anything else.

Barnes was a little surprised Kline had only nodded. He thought *Ray was never at a loss for words.* Barnes realized Ray was waiting for the bottom line to this meeting and wasn't going to commit to anything until he knew the whole reason for the meeting. Barnes then decided to just come out with it and offered him the place on the ticket only under the strictest parameters. Kline was stunned. He had thought the reason for the meeting was for Barnes to find a way to get his endorsement.

Kline replied, "I'm shocked Bill. I thought the only reason you had me come over was to get my supporters on your side. I don't know what to say."

Barnes continued, "Ray there are some conditions." Barnes went on to insist that Ray would only deliver Barnes' team approved speeches on the campaign trail. He was also to give no interviews one on one with reporters. Barnes would also have final say on any appearances Kline made.

Barnes concluded with, "If you cannot or will not agree to these things then this meeting is over."

Kline was silent. He was mulling over the conditions to himself.

Kline finally looked up at Barnes and said, "Bill, we see the issues so differently, I can't see how I'm going to help win this election. I mean my people are not mind numb robots. They're going sit home unless they hear from me. Not only hear from me but it's what they won't hear that will turn them off."

Barnes replied, "I understand that Ray. I think we both have staffs smart enough to tailor your speeches to accomplish both our goals. Besides you need to be elected first to do anything, right?" Finally, Kline agreed to Barnes's terms.

In Kline's mind however, he had no intention of following these demands. He mulled this over in his mind. *I'm not a politician, I'm an America first. Barnes was right about one thing*, Ray mused. *You have to get elected first and Barnes just doesn't get it. He doesn't know how to get elected. I do. Let them think they're in charge. I'll know who's really in charge.*

After the convention closed everyone went home and tried to figure out how this ticket could be sold to the voters. The conservatives had to swallow Barnes, the party regulars and the moderates had to find a way to play down the Kline factor. The delegates as a whole were not fired up. Conventions normally create an upswing in the polls for a candidate, but not in this case. This was one of the few conventions in history when the whole Party was disappointed.

***

Just before the grueling campaign was to get under way, Barnes's staff insisted he get a complete physical examination mainly to prevent any speculation about his ability to do the job as President due to his age. Although seventy years old, Barnes was in good shape, but some voters might question his age and they wanted to put that to bed immediately.

The staff arranged an appointment with Barnes's personal physician, Dr. Weingarten, shortly before his speech with the VFW. The staff chose Barnes' own doctor because if anything was not right, no matter how small, they would have a good chance of keeping it from the press.

Barnes arrived at the office of his doctor, and friend of 20 years, Dr. Weingarten, and was quickly ushered into the exam room. Dr. Weingarten had rearranged his other patient's appointments for that day so the office was empty except for his nurse, Susan Dillman.

"Bill I know your busy, I'll try and get you out of here as soon as possible. But I don't get you here too often so while you're here I'm going to do as complete a physical as I can. I've got some basic tests to do, and some others that at your age should be done. Okay Bill, you know the drill, there's a dressing gown, put it on and I'll be back in a minute."

"I don't have time for a lot of extras; just do the standard stuff so I can tell the press I'm healthy enough to run for President."

After a battery of standard tests and a complete physical, Barnes hesitated to dress. Something was obviously on his mind for a man in a hurry not to immediately get rid of that dressing grown.

Sensing the Senator wanted to say something, Dr. Weingarten asked. "You look like you want to ask me something Bill?"

"Well it's just I have had a little trouble…"

"A little trouble what?" asked Dr. Weingarten

"A little problem urinating, nothing to get excited about. It's a feeling I have to go to the bathroom all the time, and when I try only a small amount comes out."

"Any pain when that happens?" the doctor asked.

"NO. NO pain. There is a small amount of blood I've noticed. Not a lot."

"This is symptomatic of an enlarged prostrate Bill. That's one of those tests I was talking about earlier, especially with someone of your age. When's the last time you were seen by an urologist?"

"I don't know. I don't think I've actually ever seen one."

"Bill, how long have you had these symptoms?"

"It has been a few months now and I have to admit it's been getting worse. Can you give me a pill or something?"

"No Bill, no pills, you need to see an urologist now. You can't take any chances with this."

"What I can't do is to have questions raised about my health. My opponents will have a field day. Hell a lot of people in my own party already think I'm too old to be running now. You might as well accept it; I'm not going to see anyone now."

"Alright Bill, at least let me exam you and take another blood sample to run a PSI test. The test will help determine if it is prostrate trouble and we will know the severity. Okay?"

Barnes agreed to allow the examination and another blood test. The only question in his mind was not the results, but will the results be secure?

Dr. Weingarten put on a pair of rubber gloves and lubricated them with a tube of gel like substance. He instructed Bill to lie back and relax. The doctor inserted his index finger into Bill's rectum. Bill started to squirm and let out a groan of pain.

"Just relax Bill, I'm almost done... okay Bill you can get dressed."

"Well?" asked Barnes.

"I'm going to be straight with you Bill; I don't like what I found. Your prostrate is definitely enlarged. You really need to see a specialist right away."

"I told you I can't do that. What about that blood test, maybe it will show something else."

"Bill, the blood work will only show how severe the problem is. I'm 100% sure you have prostrate problems. I don't mean to scare you, but if you don't handle this now, it could be too late to treat it later."

"I understand. You've warned me, now let's get that blood test done, I've got to get going. You do know enough to keep these tests private, don't you?"

"Of course Bill. I'm taking a separate vile for this blood work and will personally take it to the lab. I'll use a code name instead of your own name."

"What about your nurse?" Barnes asked.

"I trust Susan. She sees a lot of celebrities in my office and has never violated my confidence in her. But to be safe, that's why I drew the blood myself and will take it to the lab myself."

Barnes exited the doctor's office quickly, through the doctor's private door to the parking lot in the back, to avoid any reporters that might be lurking.

Chapter 6 It's My Turn

This should be a great photo opportunity, Barnes thought. He was preparing to give a major speech to the Veterans of Foreign Wars at Carmel, Indiana, a large suburb outside Indianapolis.

The topic was "Defending the United States from Global Threat." Barnes had carefully crafted this speech to get the most applause lines as possible. He knew the media covered certain events by all candidates fully, those being the VFW, National Association for the Advancement of Colored People, and the Urban League.

Barnes wrote most of his own speeches, which explains why they were so boring. When his speeches weren't boring, the sharp tongued attack of Barnes's darker side came through loud and clear as barbs and jabs rather than the humor he meant them to be. Barnes was comfortable filling the valuable air time with dull legislative accomplishments that few people cared about. People were concerned with the present and future, not the past. At times his campaign manager and speech writer wondered why they were even there as he ignored their script and went off on his own.

The VFW, however, was different. He was one of them and he talked their language. I mean how could you go wrong with lines like, *we need better health care for our veterans. I'll make sure our military families have a decent standard of living, so they won't have to go on food stamps. I support spending whatever it takes to give our troops the best equipment and the latest weapons available.* These were sure fire lines to get the crowd excited. Not only did Barnes speak the part but he could also dress it. As a veteran of a foreign war this allowed him the privilege of wearing a VFW cap, what a photo opportunity this was. Barnes's service in World War II allowed him to wear that VFW cap. Something President Anderson could not do because he was never in the service. Never mind the fact that Ray Kline was not in the service and Vice President Tierney was. Vice President Tierney was even in Vietnam.

Nobody cares about the Vice Presidential candidates, only the accomplishments of the Presidential candidates seem to count.

The speech came to a rousing conclusion with Barnes promising to "Never compromise the security of the United States for political gain or to put our troops in harms way without just cause." Barnes was feeling good as he finished the typical photo session with the commanders of the VFW. He felt secure that he had pinned down this important voting block.

The motorcade was making its way to the Indianapolis airport with Barnes and his staff congratulating each other on a job well done. For some strange reason, Barnes reached into his coat pocket to find his cell phone. He normally didn't use the phone and seldom looked at it for messages. In fact, he rarely carried it. That task was assigned to his aide Dan Reilly. Barnes, realizing Dan had his phone, asked him to check it for messages. Dan was not surprised to find 12 messages were on the phone awaiting a reply. Some how, people were able to obtain famous people's phone numbers and would leave a variety of messages. Some of the calls were from supporters and some were nasty calls from crackpots.

Dan went through the messages, one by one. He deleted the ones that had an unrecognizable caller id. Dan came to a call from Dr. Weingarten. He knew that was Barnes's personal physician.

"You have a message from your doctor", Dan told Barnes. "Do you want to listen to it now?"

Barnes, anticipating it was important said, "Yeah, I'll listen to it. Put in the password Dan and give me the phone."

Barnes had received a message to call Dr. Weingarten as soon as possible. He recognized Weingarten's voice. It wasn't his secretary, it was Weingarten himself. Barnes thought it must be serious for Weingarten to call himself. The blood test must have shown something. On the way to his airplane, Barnes called Dr. Weingarten on the doctor's private line.

"Hello doc, what's up?"

"Bill, I need you to come into the office as soon as possible."

"Why? Do I really have to come in?" asked Barnes.

Dr. Weingarten's voice was stern as he said, "its important Bill. You know what I'm talking about. I don't want to discuss it on the phone."

Barnes was flying back to Washington, D.C. anyway, so there was no need for anyone to know of his important meeting with his doctor.

"Ok doc. I'll give you a call when I get in."

Knowing people in the car had heard the words doctor and do I really have to come in, Barnes was searching for an answer.

Dan questioned, "Everything alright Bill?"

Barnes laughed "Oh yes Dan, my doctor says during that physical last month he forgot to do some kind of test I need to complete the physical. You know those reporters; if you don't do a certain test they will write a piece speculating something must be wrong with you. I'll set something up with him. He says it will only take 5 minutes."

The next day Barnes called Dr. Weingarten for an appointment and asked if he can come in early like 5 o'clock. He had hoped to make the trip without his staff. Barnes was an early riser and his staff generally worked late in the night. Dr. Weingarten agreed to meet Barnes that morning. Barnes called his driver and requested he be at the apartment where Barnes lived in Washington D.C. at 4:30 am. He told his driver he needs to pick up a prescription from his doctor for a slight case of sinus.

Barnes's car pulled into the doctor's parking lot and headed towards the back. Dr. Weingarten had a private entrance that his more famous clients used to enter the office. As Barnes opened the door, he was greeted by Weingarten.

"Good morning Bill."

"Good morning doc, blood tests come back?"

"Sit down Bill; I'm afraid I have some bad news. I need to run some more tests, but the original findings I told you about were confirmed. Bill I think you have cancer. I need to run another test to be sure."

Barnes was unusually calm for a man who was just told he had a terrible disease. He seemed to be calculating a strategy to attack the disease and did not look like a man in shock after receiving the devastating news he had a disease like cancer. He suddenly looked up and asked, "What kind of test are you talking about?"

"We will need to do a small surgical procedure to get a biopsy of tissue from your prostrate gland. That will tell us for sure if the tumor is malignant."

"Is there any treatment? I mean something that could be done outside of going to a hospital."

The silence displayed by Dr. Weingarten gave Barnes a clue that there was no other choice available, it didn't look good.

Dr. Weingarten explained, "If I'm right Bill, it's a form of prostrate cancer, a tumor on your prostrate gland. As far as treatment, for the most part there isn't any known treatment except for surgery at this stage. We can start some chemotherapy, but Bill I have to be honest; there hasn't been much success with just radiation. There are some specialists I can recommend; this is not my field of expertise. I wish we would have caught this earlier."

Barnes was now stunned, but not so stunned as to quickly ask, "If I didn't do anything, what would happen?"

Dr. Weingarten said, "The test will help determine that. Sorry Bill but from what I know about this form of cancer; six months, maybe a year tops at this stage."

"I see", said Barnes accepting his fate. Barnes then changed his persona and went into his politician mode. He was now thinking of the race for President. He continued, "When will I start to feel sick? Hell I feel fine now, a little trouble going to the bathroom, but that's about it. Are you sure about this?"

Weingarten repeated, "We need to take that biopsy before I can be absolutely sure. I've only seen this one other time, but this test is pretty conclusive. If I'm right about what stage you're in, you should feel relatively normal for about 4 to 5 months. It then goes quickly after that."

"I should make it then through the campaign then."

"Well yes Bill, but are you really going to continue?"

"Doc, I've worked my whole life for this. I'm so close. Do you have any idea how close I am to being President of the United States? Hell, I'm leading the polls for the first time. We're really starting to gain some momentum."

"But Bill, if something happens to you what about Kline? I mean how could you let a man like him be President?"

Barnes was getting mad. He realized it was becoming a matter of his personal wants and dreams and he was coming across as not caring about the country.

"Doc, I care about my country. That's why I went to war for this country. I toiled in the Senate for years to give this country good legislation. I'm what this country needs now. Kline's not as radical as most people think. It's somewhat of an act. It gives him a platform to get supporters. He's assured me if he had to take over the office he would be more moderate than his rhetoric. It's politics Doc. You do and say what you have to get elected. Then you govern for the best interests of the people. I'm begging you Doc, let me do this."

Dr. Weingarten was worn down by Barnes's plea. His friendship with Barnes, over 20 years, was weighing on him.

"Alright Bill, I give you my solemn oath I will keep this secret. You can rest assured if it leaks it won't be from me, no matter what."

"I promise win or lose, when the election is over I'll have that biopsy done. I thank you my good friend. I know you only want what's best for me. Oh yeah, I promise to talk to Kline again and keep close tabs on him. I'll also make sure my staff is on top of him. God bless you."

Dr. Weingarten grasped Barnes's hand firmly and said his goodbyes. He knew the next time he would see his friend, his friend wouldn't be seeing him.

***

Senator Damon Larson, Republican moderate, was quite the power broker in the Senate. Ralph Sampson, the RNC chairman, and Larson were a lot alike in the power that they both held in their respective areas. Senator Larson had been in the Senate for 24 years, the same as Barnes, but he had no ambition to be President. He was happy taking over the Majority Leader position of the Senate from Bill Barnes. He had a safe Southern state seat, and was looked at by his fellow Senators as someone who gets things done. He was the ultimate compromiser. He got along with everyone, Democrats, moderate Republicans, and yes even some conservative Republicans. Most of the conservative Senators were not happy, however, with his constant watering down legislation to appease the Democrats just to get a bill passed. Senator Larson often said that the definition of politics was the art of the possible. Senator Larson held a high opinion of himself and rightly so. The rest of the Senate, including the Democrats, had a great deal of admiration for Larson. If there was anything that needed fixing to get a bill passed, compromising, or vote trading, he was the man to do it. He had that belief that you could find in a lot of key people everywhere; the place just couldn't get along without them.

Larson had returned from the convention quite depressed with the Republican ticket. He was a good and loyal friend of fellow Senator Barnes, but totally opposed Barnes's Vice Presidential choice. Larson's loyalty to the party was true, but he was not an ideologue and didn't care what the national platform said. He admitted the platform was only a tool to keep the conservatives in the party happy. A bone to the dogs to help them justify what they thought the party stood for. It was all a game to Larson. It was a serious game to be sure; but a game none the less. The big prize was the Presidency, control of the Senate, and the House. That's all that mattered to Larson.

Being the leader of the Senate gave Larson tremendous power, prestige and patronage. A position he would do almost anything to keep. Still smarting over the Kline pick by Barnes, Larson felt he needed time to think. Even with the polls showing the Barnes/Kline ticket ahead, winning meant Kline in the White House and Larson couldn't fathom that.

After graduating from law school he found himself working the State Attorney Generals' office as an assistant prosecutor. He was anxious to break into politics with the goal of some day being a United States Senator. He was young, smart, and ambitious. He lacked only one more thing, money. He sure wasn't going to get rich as an assistant prosecutor. His break came when he attended a birthday party for the Governor of Arkansas.

The same party was held every year. Larson attended every function where he could meet the right people. He always came home disappointed. This time was different. The band started up and people were moving to the dance floor. Larson, seated at the assistant prosecutor's table, looked around for a possible dance partner. As he turned, one side to the other, his eye caught the Attorney General and a group of people moving toward his table. Larson noticed the Governor was with the group. He decided to wait and see if they passed by or would stop to make introductions.

The Attorney General gently grabbed the Governor's arm and moved him toward the table. "Governor, I'd like you meet the hardworking attorneys at our office. They are the ones who do all the work and get none of the glory."

Larson standing up to shake hands with the Governor thought to himself, *you got that right.* The Governor thanked all of them for their service.

Larson again thought to himself, *he didn't even introduce us by name.*

The Governor moved to his right a little and said, "Ladies and gentlemen this is my daughter, Irene."

Larson, being the closest to her, put out his hand to Irene. It is not proper etiquette for a man to offer his hand. A lady must make the offer of a hand to shake first. Irene wasn't fazed by this breach of etiquette and shook Larson's hand. While nodding to the rest of the table, she kept holding Larson's hand and asked him, "Are you enjoying the party?"

"Yes, and are you?"

Irene smiled and said, "I would be enjoying it more if I had someone to dance with. It seems I must scare everyone, nobody has asked me to dance yet."

Larson jumped at the invitation, asked the Governor's permission, and after receiving it proceeded to the dance floor with Irene.

Sad but true, Irene was not what you would consider a looker. Overweight and self confident about her lack of beauty, she didn't enjoy many male suitors. Larson saw her as his stepping stone to bigger things. They dated for only three months when he popped the question. Irene accepted and they were married six months later. It didn't take long, with the Governors influence, status, and of course funding, Larson was a United States Congressman.

Once in Washington D.C., Larson quickly learned the ropes and how to maneuver into influential positions on the important committees. He had a lock on his district. Making sure he had top-notch aides to help the locals back home, he stayed in the capitol almost year round. He came home enough to give Irene three children. That also was calculated.

Irene was a good mother and enjoyed spending all her time raising the children. Larson, like any man, needed those physical encounters with the opposite sex to satisfy him. He found a number of women at the Capitol ready and willing to be the mistress of a powerful up and coming man like himself.

Larson didn't have much of a marriage. Fact was it was a marriage of convenience some 40 years ago. He had a number of extra marital affairs in Washington. Irene chose to look the other way and spent her time raising their children.

The latest of these affairs was with Susan Dillman, Dr. Weingarten's nurse. After a long week at the Convention, Larson decided he needed to see Susan. He looked forward to being with her. When they were together he felt like he and Susan were on a deserted island. No politics, no problems, no worries, just time with Susan.

Chapter 7 How to Defeat Our Man

Larson arrived at Susan's apartment. He didn't need an invitation. He trusted she was only committed to him and felt confident he wouldn't find anyone else there. She was his lover, and his alone. They had developed a relationship that seemed more like a marriage than an affair. Larson trusted Susan as you would a wife. When they were not physical, they actually had conversations, but not about politics. That was a strict rule Larson had and Susan knew it was something she adhered to.

Sen. Larson was greeted by Susan in a way he thought a bit strange. She normally opened the door and welcomed him in with a smile. Today, after opening the door, seeing it was Larson, put her arms around him, giving him a huge hug. She released her hold a little and kissed him hard.

"What's this all about?" Larson asked.

Susan walked him in, closed the door, and moved both of them to the couch.

"Sit down. Have I got something to tell you", she gushed. "Guess who was in to see Dr. Weingarten?"

Larson said "I don't have the foggiest idea, who?"

Susan Dillman couldn't wait to tell Larson her big secret; she was bursting at the seams. "Senator Bill Barnes" she revealed. "Bill Barnes, so what, that's his doctor, isn't he?" Larson replied.

"Yes. But I know why he was there. Do you?"

"Probably had something to do with an exam he took. All the candidates have an exam. It calms any fears people might have, especially with someone Bill's age."

Susan continued, "Listen, I had to come in early that day. I had to be there at five in the morning. Weingarten wanted me to take some blood samples over to the lab when they opened at six."

Larson said, "So?", still waiting for some relevance to Susan's story.

"Just wait. I'm getting there." Susan honestly felt it was important to get every detail correct. She was going to tell her story point by point whether Larson liked it or not.

"When I pulled into the parking lot, I saw him leaving the office by the private door and get into his limousine. I knew it was Barnes. I then walked around to the front door. I'm not supposed to use the private door, even though that's the quickest way to get the samples."

Larson was getting frustrated. "So far you've told me nothing."

"Okay. Okay. I went to the back and saw Dr. Weingarten crying. I asked him what was the matter and he said nothing." Susan took a deep breath, getting herself ready to finish her story. "He told me to forget about the lab samples. That he had to go to the lab anyway and he would take them. My first reaction was that I was mad; I didn't have to get up so early after all. He then picked up a vile on his desk, went to put that one sample away, picked up the rest and left."

Susan took another deep breath. She saw Larson was really getting flustered with her. "Now here's the good part. I mean the sad part. I noticed a patient folder was opened on his desk where the vile was. I walked over and took a peek. The last notation said he informed the patient that he had cancer."

Larson was now even more curious. He asked, "Cancer? Who was the test for?"

Susan said "the folder was for John Pine. Now I happened to know John Pine is the doctor's code name for Senator Barnes." Susan was one of the people who, after years of dealing with Dr. Weingarten, knew the code names he had for some of his patients.

"What exactly are you saying Susan?" Larson asked.

"I'm telling you Senator Barnes has cancer, Damon."

"Do you know what kind of cancer?" Larson asked.

Susan had been a doctors assistant long enough to know all the medical shorthand used in writing lab scripts. She revealed to Larson, Bill Barnes's terminal illness and the fact he would have about six months to live. She also thought Barnes had sworn the doctor to secrecy because he didn't mention it to her. He always talked to her after telling patients this kind of news. A way the doctor used to release some stress and express his sorrow, especially when he knows the patient well.

In a tinge of conscious, even with it being Susan his lover, Larson thought *you would think those people in charge of confidential medical information would hold to the high standard expected from them. But gossip, especially in Washington, D.C., is alive and well and could teach a small town a thing or two about not honoring an oath of secrecy.*

After hearing this, Larson was in no mood for sex; it was the farthest thing from his mind. The political instincts kicked in immediately. What would happen to the party, was his first concern, not what about poor Bill Barnes. What would happen to the election? What if Bill dies on the campaign trail? If we win and Bill dies, then Ray Kline would be President!

He thought of all the consequences if Kline became the candidate or worse yet if Kline became president. He thought back to the promise Sampson said Barnes had made with Kline to behave on the campaign trail and how lately, Kline was continuously not sticking to it. In fact Kline was speaking more radically.

It was just yesterday Kline was speaking to a group in Texas about immigration. Kline was at a small border town. He was speaking to a group of farmers and ranchers who had unpleasant experiences with illegal aliens crossing the border. The speech was tough, but didn't cross the line Barnes had set for him. The problem came with the question and answer period. When it was announced that Ray would now take questions, a dozen or so people jumped up to form the line behind the floor microphones. The questions seemed benign enough, more statements than questions. Kline just nodded his head as the people vented. He was determined to stay on his best behavior.

A man wearing a cowboy hat stepped up and cleared his throat. He was a rugged man in his 60's with an obvious bulge of chew in his cheek. "Ray." he started out. One of Kline's qualities was the ability to have people feel comfortable with him enough to call him Ray. "I have been ranching here for 40 years and have not seen anything like this. These wet backs are crossing over like fleas. They steal from our homes. Look like gangs roaming over our land. My question is what are you and Barnes going to do about it?"

Kline saw that the man had a tear in his eye. He immediately felt for him. Kline looked around the room for television cameras, and anyone who looked like a reporter. He was assured there wasn't going to be any reporters. He was invited by this group as a neighborhood meeting before he was even a candidate. Truthfully, Kline was traveling through on the way to a scheduled event by the Barnes people. This town was on the way and Kline decided to spend the night and fulfill his commitment he made to speak to them last year.

"Sir, I don't know what Barnes's going to do. He has never really been in favor of doing anything I know of. But when I get to that White House, you can be assured I'll send the Army Corps of Engineers and start building that wall I talked about." This was the raw meat these people wanted to hear. The whole room erupted in applause and you could hear the hoots and hollers all through the room.

Unknown to Kline there sat a local reporter in the audience, who had a tape recorder hidden in his jacket. This was the stuff every reporter longed to get, a story that would put him in the national news. Right after the meeting was over; he made a bee line to his office. First thing, find the phone number for the *New York Times*.

"This is the kind of stuff that'll sink us", Larson told Susan. "Nobody can control Kline, especially Barnes. I told Sampson not to give in to Barnes. I've got to think." Larson said, pacing the floor.

Then the thought slowly seeped in his brain, *what if we lose?* He started walking around the room, with Susan sitting there half dressed, talking out loud like he was pondering a great solution, *okay, okay what if we lose?* He stopped short and came to the reality, but we are winning in the polls! Larson started to lay out a plan verbally, ignoring Susan; he spoke as if to only himself. "I need to meet with the right people, people I can trust to keep this quiet. We can't let anybody know about Barnes. Kline might get the spot. I need to talk to Ralph at RNC, Fred at CIA, yes. No wait, I'll need to talk to Mitchell first, there isn't a better political mind out there." Larson walked to the door.

"Susan, I've got to go; you cannot tell another soul about this. Not just for me, this is for the good of the entire country, maybe even the world. Mitchell will know what to do."

Joseph Mitchell had been involved with the White House for sixteen years. He was Vice President for two terms. Defeated for President in a close election and then came back to win two terms as President four years later. In addition to that, he had served eight years as a Congressman from Ohio. He became best known for his foreign policy in which he had successfully arranged the end of the Cold War. He also was well known in inter-party circles as one of the best political minds around. A person certainly that Senator Larson felt he could trust with the Barnes Kline situation.

Larson made a call to Mitchell's home and after securing a meeting with him, rearranged his schedule and made a flight reservation to California. He told his staff he has to go out to the Barnes headquarters in California and help with organization. Larson always flew first class. His staff was a little surprised when he insisted on a round trip coach ticket. They inquired about transportation from the airport to Barnes's headquarters.

Larson said, "Don't bother; I took care of that myself. They will be there to meet me." The staff was unaware that Mitchell would provide the transportation.

"Oh, one more thing, if you need to get a hold of me; call me on my cell phone. Barnes's people tell me the phones aren't all set up and the ones they have aren't reliable yet."

Arriving at LAX, Larson looked for his driver. He saw a man holding a sign that simply said, *"Senator."* He knew that was his ride. Driving to Mitchell's, he had time to relax, it was over an hour long drive. Larson thought to himself; *now don't go in half- cocked. Mitchell might laugh this whole thing off. He's probably got a simple solution to all of this.*

Larson was escorted into Mitchell's private office. After the usual pleasantries, how are you? How's the family? Etc. Larson launched into the problem with such excitement and concern, Mitchell was taken aback. Mitchell was very intrigued with the emotion in Larson's voice. Mitchell had known Larson more than thirty years and always thought of him as a cool, calm, and collected man.

Larson started the conversation with, "We have a crisis of major proportions Mr. President." Every one in the party called Mitchell Mr. President out of the respect they had for him. Larson knew Mitchell had vast experience and expertise in the areas of geopolitical affairs and national politics.

Of course, Mitchell already was aware of the Kline effect on the election and future of the Republican Party. Larson never let Mitchell get started on Kline as the problem the party had was bigger than Mitchell knew. Larson wanted to get to the major reason for the visit. Up to that point, Mitchell thought the meeting was to ask his advice on campaign strategy given the Kline problem.

When Larson told him of Barnes's terminal illness, Mitchell didn't blink and began to lay out the worst scenario, that being Kline as the President of the United States, from a national and global perspective. Larson was puzzled that Mitchell didn't seem surprised about Barnes's illness. He thought *maybe he already knew, but how?* Larson thought, *if Mitchell knows, who else might know?*

"Excuse me, Mr. President, but did you already know about Senator Barnes?"

"No, Damon, I didn't know. We need to stay calm and think it through. I have learned, along time ago, not to show emotion, it only muddies the thinking process."

Mitchell methodically continued to lay out a disastrous picture of foreign relations with China and Mexico, along with the fall out to the Republican Party. Larson sat stoned faced as he listened to Mitchell, all the time thinking *something must be done to stop Kline. I know the problem. When's he going to give me a solution?*

Mitchell then threw out a bold suggestion to Larson. Suggesting, if he were to include Anderson on the situation to stop Kline, this might give Larson even more power with the next Anderson administration. Mitchell was all about making complicated deals to gather power for him.

Mitchell went on to say, "Find a way to defeat Kline at the polls. You may need to gather a small group of trusted people to formulate a plan."

That was it? Larson thought. *I could have come up with that.* Larson had to ask, "Mr. President we both agree we need to find a way to defeat our own man. The question is how?"

Mitchell said nothing. He decided to let Larson think it through for himself.

Larson thought about it a minute and said, "I know I can trust Ralph Sampson, the RNC chairman, and I would definitely need Fred Clayton."

Fred Clayton was the CIA director who Larson was able to get Anderson to appoint by exchanging his appointment for a positive vote on Anderson's welfare bill. Fred Clayton was not only a long time friend of Larson's, but had been a former CIA covert operator who had worked under cover for Larson over the years to secure information for Larson. It didn't hurt that Larson had over the years obtained enormous funding for the agency and was well liked by the previous CIA directors. Larson just couldn't bring himself to include Anderson in on any solution at this point, worried that the Democrats might hold this over the Republicans for years to come.

Mitchell interjected, "You cannot include or exclude anybody until you come up with a plan."

"Yes, I agree", Larson nodded. Larson, still trying to get some ideas from Mitchell, asked again, "What are all our options as you see it?"

The two laid out their possibilities. Just what could they do with the future of their country and party at stake? Option one, do nothing. It is possible Anderson might win and they would not have to be involved in anything unseemly. Option two, appeal to Barnes to help get rid of Kline from the ticket. Option three, campaign for Anderson behind the scenes and hope he is re-elected. Option four, try and work with Kline if he would become President. Option five; find a way to defeat Barnes/Kline without working with or for Anderson.

Larson then went back to a comment Mitchell made early on; that we must find a way to defeat Barnes/Kline at the polls, but it would have to happen without anyone suspecting what was going on. One thing they both agreed on with this solution was that affecting a national election would be easier said than done.

Mitchell then came up with idea that would turn out to be the beginning of the end of fair and free elections in the United States. He commented to Larson, "Since the election is so close, where a state or two might swing it one way or the other is there any way to concentrate on one of those states to achieve your result?"

Larson immediately thought of the new computer system. It had been successful in its trial run. Larson also knew it had been approved for the Presidential Election this year in key States. Larson had integral knowledge of the system. He was the man who helped steer it through the Senate.

Looking at the five states involved; Texas stood out like a sore thumb. Larson looked at Mitchell and said, "Normally, Texas would be in our column. With a higher turnout of Hispanics, we could sway it to

Anderson. We could use the excuse it was a back lash to Kline that brought out more Hispanic voters for Anderson. I know Anderson has the Justice Department and others down there now working on Hispanic turnout. I think part of the computer team that worked on the election system works at the DOD headquarters. Fred Clayton could find out."

Larson was formulating his plan as he thought about it. That plan would be to fix the election. Mitchell was thinking the same thing.

Mitchell looked at Larson and said, "That might work, probably your best bet, but at this point you're on your own, and I don't want to be involved anymore."

Larson got the message; Mitchell didn't want to be involved any further. Larson would have to make that decision himself. As he left Mitchell's house, he knew while Mitchell washed his hands of any further involvement, Larson was somewhat comfortable in knowing Mitchell agreed this was the best possible plan. *After all,* he thought, *it was for the good of the country. Wasn't it?*

On the drive back to the airport, Larson started to outline his next moves. First, he would contact Fred over at CIA and arrange for a meeting.

1. Feel out Fred on the plan.

2. Give Fred the task of finding the right computer expert who could not only pull this off, but could be trusted.

Then if all went well he would meet with Fred and Ralph. Larson's decision to include Ralph Sampson would give him some personal comfort. Larson concluded he could trust Ralph; he was a good friend. He needed someone on his side, someone to watch his back. He also needed an insider at the Republican National Committee. The RNC had all the latest polling numbers, even better than Barnes's polls. He would need to know the status of the election every step of the way.

That would limit the group to only four that would know what was going on. He decided not to wait until tomorrow and put in a call to Fred at CIA, using his other cell phone. Larson had purchased a private cell phone some years ago under a different name and it was not traceable back to him, another perk of being a friend of a CIA operator and now a Director.

We have to have a safe meeting place, Larson thought. *We cannot meet at CIA Headquarters or my house.* Fred will know where to meet.

Finding a meeting place was first on Larson's mind when he called Fred. His call went directly to Fred's private number. Larson asked Fred for a private meeting location.

Clayton responded, "That's not a problem. What's so important that we have to meet right away?"

Larson went on to fill Fred in, about Barnes's illness, the Kline problem, and the fall out nationally if Kline were to become President. Larson used some of Mitchell's opinions about international consequences. It added to the urgency of the situation. He also explained to Fred why they needed to bring Sampson on board.

Larson thought *Fred, being a CIA guy, would readily pick up on the international implications. Besides, it gave him more stature with Fred.* Larson went on to give Fred the plan that he had thought up at Mitchell's house, leaving out the fact that Mitchell was involved. Larson was not leaving out Mitchell's name to protect him; he just wanted Fred to think this great plan was all his own.

Fred seemed concerned as Larson laid out the plan. He was not shocked however, having been involved in other covert actions throughout the years, but this one he knew had a greater impact on the future of the country. Larson sensed this right away and started to spin this as necessary, not only for the country, but also the impact on world affairs it might have.

Fred finally agreed to seek out the computer people involved in the election system and do a background check on them. He would get the information by the time he and Larson would meet.

Fred concluded the conversation with, "I'll send a driver for you and Sampson tonight. Say 9 o'clock. Call Sampson and let him know to be at your office."

Larson agreed, but had a question. "Are you going to be able to get all the info we need by tonight?"

Fred snapped back, "Damon, this is my area of expertise. If you don't trust..."

Larson, sensing Fred was insulted said, "No, no Fred I was just surprised you could find out so much so quick."

"Alright then", Fred said. "Let's see where this goes." He hung up the phone.

Larson, still holding the disconnected phone to his ear, mulled over Fred's last words. *Let's see where this goes*. He wondered how committed Fred really was.

It was now September and only seven weeks until the election.

Chapter 8 Electronic "Coup d'Etat"

Sampson and Larson sat around Larson's office waiting for Fred's car to arrive. There was silence as the two men looked around the office walls. Pretending to look at photographs, the two men were really contemplating the seriousness of the journey they were about to embark on.

Sampson broke the silence, "Damon, how well do you know Clayton? I don't know him at all."

Larson, trying to alleviate Ralph's obvious fears replied, "Fred's alright. He knows how to get things done that nobody else would, besides, who better to put your confidence in than the CIA Director? He can get the right people for the job. Look at tonight's meeting. You can trust Fred knows where and when to meet without being seen."

Larson was talking fast and furious. Sampson, instead of being comforted by Larson's answer, was thinking, *sounds more like Larson is trying to convince himself.* Sampson was not about to get Larson wound up again.

He changed the subject a little by asking, "Do we have to look for the driver out the window, or is he coming up to the office?" Larson answered, "I don't know. Fred didn't say." Larson realized by that answer he had found a chink in his knight's armor. He knew Sampson would pick up on it too.

He quickly added. "I'm sure Fred told me but I must have forgotten. Let's watch the street. If a car stays there running, it must be him. Otherwise, he'll come up to the office." Arguably two of the most powerful men in the country stood vigil, waiting for the car to arrive.

"What time you got?" asked Sampson.

Larson glanced at his watch and then looked at his office clock to be sure and said "I've got 8:58".

Sampson gasped, "There's a car."

"I see it Ralph. Nobody's getting out. Should we go down?" Larson said awkwardly.

"Let's wait another minute and see what he does." Sampson wanted to make sure. The minute Sampson asked for came and went.

Larson took charge. "Let's go".

Down the elevator, past the security guard, right before opening the front doors, they heard, "Wait a minute, Senator." Larson turned to see where the voice was coming from. It was the security guard.

The guard smiled and said, "I need your guest to sign out Senator."

Larson was relieved. "Sure thing. Ralph come over here and sign out."

They went out to the sidewalk. Moving slowly, not sure if this was the right car, they both stopped as the driver's side door sprung open. A huge form of a man stepped out and waited by the opened car door.

"Gentlemen, I'm here to take you to the meeting. Please get in."

Larson and Sampson were used to being chauffeured around Washington and were at odds with the situation. They didn't know where to sit. Larson, realizing this was not a normal situation, took the lead and went to the passenger's front door. Sampson got in the rear door. No one spoke. Larson and Sampson were certainly not going to start some chit chat with the driver unless he did. The driver sat stoically behind the wheel and said nothing.

Larson noticed, after 15 minutes of traveling, they were in a part of town he didn't recognize at all. He wanted to comment on it, but didn't. They slowed down in front of a series of two story buildings. Larson thought, *they don't look like warehouses, or office buildings. They aren't old but not new either.* He gave up trying to guess where they were.

The silence was broken by the driver. "Here we are. Gentlemen, please go into the door that has 104 on it. Thank You."

With that, Larson and Sampson got out of the car and went to the door marked 104. They heard the car speed off and looked back a second. Instead of knocking, they decided to follow the driver's instructions exactly as they were told, opened the door, and walked in.

There was only one visible room with a light hanging over a table. Chairs, comfortable looking ones, were scattered around the room close to the table. A man stood up from one of them. He was not readily recognizable. The light cast him as a black silhouette.

"Damon. Good to see you. Come over and grab a chair. Mister Chairman I presume?"

"Yes" replied Sampson.

"Ralph Sampson. Fred Clayton. I don't think we ever met?"

"No. I don't think so."

Larson was glad to see Clayton, but was curious who the other man was sitting at the table. He wasn't about to say a word until Clayton introduced him.

Clayton opened the meeting, "I've invited someone to this meeting who will be essential to accomplishing the mission. This is Carl Minster. Carl's in charge of Information Systems at the Department of Defense. All the computer systems at DOD go through Carl. Oh, and one more thing about Carl. He's one of us. Carl does most of our recruiting for computer people." It was understood by all that, one of us, meant CIA. "Carl's got our man identified. The one we will need to handle the election computer system. I've talked to Carl about your plan Damon. He thinks it will work."

Larson interrupted, "Thinks it will work? I'd like a little more assurance than that."

Minster leaned over the table, "Senator I'm in charge of the presidential election system. The team doing that project reports directly to me. By the way, the system has proofed itself in the last election. We will have the tool that we will need. I'll leave the politics to you people, but let me assure you the system can be, how should I say it, adjusted to our needs."

Larson wanted to throw out one of the other possibilities that he and Mitchell had talked about, before jumping into the computer option.

"Fred, before we commit to the computer option, I want to ask your opinion about another approach."

"Go ahead Damon what are thinking of?"

"How about trying to feel out Anderson on this? I mean if we could talk to him about our concern for Kline we could offer to make him a deal. Something like, if Ralph here would give the Anderson people all of our campaign strategies each step of the way that would help him get elected."

Sampson asked "What would we get in return?"

Larson replied "We could get some appointments we want, some legislation through without a veto, any number of things that would be good for the Party, long term."

Clayton jumped in "Hold it Damon. I've gotten to know the President pretty good. He may be a lot of things, but one thing he's not is dishonest. He's not that desperate to get reelected that he would be involved in such a scheme. Besides what kind of Presidency would he have if this thing were to be found out? It would be Watergate all over again. No, that's out of the question. It's bad enough fixing an election; taking down the country and both parties would be a disaster. God knows what would happen to the country then. Look we are all here to do what's best for our country. And what's best for the country is to not have Kline as President of the United States. If the Republican Party has to take a hit for four more years of being out of the White House, then so be it. The computer approach, especially being only in Texas, is the correct solution. We will have a small group of people involved and only one state to deal with. Our chance of being discovered is slight. Ralph, this is your area of expertise, will Texas do it, or will we need other states?"

Sampson pulled out a notebook from his suit pocket and flipped through several pages, pausing momentarily to read some figures. "Yes, according to the latest polls and our campaign plan, giving Texas to Anderson, along with their Hispanic strategy, would do it."

Clayton piped in trying to move the meeting along, "Okay then it's settled. Carl, tell them about the Captain."

Minster addressed the group, "Fred's referring to Captain Gary Hallstead. Captain Hallstead is not only the Senior Project Manager on the presidential system; he was the manager on the Congressional system that was the basis for it. You remember, that was basically the trial run for this. He not only is a top notch manager, but he has also designed and even coded some of the more integral parts."

Larson interrupted, "But can he be trusted?"

Clayton said, "We're getting to that, hold on and listen Damon. Carl, tell us about the Captain."

"The Captain comes from a long and impressive military family. His grandfather George was in the original OSA, Office for Strategic Affairs in World War II and accomplished a number of covert missions for us in

Germany. His father was involved in our psychological warfare unit just after Korea. Both his grandfather and father were volunteers, and always obeyed orders. I can't tell you what they were really thinking at the time, but when asked to do their duty, even on some questionable missions, both of them never hesitated. These things tend to run in families. We brought the Captain on board after he graduated from the Point. He showed not only a great aptitude for computers, but a psychological bent to follow orders and do his duty when called on. He's the best possible candidate. We're going to have to trust him. I'm sure he'll come through if it's explained to him in the right way."

Clayton took over, "That job gentlemen, is going to fall on all of us tonight. It's going to be up to us to sell the Captain on this. Carl has ordered, well let us say, asked the Captain to attend an important meeting here tonight, presumably having to do with the computer project. My driver is bringing him here at 11 o'clock."

Everyone was silent, sitting and staring at each other, each waiting for the other to come up with the right words for the Captain. They all knew orders or not, this was going to be a hard sell to anyone. Larson even wondered about Sampson sometimes, if he will be up to this whole scheme. Larson's concern stemmed from his workings with Sampson over the years. Sampson was a very reserved man, never one to take chances on anything.

Larson turned to Minster and asked, "Is the Captain political at all? I mean does he talk politics or express any opinions?"

Minster, who rarely came down to the Captain's office, hesitated to offer an opinion. He searched his memory for any examples and could think of none. "No, I've never heard the Captain talk about anything outside of normal work related things. I am told there is someone on his staff that does. Is that a concern?"

"Is it someone close to the Captain?" Larson asked.

"Hallstead is close to all his people. That's what partially makes him a good manager, but I don't think this is anything that we can't handle. He and others of his staff can be found daily on the smoking patio. There is some political talk that goes on, but nothing to get excited over."

Sampson, trying to be part of the conversation, asked, "What about the man himself? Does he have a family? What does he do outside of work?"

Minster wasn't impressed with Sampson's questions, but felt compelled to give an answer. "Captain Hallstead is married and has two young children. The last couple of years he hasn't had much of an outside life, what with the two systems he has had to implement. His wife, Sally, is a home body. She spends all her time with the kids and activities at her church. Nothing unusual here."

Larson was half listening to the conversation working to come up with some questions himself about the Captain. He let out a sigh of relief and spoke. "I think the only approach we can take is to make the Captain understand that it is his patriotic duty to help us. No, help his country. Carl, as his boss can order him, but that's not going to good enough. All of us must frame the situation in such a way as to make the Captain feel it's his duty."

"I agree", said Clayton.

It was now 11 o'clock and every one anticipated my arrival.

I arrived at the meeting place. The driver who picked me up told me to knock on the door of number 104. *This is a strange place for a system meeting,* I thought, knocking on the door.

Minster answered the door and only greeted me with "Captain, come in."

I did a quick search of the other men there, coming to the conclusion; no I didn't know any of them. *Wait. Isn't that Senator Larson, one of the heads of the Senate? I'm not going to say anything. I'll wait for introductions.* Carl motioned me to sit down at the only vacant chair at the table. Minster continued standing. He looked like he was in charge of this meeting, but I expected that.

Minster said, "Captain, let me start this meeting by telling you what you are about to hear must stay here. Understood?"

I nodded in the affirmative.

Minster continued sternly, "Captain, we have brought you here to tell you about a crisis of major proportions that is looming on the horizon. We have a situation developing that affects not only our country, but the world."

I was getting scared now. What did I have to do with this crisis? Had I done something?

Then, Minster continued with "we need your help".

I knew I didn't do anything wrong. They wouldn't be asking for my help if I did.

Minster followed with, "I don't know how much you follow the campaign for President, Captain. Let's assume not at all. Now understand we are not here to take sides. Yes, we have Mr. Sampson from the RNC. He's the Republican National Committee chairman. Senator Larson is the Republican leader of the Senate, but we also have Director Clayton of the CIA, who was appointed by President Anderson." I made sure my facial expression didn't change. I was trying to portray an image of understanding, when I still didn't have a clue what was going on.

Minster waited to see if anyone else had something to say. Hearing nothing, he continued, "I guess it's time to get to it. We have been informed that Senator Barnes has a terminal illness. The best guess we have is he may not last through the election. If he does, it will be only a matter months until he succumbs. That will mean either Mr. Kline will be the standard bearer through the election or if the Barnes/Kline ticket wins; Kline will become President."

I was confused. *So what,* I thought. *Hadn't these guys been following the campaign? I feel bad for Barnes personally, but what's wrong with Kline? He's the only one I found worth voting for. There must be more to it than that. Maybe they just don't like Kline? But if that's the case I don't know if I want to get involved with what ever these guys might be talking about. I was back to being scared.*

Minster then answered my question. "You may be wondering about now, what's wrong with Mr. Kline? Senator Larson will speak to the domestic issues. Director Clayton can tell you the more serious international implications we face with Kline as President. Mr. Director, you want to start?"

Minster still had that formal air about him. He called everyone by their title. I'm surprised he lets me call him Carl.

Minster sat down and Director Clayton took his place, standing up, he said. "Ever since President Mitchell opened the way to relations with China, the public has been steered away from seeing them as a military threat. I'm going to relate some information that very few people are privy to. The agreements signed with China during the Mitchell trip there, included a strong statement regarding trade. While we tend to sign anything we think is benign, other countries take these agreements more seriously. We have basically said to them that in exchange for their nonaggression internally and externally; we will drop our trade restrictions against them. I have received intelligence that the Chinese leaders are very upset with remarks made by Kline. These statements are not the usual campaign rhetoric. Mr. Kline has written extensively over the years that given the opportunity, he would shut down all trade with Communist governments." Clayton paused to view my reaction so far.

Clayton then continued. "Last week at a rally in California's Chinatown, Kline reiterated the same line. Two days later I heard from my counterpart in China. He said if the trade agreement is going to be broken, then they would no longer be required to keep their part of the treaty. I know Premier Zhang. He was not bluffing."

I guess politics was not all that simple as I had previously believed. You're not given that kind of information on C-span. I felt really stupid. Here I was watching and listening to the candidates, thinking I was an informed citizen. I didn't know anything.

Director Clayton wrapped up with "So you see Captain, there's more to campaigns than just domestic issues. We need a President who can keep a lid on potentially explosive issues, a man who can be a peace keeper, without of course sacrificing American interests. If Ray Kline is allowed to become President the Cold War will get hot, real soon. Senator Larson."

It was now Senator Larson taking the floor. "Captain, the big issue today is the economy. You must know unemployment has been on the rise. Kline has used this issue to continue his attack on immigration, especially Hispanic immigration in the Southwest. His remarks border on a new racism. Yes, we have a problem with illegal aliens; but the answer is not building guarded walls and shooting people trying to cross them. Our economic troubles are cyclical in nature. There have been booms and busts throughout our history. This is exactly what we are going through today. It actually started with some bad assumptions in the Treasury Department and, well it gets too complicated to explain here. I want you to know Mr. Sampson and I pleaded with Senator Barnes not to take Kline as his running mate. But he assured us that Kline was manageable and he gave Barnes his word he would be on board with Barnes's position on the issues. He has broken his promise numerous times during this campaign. As President, more than that, as Commander in Chief, I fear for the stability of this country. Kline will turn back the clock on domestic and international affairs, and return this country to a state of isolationism. We can't let that happen!"

I felt compelled to respond now. All I could stumble out was "Yes, I see." I really did see the problem. Ray Kline must not be allowed to be President. I came to that conclusion as quick and easy as I had in selecting Kline as my man.

"Good." Larson said. "Now you can see why this must be kept in this group only. Otherwise, we will have a national disaster on our hands. We need your help. I have a plan of action that will, God willing, solve our problem. We implore you to help us. Yes, we are appealing to your sense of country, your patriotism, your duty as a military man to protect your country just as your father and grandfather have done. We can't make you or even order you to help us. But we are counting on your sense of duty to help save your country, Captain."

Larson, having finished, everyone was looking to me for my response. The silence was deafening. I knew I had to agree to help. But while I was summoning up the guts to tell them I would do my part, I was also going to let them know something else. "Gentlemen, I have always served my country. I will always protect and defend it. But I also took an oath to protect and defend the Constitution of the United States. I realize these are unique circumstances and sometimes there needs to be sacrifices by some for the many. I just want you to know I will do my best but something bothers me. Is whatever you want me to do have any authorization, I mean by someone higher up? No offense to you gentlemen, but is the President asking us to do something?"

Clayton spoke up. "Yes, the President has given us the authority to handle this potential dangerous situation. He, of course can't be visibly supporting us as it will only look like a campaign ploy."

Larson, Sampson, and Minster all knew Clayton was lying. That's what Clayton did best, doing whatever it took to get his way.

Larson being the politician responded sympathetically, "None of us feel good about what we have to do, Captain. We all have racked our brains for another answer. There just isn't any. We appreciate your help. Your country appreciates your help."

I thought, *well if it's the President, my Commander-In-Chief, making the request* I guess its okay.

The cast of characters for the *Coup d'Etat* was set. Sampson from the RNC, Clayton from CIA, Minster from DOD, Sen. Larson, and last, but not least, me, Capt. Gary Hallstead, had cast our fate to the plan. Now it was time to get down to details.

Sampson agreed Texas would be the best target for arranging a change in the election. Sampson was familiar with people in the election's bureau in Texas, having spent his college years interning at that department. He knew the Governor as well, but cautioned he didn't think the Governor would be with them.

Clayton told Sampson, "Hold up with those kinds of details. I think the Captain needs to give us his thoughts on how this is to be done. Then, we need to support that plan. Captain we need a way to make sure Texas goes to President Anderson. Carl thinks your system might be our best bet to make that happen. What do you think?"

I was hesitate at first, feeling almost traitorous, but I knew they were waiting for a statement from me. "The most feasible way would be to change votes as they happened. It would be a lot easier to manipulate voters from select counties with heavy Democratic population to keep it from being discovered. If we can intercept on the network, the totals going to the State and National Election Bureaus, as they occur; we can adjust them before they are received. Also we will have an exact number that will have to be adjusted at the county level."

Larson questioned, "How is that possible to adjust at the precinct level?"

I replied, "All the precincts in the five electronic states were given new voting machines tied to the state and national network. The Senate insisted on this to make voting fair and consistent. The Senate ultimately wants these machines installed across the country. So it's a simple matter to boost the vote and send it out where needed and reverse the process and add the votes back to the local precincts."

Larson asked again, "How is it possible to have a system that allows input back into the local machine? Who would approve of such a thing?"

I was quick to respond, "The system doesn't allow it today. We will have to develop a piece of code, sort of like hacking, and enter it into those local precincts. Rest assured it can be done."

Sampson interjected, almost with a joyous tone, "That kind of leaves me out it; I mean what do I need to do?"

Larson responded to Sampson, "You need to make sure that any possible move to look at those Texas precincts by our people is discouraged. There maybe those who study these numbers who smell something. Make it a discrimination issue. Use that power you have at the RNC to keep that from happening."

Larson continued giving out orders, "Minster, you will need to cover for the Captain, give him some sort assignment where his absence from the team for a few days is not noticed. I'm sure he will need an isolated place to work; also give him any equipment he needs."

Larson suddenly thought of something else. "Captain I'm sure you know what things you'll need equipment wise, but what about other staff? You can handle this by yourself can't you?"

I thought about it and replied, "I may need another person, Larry Davis. He is on the team now and helped develop a large part of the code."

Larson was immediately concerned. He didn't want another person in on this. It could be a source for the whole project to be found out. Larson asked me, "Are you sure you need this Larry?"

I didn't hesitate at all and responded with a firm yes, but not an ecstatic one, noting my reservations.

Larson said, "I'll have to give it some more thought, but lets get started with what we know we have to do for now."

"Fred. Is your driver here?" asked Larson.

"Yes. I asked him to wait after bringing the Captain."

Larson dismissed Sampson and me from the meeting but motioned Clayton to stick around.

He walked over to Clayton and said "Can you have him take everybody else home and come back for us?" It was said in a half whisper, but loud of enough for me to hear.

Clayton didn't say anything but immediately went out to the car. When he returned he announced "Okay everybody the car's here." We all left except for Larson and Clayton.

***

"I'm concerned about bringing another person in on this," Larson said to Clayton. "How do we know we can trust this Larry? Do you know anything about him?"

"No." replied Clayton. "But I'll get right on it."

Larson continued. "Another thing Fred, is there any way to keep tabs on what's going on in the Captain's area besides Carl? I mean, I want a way to make sure the Captain doesn't get cold feet."

Clayton said, "If you mean a little insurance, I have an agent, Diane's her name. I've used her in the past. She's not only pretty, but has a body to die for; she knows she's expected to use it in her assignments. She's one of my most trusted agents. The Captain is a happily married man, but his wife is what you might call a plain Jane with a rather unimpressive body. Diane's also smart and I think we can brief her enough to get by. I don't think she has to know everything. I will introduce her to the Captain as my liaison to the group, someone I trust and will use to communicate between the Captain and me. She does have computer experience. I think he'll buy that."

Thinking further Clayton smiled and said, "I'll instruct Diane to get the Captain to have sex with her and we'll arrange to get it taped."

"That should work." Larson said. "But we really need to know more about this Larry."

Fred said. "Consider it done."

Chapter 9 Assured Commitment

Minster opened the door to a new office down the hall from my regular office.

He said "Here's your other office, Captain"

I knew what he meant. This was where I was to alter the software to give Texas to Anderson. I looked around and acknowledged to Carl that it looked like I had everything I needed. I asked him what security clearance I had.

Minster said, "You have all you will ever need."

I no sooner returned to my normal office when Minster appeared again. He told me, "Fred called and he wants to see you tonight. You can use the regular way to get there. The car will be here to pick you up at 8 o'clock. Be ready."

"Yes sir. Carl? Do you know what it's about?"

Minster looked around to see if anyone could hear him. He saw no one. "He needs to talk to you about Davis. That's all I know."

I knew what this is about. I asked for Larry's help last night. They probably don't like having another person in on this, especially Larry. He does talk a lot and has an opinion on everything. These guys don't mess around. I'll bet they know Davis better than I do. I might be able to do this without Larry, that would save him from getting involved. Besides, I really think Larry would object to what we are planning. No, that wouldn't work. Larry did all the local modules. When I change them, I'd have to resubmit them through the network. Larry watches that traffic through the network like it was his own child. I do need to see Clayton and talk this over with him.

I was driven to the 104 building. It was my second trip, but it already seemed like a routine had set in. I felt a lot more confident now that I knew what was expected from me. Expecting to see Clayton only, I was understandably surprised to see another person there with Clayton.

Clayton said, “Captain I want to you to meet Diane. Diane, this is Capt. Hallstead.” I shook her hand without even noticing there was no last name given by Clayton. I didn’t take notice of her physically until we all sat down. I was trying to think of an excuse to say something to her so I could get a better look at her.

Clayton did it for me. “Captain, Diane works for Carl in the DOD. She is not only on his computer staff, but acts as a liaison to my office.”

I thought, *funny, I’ve never seen her before. She must be one of Carl’s phantom people on his resource budget. He had told me that when we started the project, he padded the resources needed. He did that to justify more money for his department. Now I knew why he really did it. So he could have people reporting back to the CIA without directly doing it himself.*

I took the moment Clayton was explaining about Diane to have that look at her. She was young. Probably mid 20's at the most. She was very pretty, that kind of pretty that didn’t have innocence, rather one that was seductive. She was dressed very professionally in one of those women’s business suits. Not the kind a librarian would have, but one that fits tight, one that shows off her body in a way that any man is going to take notice.

Clayton explained how Diane will be his way to communicate with me and vice versa, without going through Minster. He said something about how Minster had to keep his distance from the CIA or something like that. I was still looking over Diane. She had sat next to me and moved toward me. This made it easy to size her up.

Clayton quickly moved onto Larry Davis. “You know Captain, Larry will have to know what’s going on if he works on this. You told me you needed him, and that there was no way around it. I’ve looked into his background and it tells me nothing about the man. I know he has some friends involved in politics and he is interested, if not active, in it himself. I do find that a little disturbing. What can you tell me about him?”

I explained that Larry was a solid computer man and can be trusted to do his job. I went on to say, “I really need him to code some of the modules that we need to accomplish our task. I was thinking today, if I could do it myself Larry wouldn’t have to know anything about our plan. I came to the conclusion that Larry will know something’s going on whether I did the code or not. I do know one thing for sure, we really need to get going on this or we won’t make our deadline.”

Clayton thought for a moment and said, "Okay. Let's bring him on board. You tell him only what he needs to know. If you have to, make up some excuse about top secret and that's why you can't tell him more." Clayton wasn't that naive, he wanted to get the project going, knowing full well he would have to handle Mr. Davis when the time came.

Diane was at my office the next day. I called Larry in. I took them down to the new office. Our special team, that's what I called our little group, were the only people permitted in the new work area. I introduced Larry to Diane. He looked at me and raised his eyebrows and just smiled. He gave me that kind of look that says I don't mind working with her at all. I explained to Larry she was part of the special team that was needed for some unique work.

I had come in early that morning to script out what I was going to tell Larry about why we were working out of a new office. I explained to him we needed some special subroutines that the clients had requested and Diane was here to help us out.

Davis couldn't help, but stare at Diane. She was easy to look at. Larry being the typical red-blooded male had temporarily forgotten what it was he was asked to do. All he knew at the moment was that he was going to work with Diane and see her everyday. I could see he was smitten with her physically just as I was.

As the days passed by, Larry was coding modules under my direction. I could tell they seemed puzzling to him, but he didn't say anything yet. I think he was satisfied, for the moment anyway, that I knew what I was doing. I was getting nervous when Larry started questioning me about the specifications I was giving him. I knew it was just a matter of time before he would confront me about these strange specifications. He trusted my integrity and decided to let it go for now.

Larry noticed Diane seemed to be trying to get friendlier with me, almost could call it flirting. I don't know if it was jealousy or the fact that Larry had enough of this top secret stuff, but he asked to talk to me.

"Gary. Look, I've coded these last couple of modules and said nothing. But you and I both know this is bull crap. What the hell is going on? If these clients are trying to pull something I want no part of."

I was now going to have to use every skill I could to convince Larry these modules were necessary. "Larry, I couldn't say anything before; I gave my word not to. I know what this must look like, but you've got it all wrong. Carl, you know Mr. Minster, came to me last week with the clients wanting to go over some enhancements. When I heard what they wanted, believe me, my reaction was the same as yours. Then they explained to me why they needed them and made me promise not to tell anyone. Larry, you know politicians and how they always want to cover their collective butts. That's what this is. They're afraid if something went wrong with the system, they wanted to be able to make corrections as we find them, and not let anyone know. That's the reason for the ability to do uplinks through these new modules."

I hesitated to see if Larry was buying this or not. He said nothing giving me the indication he might just be satisfied with my explanation.

I continued, "That's the reason Diane was brought on board. She works for the House Committee's computer staff and reports back to them. You could call her their spy." I started to laugh hoping to encourage Larry to see the irony in his adoration of Diane. I had hoped to put to an end to Larry's questions and jealously at the same time.

"I have to admit," said Larry. "Now that I know she's a spy for the clients I feel a little foolish, but if you want to know what was really bothering me. It was you Captain."

"Me?"

"Yes, you were bothering me. I was worried you might be putting your marriage at risk. It was becoming obvious to me; Diane was coming on to you. I didn't want you to do anything foolish."

"Thanks Larry. No, I was just looking. You quit looking you might as well be dead." We both laughed.

Larry looked at me seriously and said, "Just remember this. I was in a store one time looking around the power tools. I was actually just killing time waiting for some paint to be mixed. A salesman came up and asked if he could help me. I said no I was just looking. Then he said well, looking is the first step to buying." I got the message.

Working closely with someone on an intense project, especially a project with as much pressure as this one brings people together in a strange way. A common bond develops under the strain. An unspoken support mechanism starts to unfold. When all men are involved there's a lot of swearing and complaints about physical stress on their bodies. This type of bonding makes each man a buddy of the other. Even if one of them had problems with one of the guys before, under stress, he's your buddy now. That's how men work it out. Men don't talk about their feelings. That's a woman's thing. It would lower your masculinity in the eyes of your buddies if you did.

Working under similar conditions with a woman is something totally different, especially when the woman is single, good looking, and just plain physically attractive. It makes one's resistance start to fail. At the end of long and stressful days, Larry, Diane, and I would sit around the office trying to unwind. Larry and I would do our buddy thing, filled with slang and men speak. While Diane would sit in a chair, push it back from the desk, to show off her whole body, legs and all. She tossed her hair back with a flip of her head. Then, she would interlock her fingers and place her hands behind her neck; arch upwards, pushing her chest out. She never said I need to sleep or I'm tired, she would always say it in more suggestive terms like I need to go to bed, or I need a nice hot bath. The things that she would say always brought up images in my mind that I didn't need to be thinking about. Diane was becoming more suggestive to me and I was starting to notice.

Larry, Diane, and I had been working almost around the clock together. I had told my wife, Sally, I was working on a short, but important project for seven weeks and not to expect me home much. Sally always understood my work was important and sometimes on the secret side. She had learned over the years not to ask me too much about my projects. I guess some would call her a simple housewife. That's true, but I wouldn't have it any other way. She was a good woman with Christian morals. She lived for me and our children to make us happy. Sally trusted me.

The project was close to being finished and ready for testing. In fact, a trial run by Larry confirmed the major parts were working as expected. All that was needed was a clean up and some bells and whistles added to the code. All five states were reporting good results on their testing.

The only thing left to test was our special code. This was going to tricky. We needed to run the tests, but by doing so it might bring up questions by Larry again. I was trying to think of a way to run the tests myself without Larry. I wondered if Diane was as smart as she was beautiful. She might be able to help me pull the tests off.

After Larry left for the night, I approached Diane about helping me. She agreed. Turned out she was a pretty good programmer. Actually, I think she was as good as Larry. Together, we finished the critical portion of the test and I was satisfied we were to ready to go. A strange feeling came over me. I should be pleased with how the system was working. After all, we accomplished our two tasks. One, we could be assured we had a good system to ensure a fair election. Finishing our second task would ensure a fixed election. Two nights later a final parallel test was to be done to confirm we were ready. The parallel test went exactly as planned. The team had done a fabulous job. Yes, we were ready, but ready to do what I kept thinking.

I sat alone in my office. I couldn't help but dwell on the consequences of our successful system. The rest of the team was putting together a make shift party to celebrate their hard work. I knew I had to make an appearance, but not right now. People, who haven't worked on a stressful, complicated, piece of work don't understand. All during the time you are developing, correcting problems, running into challenges, it's exciting and the adrenaline is flowing. When you're finally done, even successfully done, there is a feeling of a let down. A feeling of remorse, sad, that it has come to an end. I've done a dozen major systems in the past and I know this feeling well. But on this one, it was a different kind of remorse. I felt physically sick, mentally depressed. I felt like crying not celebrating. I had to go out and join the team and congratulate them on a job well done. This was my duty. They thought they were doing the country a service. They had worked long and hard, and they deserve my praise, regardless of how their work will be used.

I joined the team in our conference room, where someone had ordered pizza and beverages. It was unusually quiet; probably due to the fact everyone had their mouths full of pizza. I looked for our secretary, Evelyn, figuring she had ordered the food.

I found her and asked, "Who do I owe for the food?"

"No one", she replied. "It was delivered already paid for. We just thought you did it."

I just said "Oh yeah." I didn't say it for everyone to think I paid for it. I figured Minster did, and he didn't want anyone to know, so I just left it at that. Funny celebration I thought, awful quiet. The group celebrated their success by relaxing and speaking proudly of their accomplishments. I walked around to each person starting with Dale, and congratulated them individually. I didn't like giving speeches in front of a group. It was getting late and I could tell everyone was tired.

One by one they cleaned up their plates and cups, putting them into a small trash can that was starting to overflow. As the team left, they were having a hard time pushing down all the previous garbage. I went out to find another trash can for them. I picked one up from someone's desk, and ran into Larry. He was coming back from the restroom.

I said, "Larry, you can take off. Diane and I are going to clean up a little documentation and take off soon."

Larry took this as a subtle signal I wanted to be alone with Diane.

"Sure, Captain." Larry said sarcastically.

I was going to straighten out Larry, but thought *no, I'm not getting into that with him tonight. It was ridiculous.* I really wanted to go over the documentation with Diane to see how we could hide the special modules that were available in the system. Clayton only wanted Diane and me to be aware of them. I knew Larry would question why we left them out of the official documentation for the clients, when they were the ones who asked for them. I thought, *out of sight and out of mind for Larry*, and since I was going to be the only one who would actually use them, nobody else needed to know why they weren't there.

Larry said goodnight and left quickly. The rest of the team had also left for the night, leaving Diane and me to work on the documentation. I asked Diane to meet me for a few minutes at our office down the hall. The place we did our special work.

I sat down at the desk and pulled up the documentation. It was written using our word processor. I wasn't a very proficient typist, so I asked Diane to pull her chair over to the screen, next to me. Diane rolled her chair slowly over to the screen. I couldn't help but notice when she sat down and crossed her legs, her skirt rode up beyond her thighs and she made no effort to pull it back down.

Diane said, "You want to dictate and I'll type?"

"Yes, that's what I thought we could do. We only need to clean up the area Larry wrote about the special modules. It shouldn't take long."

"That's ok", she said, "I'm in no hurry."

We proceeded to rewrite those areas where Larry had questioned why those modules were there in the first place, trying to make it look benign to anyone who might read the documentation. It isn't often people outside data processing ever bother to read a system's documentation. It needed to be rewritten as to not cause attention, but also not look suspicious. We then deleted any reference in how it could be used or even how to access it. This would be our secret.

We finished in about two hours. It was now close to midnight. Diane excused herself. I assumed she needed a restroom break. She returned with some noticeable changes to her attire. I could say I was shocked, but that would be lying. Diane had left her suit coat off and the first two buttons of her blouse were unbuttoned. I admit I was excited. My resistance was lowered and I was vulnerable to any suggestions she might have.

Diane walked over to me in a slow and sultry manner. She didn't sit back down. Instead, she leaned over, putting her hands on the desk, looked at me and smiled. I could see down her blouse. It became obvious to me this was on purpose. She leaned farther down, next to my head.

First looking at the screen and then turning her head to me she asked, "Are we done?"

I turned my head away from the screen toward her, where our lips were only a fraction apart. Not a word was spoken. She closed her eyes, pouted her lips, and we kissed. Diane positioned herself into my lap where our bodies were pressed together. I was lost in another world. She suddenly moved away from me and whispered, "I'll lock the door."

Diane walked over to the door and locked it. Then, she turned out the lights. The only light left in the room was that of the computer screen. She walked back to me, I stood up, ready to receive her. She hesitated a moment about three feet away; I thought maybe she's having second thoughts. Maybe this is the break I needed to come to my senses.

Instead she said "Gary, I've dreamed about this for weeks." After hearing her say that, all my inhibitions melted away. What I didn't know was that when she had hesitated at that moment, she had arrived at the place where she could turn on the videotape machine set up by Clayton's people. We both proceeded to have the relationship Diane had been maneuvering for weeks, all the while being recorded for Clayton's purposes.

The next morning Larry arrived early, as usual. Larry started work at 6:00 a.m. and usually left at 3:00pm. He stayed late on this project and sometimes didn't leave until midnight, which didn't prevent him from coming in early the next day though. He was 66 years old and there were times I wondered how he could do it. Larry had told me once, he came in early because it was quiet and he could concentrate better. He was a very detailed, solid computer programmer who always saw the little flaws in computer code that no one else did. He passed up numerous promotions to management, preferring to stay out of office politics.

Larry decided to go down to the special office and see if Diane and I had wrapped up the documentation we talked about last night. I think he was still jealous about Diane's attention to me and wanted to check up on us. If so, his instincts were correct.

He tried to open the door, and found it locked. I was scared it might be Minster, so I got up quickly. I put my clothes on and straightened them up as best I could. I motioned Diane to do the same. I waited until she looked appropriate. We both still looked disheveled, but I couldn't wait any longer. I unlocked the door. It was Larry standing there. I was relieved. At least, it wasn't Minster. Larry stared at Diane and me. It was obvious what we had been doing all night and it wasn't only documentation. He could tell we had spent the night there.

Larry just said, "Good morning" in a sheepish tone of voice and stepped back into the hall. I moved back to the door to close it for some privacy. Diane said she needed to go home to change clothes and shower. She left. I motioned Larry to step into the office and close the door. I knew I would have to say something and I didn't want an audience.

I turned to Larry and said, "I know this looks bad. I don't know how it got started, but I can assure you it was only a one time thing."

Larry said, "That's your business, don't worry. I wouldn't say anything about it."

Larry continued. "Say Gary, while we're making confessions. I didn't sleep at all last night, thinking about this project. What bothers me is that I was thinking how this special code could be used. It looks like someone could actually alter the vote tallies in Texas with this. Frankly, if this is what it's going to be used for, I want no part of this. I'm really disappointed with what I have already done."

Larry spoke openly not knowing a video recorder with a 12-hour capacity was still recording what was going on in the room.

I told Larry, "That's one way to look at it, only you would think of that. I assure you Larry that is not the real use of this code." Larry was a smart man and not easily persuaded that I was telling him the truth.

Then he made the comment that I thought at the time Clayton wouldn't be happy hearing. Larry said "if that's how someone is going to used it, I'd have to tell someone. I bought your explanation before, but, well, I don't believe it Gary. These modules could be used to fix an election."

I tried again, "Larry I'm telling you, honestly, no one is going to use this to fix an election." I was getting nowhere. Larry was not easily convinced.

"Captain, I'm telling you, I am going to personally monitor that code and if anybody tries to use it to change any votes without a good reason, I'm going to blow the whistle on them, no matter who it is!"

I didn't know what to do. Should I tell Diane about Larry? She could talk to Clayton and give me some direction. I eventually decided to use the first rule of management I was taught in project manager's school when presented with a problem, that being, to do nothing. It might just solve itself.

***

Later that night after everyone had left the office and went home, the video tape was retrieved by Diane and given to Fred Clayton at CIA Headquarters. He reviewed the tape with Diane looking on.

Clayton said, three quarters of the way through the tape, "Good job, Diane this is exactly what we need. I need you to go back to the DOD. This time just observe the Captain, and let me know anything that looks out of place, especially with this Larry guy."

Diane agreed and left Fred's office with the tape still running.

Clayton walked over to turn off the tape, when he noticed Larry and my conservation was just starting. Clayton watched and listened as Larry all but said he knew the purpose of the project and was not going to be a part of any election fixing, no matter what. Clayton was a man of action.

His saw this as a direct assault on what we were trying to accomplish. He immediately knew what he was going to have to do to protect the mission.

Clayton put in a call to one of his operatives, one of those people that don't show up on anybody's staff or payroll records.

He decided Larry would have to be dealt with.

Chapter 10 Deadly Consequences

Election Day was coming fast. The team and I were spending our time cleaning up loose ends on the system and getting ready for a final download of the computer code to the five states involved. I was giving the team time off if they requested it to catch up on things they put off, having working so many hours. Larry even wanted a day off to get some things done around the house.

Larry lived alone in a large house he had shared with his wife, before she succumbed to cancer five years ago. They had one child, a son, who had moved to New York because of his job. Larry was always complaining about the little repairs on his house that he was neglecting because of working so many nights and weekends. I was glad I was able to give him the day off.

It was good not to have to spend all my nights at work. Good for me, but better for my family. I still felt the guilt of that night with Diane. I was trying to be a good husband and father now. I played with the kids. We played games together as a family. No more C-span or news that talked about the elections. I brought home family rated movies from the video store that we could watch together.

I must of been doing too good of a job at playing family man because I caught Sally looking at me, with a curious stare now and then. Not a look of, he's hiding something, but more a look of, why the big change. Every once and awhile, during a conversation with Sally, I would throw in a comment about how good it was to be home for a change. I had hoped this would satisfy Sally's curiosity.

One of my rituals I was now able to pick up again was sitting down to read the newspaper. I stopped watching television because of the election coverage. I had enough of that the last six months. It amused me that I searched the paper for any news that wasn't politically related for a change. Even bank robberies, local school articles and traffic accidents were welcome sights, as strange as that might sound.

I picked up my local paper and sat down to go through the mundane news of the day. My eyes scanned the headlines of the middle section of the front page. I knew the top of the paper would have the election coverage and I didn't want to see any of that. For some reason, I was drawn down to right side of the paper. Maybe it was the bold type there, or maybe I had a sixth sense about what I would find. My eyes focused in on a short, bold headline.

"Local Man Found Dead."

When you see the word "Local", it grabs your attention; it could be somebody you know so your inclination is to read the story. The story started out describing that a local man, employed by the Department Of Defense, was found dead at home. This certainly grabbed my attention. As I read further, now hoping it wasn't someone I knew, the name of the person was revealed. It was LARRY DAVIS. *No. No.* I thought, *Not Larry.* I needed to know more, but didn't want to at the same time. I read on.

The initial report by Mark Fleming, Arlington Police Chief, was that it was a suicide. Mr. Davis was found by his son, Richard Davis of New York City yesterday afternoon. The son confirmed he found his father in his car, at home. The car was idling in the garage with all the doors closed. I was shaken. My first thoughts were of Larry and his son. His son was his only family I knew of. Larry might have had brothers and sisters, but he never mentioned any. I do remember him saying at the funeral of Gloria, his wife, that Richard was their only child. I could not picture Richard, although I met him briefly at Gloria's funeral. I wonder if he was staying at Larry's. I needed to talk to him.

I knew it would be my duty as Larry's boss to get the arrangement details for the rest of the staff. First, I needed to tell Sally. I called out to Sally. She was busy in the kitchen putting dinner together. I hated to give her this news. She was happy, singing as she cooked dinner for a husband at home for a change. She finally didn't have to make up a separate dinner for me to put in the refrigerator for when or if I was coming home. Sally heard me call out to her. She put down the pot of green beans and came into the family room. She was smiling, looking so cheerful. Now I had to give her the bad news.

"Sally. Sit down. I have some bad news." I said in a manner that she knew was my serious tone.

"Gary, you're so pale. What's the matter?"

"Sally who remember Larry Davis, don't you?"

"Yes, you work with him, right? I remember his wife died a few years ago?"

"That's right. Well I was reading the paper and well… here, read this." I couldn't tell her myself. I chickened out. I handed the paper for her to read it herself. I could see tears welling up in her eyes as she read the story.

"Oh, no, that's terrible. What do you think happened?"

"I don't know Sally. He seemed alright to me. I mean he seemed happy. Just the other day..." I stopped short. I thought of our conversation about the special code. Larry was pretty adamant about what he thought might be done with the software and he wasn't going to stand for it.

Larry rarely talked about his son Richard. Even holidays, he never talked about going to Richard's or Richard coming to his house. I remember thinking at the time that *it seemed strange especially only having the one child. Maybe they didn't get along, that happens in families. I was really trying to rationalize why Richard came to his house now. I was afraid to admit to myself that Larry might have taken the day off, called Richard to come there and to tell him of his concerns about our project. He did say that day; he would tell someone if he suspected someone was fooling around with the special code for the wrong reasons.*

Sally interrupted my thoughts by asking, "Are you going to call his son?"

"Yes I have to. I need to find out the arrangements for the rest of the staff."

Sally looked at me bewildered. I know how that must have sounded, cold and matter of fact. I didn't mean it that way, but she had no clue to what I was really thinking about.

I called Larry's number. To my surprise someone answered. "Richard?" I inquired.

"Yes, who's calling?"

"Richard, this is Gary Hallstead."

"Oh yes, Captain Hallstead. My father spoke of you often."

"I'm so sorry, Richard. I just read about it in the paper."

"I'm sorry you had to hear it that way Captain. I was trying to find dad's phone list to figure out who to call."

"That's alright. I'm just so sorry to hear about your dad. He was a nice man. He will be missed by all of us. I called to express my condolences and see if there were any arrangements yet?"

"Well you know that's funny. Dad had it all laid out some time ago. You know dad was very organized, even down to his funeral. He had it all written down here in his private papers box. I'm going to contact the funeral home and when I do, I'll be sure to let you know. They have dad at the hospital now; I think the police said the coroner's office had him."

I interrupted Richard. "This is probably not the time. The paper said it was suicide. Did he give you any idea that, well you know... that it was a possibility?"

Richard knew what I was trying to ask so clumsily. "No. To be honest, we didn't talk that much since mom died. I was busy with my new job and he was busy at work. We just sort of lost track of time. You know how that goes. You probably knew him better than I did these last five years. The police asked me the same thing. They were a little curious why there wasn't a letter. I told them I also looked for a letter, but didn't find one. The police did say, contrary to people's belief, suicide victims don't always leave a note. Did you see any signs why he might have done this?"

"No.", I quickly jumped in. "He seemed perfectly fine to all of us. We were working long hours on an important project lately, but he gave no indication of being down or depressed about anything. The project actually just wrapped up and looks like a big success. Everybody was happy about that. Well, if there's anything I can do Richard, please let me know. Do you have my number?" Richard confirmed my phone number and agreed to inform me of the funeral plans when they were settled.

A more practical thought entered my head. *I will need Diane now more than ever to help with the project. I don't like it, but she was the only other person on the team that knew the special functions.* I told myself, *I've got to make sure there is not another incident with her. I've got to make that clear from the start. It takes two to tango so it's up to me.* I forgave myself for the first time. I prayed to God to help me overcome another temptation. I keep thinking of Sally and her blind trust in me.

I came back to thoughts of Larry. *God, please don't let me have been a cause of his suicide. Driving a man to take his own life over something as insignificant as an election? There's nothing more significant than a human life. Nothing is more important than that.*

At this point, I didn't care if the country was at risk. *I mean how bad would it really be for Kline to be President? There are all kinds of people who surround the President. There has to be someone there to help him and keep the country out of trouble, right? I don't really know for sure.* These thoughts were driving me crazy. I felt scared and mixed up all at the same time.

Then I thought of something else. *Why wasn't there a suicide note? There's always a note having some explanation. At least on television there is. Right now, I needed to talk to Carl or Clayton about getting Diane to stay on. I could talk to Diane, if she comes in tomorrow. I remembered Clayton saying Diane was his communication source because he didn't want Carl getting involved with his office. This leaves out Carl,* I thought. *I better go and see Clayton myself and get this over with, talking to Diane might be awkward.*

***

Feeling distraught and confused, I went to CIA headquarters. I had never been there before, not even for this project. I really had no need to go there and besides I got the distinct impression I was not to go there at all during this project. I didn't care. I needed to talk to someone about the project and Diane, and the Director was the only logical choice. If they wanted the project to succeed, they had to see me.

I drove up to the front entrance. The road narrowed down and forced you to stop at a checkpoint. There was no other way in. The whole place was fenced off. There wasn't the normal railroad crossing type of gate that would go up and down to allow access to the headquarters. It was a high, permanent looking fenced gate that was operated by the guards. A huge stop sign greeted me as I slowed next to the guard's station. I pulled out my military ID card and asked to see Director Clayton. I was sure that the security clearance level on my card would grant me access. The guard's eyes darted back and forth at me and then my ID card multiple times. I wasn't asked if I had an appointment, which of course, I did not have. I thought it strange the guard didn't ask that question. He turned and walked back into his station with my ID card in hand.

The guard, returning with my ID card stretching out of his long arm, said, "You don't have an appointment Captain. You'll have to make an appointment first. You can turn around over there to your right."

"Can't you call his office? I'm sure he will see me."

"I'm sorry Captain, this is our procedure. No exceptions. If you call for an appointment, we will have it on our list."

I looked in my mirror, and as most drivers know you have that feeling when someone is close to you. Another car had pulled up behind me, waiting for me to get out of the way. I pleaded with the guard again to call the Director's office, but he was having none of that and now was sterner as he repeated the procedure.

I looked in my mirror again wondering if what I saw the first time was right. Yes, it was. Although it came out backwards, I could make out SEN. LARSON.

I turned back to the guard and said "I'm with Senator Larson, he's right behind me. We're both here to see Director Clayton. I'll pull over there and you can verify that with the Senator."

I took my ID card and didn't wait for a response from the guard, hoping this was going to work. I pulled over, parked and walked to the Senator's car.

Senator Larson, recognizing me, rolled his window down. "Captain, what brings you here?"

"I need to see the Director right away. It's important, it concerns the project."

Senator Larson understood from the tone in my voice that it was something urgent.

"I can't get in without an appointment. I need your help."

The Senator then did something I'm sure the guard thought unusual. He got out of his car and approached the guard. He handed the guard his ID card and said "Corporal. I think we have a little mix up here. I'm Senator Larson and I, I mean the Captain and I have a meeting with Director Clayton today. The Captain here says he's not on the list; he must have been accidentally left off, I can vouch for him."

The guard, thinking it over a minute, nodded and returned to his station. He came back with a clipboard and had the Senator and me sign in where it said Director Clayton, 9:00 AM, Senator Larson. The Senator handed me the pen, and the guard said, "Just sign below the Senator." He handed both of us a temporary parking permit and told me to display it on the driver's side dashboard. I backed up my car and motioned to the Senator's driver to go ahead. I needed to follow him, he would know where to park.

I forgot that Senators don't walk; they are left off at the door. I kept an eye open for an opportune parking space as I followed the Senator's car. Before arriving at the entrance to the building, I saw the sign, visitors parking and turned. I was lucky to find a spot, second row, third space. Getting out of my car, I saw the Senator waiting at the door for me.

At the receptionist area, I could see people signing in. *Here we go again,* I thought, *another person to explain my presence to*. Larson signed in and said, "This is Captain Hallstead and he..." Larson didn't get to finish the story again. The receptionist spoke up and told him the guard had phoned to clear me. She handed us a badge and said for me to wear it so it was visible at all times. I complied by clipping it to the left pocket of my uniform. She smiled in approval.

I didn't have to look around for directions. The Senator walked directly to the only elevator with a guard standing in front of it. The Senator stood so the guard could read his badge. I followed his lead. The guard thanked us, entered the elevator with us and pressed the up button. When the elevator arrived, the guard said, "Please enter the reception area, straight ahead." The huge glass doors opened right into the Directors reception area. It was the only set of offices on the entire floor.

Larson greeted the secretary by name and asked her to make sure that she announces that he and Captain Hallstead were here to see the Director. She stepped to a door that said private on it and tapped lightly. She didn't wait for a response, just went right in closing the door behind her. The door opened again and expecting the secretary, there instead was Fred Clayton himself. He came out to greet us personally with a perplexed look on his face.

Ignoring Larson, he came directly to me and put out his hand to shake. "Captain, this is a surprise. Did you come with the Senator?"

"Well, yes and no Mr. Director. I'm here to talk about the project."

Clayton's face became flushed. He shook his head quickly in a negative matter that suggested I shut up. "Let's go into my office." His secretary waited at the door. She asked if the Director needed anything for his meeting, meaning coffee or any other refreshments.

Clayton said, "No, thanks. And please hold any calls. I don't want to be disturbed."

"Yes sir, but I need to remind you, you have an 11:00 AM meeting with General Holtz."

"That's fine. We should be finished by then."

Clayton motioned for Larson and me to sit down, but I did not. I was ready to take them on and needed to stand to emphasize my passion about Larry's death. He wasn't just a co-worker, he had become my friend. I decided to start out by seeing if they even knew about Larry's death.

"Have both of you heard about Larry?"

"Yes, I did. Carl Minster, your boss, called me the other day. Sad, really sad", Clayton said in a matter of fact tone.

I thought it was curious Minster had called Clayton directly. I thought Clayton had told me he didn't want Minster contacting him. I remember that was one of the reasons he said Diane was there. It also jumped out at me, why hadn't Minster called me? Of all the people at DOD, they must have known I knew Larry the best. Something didn't seem right.

Before I could dwell on this twist, Senator Larson spoke up, "Who's Larry? What happened? You're not talking about that Larry working on the project are you?"

I turned to the Senator and said, "Yes, that's the Larry I'm talking about. Larry was not only one of the top people working on the project, he was my friend. He was found dead at his home. They called it a suicide. I talked to his son last night. He's handling the arrangements."

Larson acknowledged and looked genuinely sad.

I continued, "I came here for two things. Clayton, I will need Diane to stay on. She will basically need to take Larry's place until the election is done. I can probably handle Larry's stuff alone, but she is knowledgeable on the special code and would be a big help to me."

"Not a problem Captain. She will be there as long as you need her."

"Second, I can't help it, but I've got to tell you about a conversation Larry and I had the other night. It might compromise the project." It was obvious I now had both of their attentions.

"Larry told me he was always uncomfortable with those special modules he was coding. He suspected they could be used to alter the election. He was quite upset about it when we last saw each other. I feel like I might have driven him to this." I had a quiver in my voice. My eyes were welling up with tears.

I regained my composure and continued, "One thing you should also know. Larry threatened to tell someone if this was true, about misusing the software. When I talked to his son, he didn't give me any indication that he knew anything. I don't have any clue who else he might have confided in." I finally sat down.

Clayton got up from behind his desk and walked slowly to the front. He half sat on the front of his desk, his hands grasped the edge in a tight grip. "Captain, I can tell you are upset about your friend, but this mission we are on is more important than any one man. We must stay focused to the task at hand. I know this sounds a little cruel, even hardhearted, but Captain, you must concentrate on your duty to your country. Your friend was emotionally disturbed and felt lonely after his wife's death. At least, that's what he wrote."

I interrupted Clayton to make sure I heard him correctly. "So there was a letter? I mean, Larry did write a suicide note? What else did it say?" I was waiting to see what Clayton's response would be. I had remembered Richard said neither he nor the police had found a letter!

"That's all I was told by my source. It said he was depressed", Clayton said in a tone of concern that his story didn't match mine about the letter.

I coyly asked, "Is the letter available? I would like to read it myself. I'm sure his son would like to see it also."

Clayton knew by the way I asked the question that I had caught him in a possible lie. He started to stammer and almost stutter, trying to get out his explanation. He gave up trying to waltz around the question.

"Look Captain", Clayton said without thinking. "Larry was a liability. He could screw this whole thing up. These are extreme times that call for extreme measures. I'm not about to see this mission fail on account of one loose cannon."

I was shocked. *Was he saying what I thought he was saying? Couldn't be, my God, he's almost bragging about taking Larry out of the picture.*

I asked, "But how did you know for sure Larry was going to tell anyone? Larry said a lot of stuff and never carried through on it."

Senator Larson was just as frightened as I was. He was seeing his friend, Clayton as never before. A man who would do anything and that includes possibly murder to carry out a mission. It never was a game to the Senator, but murder? That went too far even for the Senator. However the Senator sat quietly, I think out of pure fear.

"Captain, I want you to see something" Clayton said. He walked back to his desk and faced the back wall. He pulled open the picture hanging there of President Anderson. The space behind the picture revealed a small wall safe. Flipping the dial quickly, he opened it and pulled out what looked to be a video cassette tape. Clayton went over to the entertainment center in the corner of his office, and turned on the VCR and TV. Before starting the tape, he closed the curtains and locked his door. The Senator and I just sat silently awaiting what mystery this tape was about to unveil.

I looked on with horror as I saw my and Diane's loving making on the screen. I was not only stunned; I was ashamed of myself. He had accomplished one thing for sure with this tape. I no longer held any moral position over him. Clayton had me over a barrel. *No more sanctimonious me*, I thought. "Okay, Okay, I've seen enough. You can turn it off."

"No, there's one more scene I think you should see", Clayton said. Still reeling from my pornographic debut, I couldn't image what else was on that tape. Then I saw Larry's and my conversation that next morning on the tape.

Clayton said, "You see Captain, I don't take chances. I've learned to trust no one." Clayton always called me Captain, like Minster did, to enforce the fact that I should follow their orders.

Clayton looked at me with a serious, stone like face and said, "You wouldn't want your wife to see this, would you?" I shook my head in a negative fashion.

I was still looking at the floor. I couldn't face Clayton or the Senator.

Clayton wasn't through, "And more to the point, Captain, you wouldn't want anything to happen to your wife or children? Would you?"

Horrible images filled my head as I thought *if something ever happen to Sally and the kids. Was he serious? What kind of man was this?* I looked to Larson for some sympathy.

Larson, catching my look of fear, finally spoke up. "Fred, let's not go there. I'm sure the Captain is impressed with your little show and..."

Fred walked over to the Senator, pointed his finger at him and said, "Show? This isn't a show Damon. You better get on board yourself or..."

Larson snapped back, "Or what Fred? You have a tape about me?" Clayton just smiled at Larson, and turned back to me.

"So Captain, we can count on you to do your duty, right?"

I was in no position to argue with this man. He would do anything to get what he wanted out of me. My only thoughts were with my family. Sweet and innocent, they had no business being part of this, but I put them in this position. I'm going to have to make sure nothing happens to them.

I slowly stood up. I couldn't stand being there with this man another second. I finished the meeting with, "I will do my duty. Leave my family out of this, please".

Clayton had to always have the last word. "Just as long as the mission is accomplished, Captain."

Chapter 11 Election Day Arrives

I was driving home from my meeting with Clayton and Larson, visibly shaken. It was only a mile to the house now. How could I face my family without breaking down? I've got to get it together, if only for their sake. Half a mile from home, I pulled into a parking lot. I needed to collect my thoughts. I was a logical person. I just need to walk through what I had to do. *Clayton seemed to indicate he'd do nothing to my family if I carried out my mission, as he called it. They should be safe, I rationalized. Diane will be available to help me, now that they have killed Larry. Maybe there's no evidence, but Clayton as good as confessed they had something to do with it.*

All Diane and I have to worry about is handling Texas. I'll assign Dale and the rest of the team to monitor a state. Let's see four, yes four states, four people, that'll work. That should alleviate any suspicions. Everyone knows we're going to be short handed with Larry gone. I wonder how it's going to be, what with Diane and I working together and all? I'm sure Clayton's told her that he showed me the tape. I laughed out loud. *How silly I'd been, thinking Diane was actually attracted to me. This time will be different. It will be all business. I'll make sure of that. There. It's all worked out. I can go home now.*

I came in the house looking emotionally drained. I was feeling physically weak and my nerves were on edge. All I need is a good night's sleep. For all the love I had for my wife and kids, I didn't want to see them right now. I just wanted to go straight to the bedroom and sleep for a month. I had a little trick when I felt like this and needed to fall asleep quickly. I'd actually plan out my dreams when I went to bed and soon I was fast asleep. Not a weird dream. I'd make up a scenario where I was involved in uncovering a great mystery that had yet to be solved, like the Kennedy assassination. I would dream about finding evidence no one had yet discovered. This actually helped me fall asleep.

Sally greeted me with a hug and kiss. "How was your day?" she asked.

"It was tiring. I just want to go to bed."

"No supper?" she asked.

"No. I'm not hungry. I just need some sleep. In a couple of days I'll be working all night. You remember right? I told you a while ago."

Sally sensed I was really tired and in no mood for arguing about little things, like whether I told her or not about having to work all night.

I walked towards the bedroom, but stopped to ask, "Any calls today?"

"Yes, Larry's son Richard called with the funeral arrangements."

"When are they?" I asked.

"I wrote it down here. The viewing is tonight, 6 to 8 and tomorrow 7 to 9. The funeral is Saturday at 10 over at St. Peters. He said the only friends he could find in Larry's things were people he worked with. He thought these times would be good for them."

For all my rant and raving about poor Larry, I didn't really want to go back out tonight. I was so looking forward to going to bed. "We'll go tomorrow night." I said. I think Sally already guessed that.

"That's fine dear. I'll get a babysitter. Goodnight."

I finally got to go to bed.

***

It was two days before the election. Driving to the office, I couldn't help but think of Diane. What was it going to be like when we see each other again? I hadn't been able to sleep since the meeting with Clayton. Between dreaming about Larry and Diane, I tossed and turned all night. Probably kept Sally up too, but she never said anything. My trick dream thing didn't work. The horror of Larry being killed and the shame I felt about my infidelity kept me in the real world.

The staff was all there. Most of them like Larry came in early, mainly to beat the traffic. They seemed eager to get started and that gave me some relief. I was going to be busy enough myself and didn't have time to oversee or manage them. They really didn't need me. They were all professionals who knew what to do at this point in the project.

The team was very sympathetic to me, not only because of Larry, but they knew I would now have to be in charge of working on one of the five states. A couple of people offered to help me, but of course I refused. They didn't know that it wasn't Larry's death that caused me to have to work on my own state; this had been planned from the beginning. In addition they didn't realize I did have help. Diane would be at my side handling Texas. The excuse I gave the staff in picking Texas for myself was plausible. They all knew Larry and I had tested Texas together when we were piloting the system.

Although it was two days before the election, the staff and I had a lot of work in preparing the system to get ready for election night. The five states the staff and I were handling, all had absentee ballots that had arrived already. We were busy overseeing the loading and verifying the absentee ballots into the system. Diane and I would be getting to work also. Texas was the only state of our five that had early voting. We not only had absentee ballots, but actual votes to consider, with the people of Texas allowed to vote days before the formal Election Day. The databases would have to be populated with every voter.

Our main concerns were to be able to spot duplicate voters, those not registered verses late registered voters, and valid counts. We had to get a jump on this with Election Day bringing in millions of votes to be handled.

Diane and I had one more duty apart from the rest of the staff. We not only had to make sure our system worked as it should normally; we had special processing to put in, based on selected counties. We had to boost the vote in those special, Hispanic counties. We had to deliver the state to President Anderson.

I hadn't seen Diane yet this morning. I was beginning to wonder if she was going to appear. I made my way down to our private office fully expecting to see her there. Pulling out my keys, I stopped and decided to try the door first. Somehow I knew it would be open and I would find Diane there. Even though I knew she would be there, I was still startled by her presence.

"Good morning, Diane." I didn't look at her. I went straight to my desk and logged onto the computer.

"Good morning Captain. Are you ready for this?"

I thought *what kind of question is that? Is she asking me if I've been talked to by Clayton? Or does she want to know if I have the guts to carry out the mission? Either way I guess it doesn't matter. I had already resigned myself to do my duty.* I looked up from my computer. Yes, I looked at her. I didn't want to. But I was comfortable in myself that I would see her as a tool, a machine that I needed to do my job. Not the temptress I had known before.

"Yes, I'm ready to do it." I told her confidently. "Let's get started. I need you to load our list of precincts from our target counties into the database. I'll fire up the match program. I'll keep a running total by precinct and use the algorithm module to adjust the totals and put in voter's names."

It felt funny talking about the algorithm module, it was Larry's baby. He had done a great job on it, but he wouldn't be proud about the way we were using it. I was looking for something else to do after we started loading data. That was going to take at least an hour, and I didn't want to sit there and talk to Diane.

Noticing the gap in actual work, Diane sat back and started the conversation. "What do the latest polls say? Who's winning, according to the experts?"

Politics was the last thing I wanted to talk about with Diane. That was a special thing Larry and I had together. I decided to be polite. "I don't know. We can look it up on the internet. Lets see, here it is. They have it a dead heat, Barnes/Kline at 48 percent and Anderson/Tierney at 46. I guess that means 6 percent will tip it one way or the other. At least that's what the *Times* poll says."

Diane chimed in. "The *Times* is playing it safe. They always do. Go to the *Lickter* web site, they know what's going on. Fact, they were more accurate than anyone the last two elections."

"Is that *L i c k t e r*?"

"Yes," she answered.

"Here it is." I had to laugh out loud. "It's exactly the same."

Diane asked me, "Go to their state breakdown and see what they say about our five states, especially Texas."

I found the page she was asking for and clicked on it. "They've got New York and Pennsylvania solidly in the Democrat column. Florida is leaning Republican. California looks to be in the Republican column and Texas is too close to call. It looks like we will definitely be needed. How's that data load going?"

"It's about 70 percent done" Diane said.

Good I thought, only a little while longer having to talk to Diane.

Diane asked, "Where's everybody campaigning?"

I went to the candidates web pages and looked for their scheduled appearances.

Looking at Diane, I said "Barnes's in San Diego, California talking to the Chamber of Commerce. I guess that's a safe place. He's probably trying to secure his base there. Anderson's in San Antonio, Texas, giving a speech to the Organization of Hispanic Descendants. That's good for us. They have had a Hispanic strategy all along. It doesn't say where Tierney is. Hey, after he's wrapped up Pennsylvania, what else do you do with him?" I said laughing. Diane was impressed with my political insights. I could tell by her facial expressions.

She asked, "Where's Kline? Idaho?" We both laughed hard. A part of Idaho was well known as a refuge for anti-government groups. There had been numerous arrests of militant organizations there. Alcohol Tobacco and Firearms had raided them and found caches of weapons and tons of ammunition.

"No. He's in Michigan!" I said. That surprised both of us.

"Michigan?" Diane couldn't belief her ears.

"Yes Michigan, Macomb County to be specific." I kept reading. "According to the story, Macomb County is a traditionally blue-collar Democratic county, but has been a maverick county to the Democrats when there has been a liberal verses conservative choice, especially if moral issues are a factor in the race. It goes on to say, that it was the deciding factor in Mitchell winning both times against liberal Democrats in Michigan, which allowed Mitchell to win the electoral vote nationwide. But, they went back to the Democrats with Anderson when the economy was the issue. That's interesting."

Diane looked a little worried. "Do you think that might happen again? I mean Kline helping to win Michigan for Barnes?"

"No, one thing I was taught about politics was that people vote for the Presidential candidate, not his running mate. They'll go for Anderson. Barnes's no conservative."

We finished loading all our files. The special modules were working fine. No need for the both of us to be here 24/7 until election night. I suggested to Diane that we split the next two days and nights between us. She agreed and volunteered to spend the night here. I would relieve her early tomorrow morning. Someone had to be here at all times and protect our nefarious doings. No one else was allowed to enter this office at any time from now on. Diane agreed. I had no concern with her. On this, I trusted her. The day and night of the election, and the next day, would require us to be there 24/7 and we needed to get as much rest as we could between now and then. I went home.

***

It was election eve, November 8th, 1996. Diane and I had agreed to work together for the long haul starting election morning. I was too excited to wait for the morning so I decided to go in that night. I explained to Sally that I just couldn't wait any longer. I needed to go into work and she shouldn't look for me for at least two days. Sally understood; she always did, God bless her. She obviously had figured out that my project was one that dealt with the election when she asked me, "I know your work has something to do with the election, but does it have to take two days, or is there more to it than just the election?"

"Well, yes it does. They're doing part of the election returns with our computer system. It's been pretty well hush, hush until now. Not the computer system, but more who was working on it and what it all involved. They didn't want everyone to know the people's names that were working on it. That reminds me, I didn't even vote. I'm not going to be able to get away either. Oh well, it wouldn't be the first time I missed voting, how about you?"

Sally replied, "I'm going tomorrow while the kids are in school. Our church had a meeting last week to discuss the candidates."

"Oh, and what did you guys decide?"

"We discussed each of the men and their stands on the issues. We broke the issues into two sides, economic and moral."

"And what did you decide?" I couldn't wait for all the details. I just wanted to know what her church members were thinking.

"We decided that Barnes was a nice man, but things, other than the employment issue, are going okay under President Anderson. The biggest thing we all were worried about was Mr. Kline. He seems so hateful. He never talks nice about anyone."

I just smiled and told her to vote her conscience. I had to laugh to myself. I was now doing the Lord's work in making sure Kline didn't win.

On the way to the office, I was curious how things were going. Had Diane been able to keep up with everything? She must be alright. I told her to call if there was a problem and I hadn't heard from her.

Arriving at the DOD parking lot, I noticed a familiar car. Parked in the VIP area was what looked like Senator Larson's limo. I had to walk out of my way to verify it, but I was curious enough to go there. Sure enough, there it was on the license plate, SEN. LARSON. It really wouldn't be out of the ordinary for him to be here. He could be seeing some General, he did serve on the Armed Forces Committee as well as Government Operations. But I'll bet my bottom dollar he's here to check on me, seeing if I was doing my duty as Clayton would put it.

I went straight to the private office. This time the door was locked. I pulled out my keys, fearing no one was minding the store. Opening the door, I found Diane there with the Senator. As I entered, they both looked like the cat that swallowed the canary. I knew he was checking up on me, but I wondered; for himself or was he sent by Clayton. Oh well, what's the difference. I had a job to do and went straight to the computer, acknowledging them along the way.

"So, Captain. Diane tells me everything is going well. You see it the same way?" asked Larson.

"I'll let you know in a minute." I said, looking up the latest numbers. "Yes, I'd say so. The counties we're monitoring are going as expected. Our algorithm module is only bumping them by 4 percent, which means turnout must be high in those counties."

The Senator wasn't impressed, "I don't know about algorithms, tell me in English." He wasn't kidding around.

I explained, "This means we only have to increase the vote for Anderson by 4 percent in those counties, giving him the lead overall in the state."

"That's great news", the Senator said. "The smaller the number we have to adjust means it's less likely they will be questioned, right?"

"You got it exactly right. And we have names to go with those numbers. That's the beauty of the system", I bragged.

Diane smiled and said "The system is working just as we planned."

This infuriated me. I thought, *she didn't have anything to do with designing or coding this system, and here she's trying to take the credit.*

The Senator turned to leave and said, "I'm going to be staying at the RNC until the election is done. They've got people all over the country phoning in key results. If you need me for anything and I mean anything, Captain, here's my private cell number. You call me."

"Yes sir, I'll do that."

Diane and I got the office ready for the long days ahead. We planned out food, rest, and a schedule to make sure one of us would be here at all times.

***

It was now Election Day, November 9th, 1996. In many ways, it had snuck up on me. In other ways, I was glad to see it finally here. Too excited to wait for my scheduled time, I had to go into the office to double check everything. Diane was surprised to see me there early, but I explained how I couldn't stay away, given the importance of the project. She caught my meaning without further explanation needed. Diane and I manned our posts in the private office, ready to handle anything we needed to. The system had been running so well, I thought to myself, *this is going to be boring,* but I knew I had to keep such thoughts out of my head and pay attention. The biggest worry I had was what were Diane and I going to talk about all day. I assumed Senator Larson was at the RNC with Ralph Sampson. They were going to have their hands full watching fifty states. We only had five, well really one that counted to me.

Over at the Republican National Headquarters things were busy. Senator Larson was constantly bugging Ralph Sampson for the latest poll numbers.

"Ralph", Larson said, "what's the number's look like?

Sampson was getting tired of hearing that same question every 5 minutes from Larson.

"Damon, they haven't changed since the last time you asked me."

Sampson took a deep breath to relax and continued "Looks like we're up 48 to 46."

Larson shot back visibly and verbally on edge, "Not the vote percent, you idiot, the Electoral College, that's the only thing that counts."

Sampson pulled a different piece of paper out of his suit pocket and told Larson, "Nothing's been called yet, but I'd say we are on track."

"That's the best you can do?" exclaimed Larson.

Sampson shouted back at Larson "I told you we have teams set up to watch their states and they will call the states one way or the other. They haven't confirmed anything yet. When they do, I'll let you know."

Larson tagged behind Sampson everywhere he went. Sampson tried to ignore him; he was busy on the phone with the state teams trying to get the very information Larson was bugging him about. Sampson had just explained to Larson that it was only 4 o'clock and the earliest state to close their polls was Delaware, and that was not until 6 o'clock. Sampson rolled his eyes at Larson and continued to call his contacts, who were assigned to the earliest closing states. Larson paced nervously up and down waiting for that first state to be declared for a candidate.

A bell rang in the center of the RNC action room. Larson asked "What's that bell mean?"

Sampson explained to him, "That's what you have been waiting for. When that bell rings, it means a state has been called and you should turn your attention to the big electronic board at the end of the room. You'll see the state name light up with the electoral vote under the candidate's name." Sampson hoped that would keep Larson busy, watching that board, and not bothering him.

Larson said to Sampson, "You're right. 6 o'clock and there goes Delaware for Anderson, 3 votes."

Sampson told Larson, "The next bunch will start to come about 7 o'clock, depending how close they are. Just listen for the bell and watch the board. Notice the total under the candidate's name. You need 270 to get elected." Sampson thought for sure he had something for Larson this time, to keep him out of his hair.

Seven o'clock and the bells were ringing. Flashes on the board caught everyone's eye. The Eastern states' results were starting to flow in. Things were going as planned with the usual states falling into their predictable voting patterns. Sampson and Larson were sizing up the totals so far. Both agreed, it was going to be up to Texas. Eight o'clock and lights and bells dominated the sights and sounds of the RNC.

"Pennsylvania, Illinois, and there goes Minnesota, all for Anderson, that's good." Larson exclaimed.

Sampson turned to Larson and said "Quiet down dam it. Don't you know where you are? Let me remind you. You are at the Republican Headquarters, not Anderson's."

Larson put his head down sheepishly and said, "I know. I know. I just got overexcited at the moment." He turned back to Sampson and asked, "Anything unusual Ralph? I mean for the Republicans. How are they doing?"

Sampson ticked off the states he expected to go to Barnes. "Let's see. Florida, yeah, Indiana ok, and Missouri, I expected to get those." Then to make sure everything was on track, he read the column of states that had been carried by Anderson, finding nothing out of the ordinary.

Nine o'clock and the plain's states were now center stage. "It won't be long now. Texas should be ringing that bell any minute", Larson said to Sampson. "That one's the key to it all."

Sampson suddenly looked puzzled and worried all at the same time. In running through his list of states that should be completely counted, he noticed something odd. He murmured out loud, "Michigan."

Larson heard him and said, "What about Michigan." Looking himself at the board for assurance, Larson was stunned also. "Ralph, how come Michigan's not lit up for Anderson?"

Sampson replied, nervously, "I don't know. Either the boards screwed up or…" He hesitated.

Larson anxiously jumped in, "Or what?"

Sampson solemnly said, "Or it's to close to call."

Larson quickly calculated they were in trouble if Anderson didn't win Michigan, a state they assumed was a lock for the Democrats. Larson, red faced with anger asked, "To close to call? How can that be? Michigan should be a slam dunk for the Democrats."

Sampson was mad. Larson was speaking too loud again. "I told you to be quiet Damon. I'm not going to tell you again. If you don't calm down, you can go to the VIP lounge and watch the returns there. Understand?"

Larson was ready to fire back, thinking how dare you talk to me that way, I'm a United States Senator. But he didn't; he realized Sampson was right, he needed to calm down. Sampson, settling down himself, told Larson to wait here. He was going down to the people handling Michigan and find out for sure what was going on.

While Larson was waiting on Sampson to come back he thought out loud, but in a whisper this time, remembering Sampson's admonishment for being too boisterous, "It still might be up to Texas. I hadn't counted on this Michigan thing screwing everything up. God, its 10 o'clock, the middle of the country is almost done. Even the Southwest is starting to come in and we still don't have Michigan. Wait. I remember Sampson telling me, even with Texas going to Anderson, a couple of states like Michigan and New Mexico could give the election to Barnes/Kline. Well, I'm not going to worry about that yet. We still don't have Texas. Here comes Ralph."

Sampson whispered to Larson, "I'm afraid it's true, Michigan's too close to call. We'll just have to wait and see." A bell sounded. All eyes turned to Michigan, nothing changed with its status. Everyone was scanning the board, looking for the results the latest bell ringing had foretold. It was TEXAS, lit up like a Christmas tree for Anderson. Larson and Sampson looked at each other and smiled. They were both a little more relaxed now.

Eleven o'clock. Twelve o'clock and Michigan was still too close to call. California was in the right column, having been won by Barnes. Hawaii and Alaska were in according to their past voting habits as expected. The fact that Texas had come through for Anderson, with the help of a little piece of computer code, didn't help Larson savor victory because Michigan was still too close to call. Sampson and Larson had more to worry about. You now had New Mexico thrown into the mix. Thirty minutes later the final tally on New Mexico saw it fall into the Anderson camp. Larson was only slightly relieved; having just been told by Sampson that with New Mexico in Anderson's column this meant Barnes Kline could not mathematically win only tie if Michigan went to Barnes.

Sampson excused himself again to Larson, explaining he was going down to get the latest raw vote count on Michigan. He returned shortly with an ominous look on his face.

Larson asked Sampson, "Well? What's the latest?"

Sampson just pointed at the board and said, "Look. They're about to post it."

Only seconds past, but it was like an eternity to Larson. He thought to himself, *I'm waiting on a little light bulb and a ring of a bell that could announce the future of the United States of America and even the world.*

It was Michigan for Barnes/Kline! The cheers went up throughout the room, but they were short lived as everyone's eyes moved down the board from Michigan to the grand total line for each candidate.

Sampson turned from the board and looked ominously at Larson and in a stunned voiced said, "We will have an Electoral College tie. It's 269 to 269.

Larson blurted out, "Oh, my God."

Sampson was silent for a moment and then a glow came over him. He excitedly said to Larson, "Damon, this isn't over yet."

Larson caught Sampson's excitement, although he didn't why, and said, "What do you mean?"

Sampson, almost breathless, explained, "We've still got a chance. There's the Electoral College. There's no law that says the electors have to vote for their guy. It's happened in the past. Don't you see? All we need is to get one elector to switch."

Larson was disappointed. He thought Sampson had some miracle he was going to be able to pull out of his hat and it would be a done deal. Not so simple.

Larson said to Sampson, "I'm going home. I have a lot to think about."

Chapter 12 Electoral College Meets

Sen. Larson couldn't wait to get back over to the Republican National Committee offices. He needed to talk to Sampson about what options they had to win the election. What was new in Sampson's plan to get an elector to switch from Barnes to Anderson? He still held out hope. Maybe one of the Barnes/Kline electors could be talked into voting for Anderson. Larson knew he was grasping at straws. He reached Sampson's office, flying by the secretary, and went right in. The secretary, having recognized the Senator, just sat in silence. Finding Sampson on the phone, Larson slowed down and nervously paced around the room, waiting for Sampson to finish his call. When Larson heard Sampson say "Thank you", he knew he was about to get Sampson's attention. Sampson hung up the phone and acknowledged Larson's presence.

"Damon, what can I do for you?"

"You know darn well what you can do for me. What about your plan last night. You know, to get some elector to switch."

Sampson said, "That's what I've been doing all morning Damon, lining up a list of possibilities."

Larson calmed down, "Oh how's that going? Got any prospects?" Sampson proceeded to go through the list with Larson.

Larson, being in a hurry, said, "I don't need a list of who isn't going to help Ralph, just get to the ones we have a shot at."

Sampson was still going to go through his plan; he was a methodical man who wanted Larson to understand all the variables. "What we have Damon, is 269 potential Barnes voters. We need for one of them to vote for Anderson. It doesn't do any good for one of them to vote for anybody else or not vote at all. Anderson would still be one vote short of the 270 needed, which is why I have been trying to draw up a possible list of delegates. It is not easy to persuade one guy to violate the sacred commitment to his party's candidate."

Larson asked, "Well then, what's that list look like?"

"After the first pass of going through the 269 possibilities, the list has quickly narrowed to only a handful, 23. And some of those are iffy at best. Look, whose going to call these people? And what are we going to say to them? What can we offer them to switch votes?"

"I know, I know" said Larson. "Do you personally know any of these people?"

"No." said Sampson, "You?"

"Not a one", replied Larson. "I will bet most of these people are more Republican than you or I. Well, we have to try. It's our only hope."

Larson and Sampson were not exactly in favor with a lot of Republicans because of the way they seemed to sit out the election, not giving the Barnes/Kline ticket any help at all. So they decided to try and call the delegates themselves. They soon found out these delegates were more Republican than both of them, like they surmised, and they were also not stupid.

The fact was they all knew under the Constitution, the newly elected House and Senate would vote on President and Vice President in case of a tie. The delegates all knew there was a chance they could win the Presidency for the Republicans.

Larson, frustrated, said, "I'm going to talk to Clayton. Maybe he can get something on one of these people."

Larson raced over to CIA headquarters to talk to Clayton, but came away depressed. Clayton was not about to open up talk about Republicans trying to elect a Democrat to the Presidency. Clayton told Larson he feared it might lead back to the whole mission and what was really going on. However Clayton agreed to look into some of the Barnes/Kline electors and see if there was a possibility of finding a defector, but he insisted Larson do nothing until he hears from him. This would be the last Larson would heard from Clayton before the Electoral College meeting.

***

The Electoral College met as directed by the Constitution on December 14th, amid tension and speculation. The rumors were abounding throughout both political parties. There was talk of a delegate here and a delegate there that just might switch and vote for the opposite party. I didn't put much stock in those rumors. I knew if an elector did switch, that person would become a political pariah for life. We were all watching our television sets; our eyes glued to the four simultaneous pictures of four state houses, where the electors would cast their votes. This was historic. I wasn't about to miss this and settled in to watch.

The networks were covering four states at a time based on time zones. The electors were meeting in their respective state capitals and casting their votes for President and Vice President. The President of their State Senate would announce the results when all the electors had voted. All the television stations were carrying a running total of these votes.

I snickered at the anchormen trying their best to make more of a story out of it than what it was. After all, if it continued as expected, a tie in the Electoral College was a big story by itself, but they kept bringing in so called experts from both parties with stories about a delegate who was overheard saying he or she was considering switching their vote. I didn't believe it, but it kept me glued to the TV with the possibility it could happen. As the day wore on and state after state delegations came in with expected results, it became clear the vote was going to be a tie, 269-269.

The reporters were scrambling to find out what would happen next. They reported the ballot results would be sent to the United States Senate. This much they knew. They also said the President of the Senate, Vice President Tierney, would announce the fact that it was officially a tie. But that's all they knew for sure. Most of them were not familiar enough with the Constitution to even render an opinion on what would happen next.

It was funny watching the anchor people pleading for help from their field reporters to find a copy of the Constitution and tell their viewing public what to expect. You would have thought they would have been better prepared. Finally, a channel 13 reporter was ready to go on the air with "Breaking Information." He actually had a copy of the constitution in his hands.

"I'm told through my ear piece we have Tom Carter standing by with some new information. Tom what have you been able to find out?" the anchorman, Barry Winston, asked.

"Barry, I have the information on what will happen next. First, nothing new will happen until January 3rd, now that's the next important date to keep in mind, that's when the new Congress, elected in this past election will be sworn in. The new House of Representatives will then convene on the 10th of January, the next important date. They will need to meet before January 20th, which is the date the new President is supposed to take his oath. They will have the duty of electing the next President.

The anchorman interrupted to ask, "Where did you obtain that January 10th date from Tom?"

"Good question Barry. I was able to talk briefly with the Speaker of the House, George Fleming. He told me that January 10th would be the date he most lightly will set to call the new House into session."

Barry then realizing he broke Tom's chain of events said, "Sorry to interrupt Tom. I just want to get all the details spelled out for our viewers. Go ahead Tom."

"That's ok, Barry. This twist in history has us all looking for the details. The House, assuming Speaker Fleming calls them into session on the 10th, will cast their votes state by state. Each state will have one vote for President. Now let me explain that further. I guess an example would be more informative. Let's take the state of New York; I happen to have their information in front of me. The state of New York has 37 electoral votes. The way that's determined is taking the number of Representatives they have, which is 35 and adding the two Senators, that's where the number 37 comes from. It's these 35 Congressmen that will vote amongst themselves for President. The candidate who receives the majority of these 35 or I guess 18 will get that state's one vote for President."

Barry stopped Tom again, "So the obvious question, Tom, is how many Republicans and how Democrats are there in the 35? Assuming they vote their party lines."

Tom replied, "That's a good assumption Barry. There are currently 20 Democrats and 15 Republicans. One could make an educated guess the state would go for President Anderson."

"Thanks Tom. Ladies and gentlemen looks like January 10th will be the day of decision for the 1996 election. We will continue to cover this historical breaking story, and we ask you to stay tuned for all your election coverage to USB."

***

January 10th, the day of decision had arrived. I was just as excited as the rest of the country. This was history in the making during our lifetime. Every once and awhile I thought about Larson and Clayton, wondering what they were up to. I had done all I could, and God knows Larry did. He gave his life for his country. It's funny how you justify sacrifice even under these circumstances. I still believed in the project. I still believed in stopping Kline, but what if Larry died for nothing? I couldn't help but feel isolated, all alone, nobody I could talk to. I could stay home today and watch TV with Sally, but even with her, I would still feel alone. I'm going to the office and watch it.

Still wanting to be alone, I acknowledged the team and went straight to the private office. I figured I could watch the Congress on the Internet. I tuned into channel 13 through the Internet and anxiously awaited the vote. I felt like a kid on Christmas morning, seeing the presents in front of me and waiting for my parents to give me that nod to start opening. Ah, here comes Barry.

"Good afternoon everyone. USB news welcomes you to our coverage of the race for the Presidency of the United States. I'm Barry Winston. Our reporter in the House gallery is Tom Barrett. Let's go to Tom and set the scene for you. Tom, that's a pretty impressive sight down there."

"Yes Barry, not only on the floor, but up here in the gallery. You have news organizations from all over the world watching a procedure none of us have ever seen in our lifetime. Barry, let me recap for the viewers what they can expect to happen in the next few minutes. First, a little housekeeping is needed. The vote by Congress for President is again, not a direct vote. Under the Constitution each state gets one vote, and a majority of 26 states is required to select the President, one more than half of the number of states. The new House of Representatives was convened by the Speaker after being sworn in. The Speaker will preside over the House and will at some time soon ask the clerk to call the state rolls. I'm told they will be called in alphabetical order, which will make Alabama the first to be called. The states presumably have already caucused to decide their vote; they will then announce that vote to the

Speaker. Barry, I'm told the states will be able to pass two times. The third time they are called they must cast a ballot or be recorded as not voting."

"Tom, I have to interrupt you. I see Speaker Fleming ascending to the podium."

Speaker Fleming began hammering the gavel. "Will the members please take their seats? Members in the aisles please clear the aisles and take your seats." He paused, waiting to see if anyone was following his orders. A few people started to move toward their seats, but not enough for the Speaker. "Members will take their seats now and clear the aisles." He continued to bang the gavel. It was becoming more frequent now. The noise you could hear on TV began to subside like someone was turning the volume down on the television.

Speaker Fleming began the proceedings, "Fellow Representatives, this body, the duly elected Representatives of the United States of America, is convened today to carry out its Constitutional duty to elect the next President of the United States. I now officially declare the whole House to be in session and a quorum present. Under the House rules and agenda for this session, we will open with a prayer from the Chaplain and move to the business of the day. Chaplain."

"Heavenly Father, God of all Gods. We beseech you to give us your guidance today in carrying out the duties assigned to us. We ask You to give us wisdom and clarity of mind in determining our new President. Have mercy on us that we might be humble in our grand undertaking. No matter the outcome give us the ability to project a united front to the people of this great country. That they might go forward in confidence that we have done our best. We ask this in your Holy name. Amen."

Speaker Fleming, turning to the clerk of the House who was awaiting his command, said "The clerk of the House will now please call the roll of the states."

"Alabama," rang out the voice of the clerk, loud and strong.

"Mr. Speaker, Alabama with 5 Republican and two Democratic members of the House casts its one vote for Senator Barnes for President of the United States."

The clerk repeated. "Alabama casts its vote for Senator Barnes for President." And so it went state after state casting their one vote for President until Minnesota, when things became interesting.

"Mr. Speaker, Minnesota, due to the fact we have eight members of the House, four Republicans and four Democrats, is unable to cast a vote due to the tie amongst our delegation."

The clerk restated, "Minnesota is unable to cast a vote and passes for the first time."

Barry, the anchorman whispered through his microphone to the viewers, "Minnesota has two more chances to vote. I assume they will continue to try and find one congressman to switch. But, as we said before, that's highly unlikely."

A new wrinkle had made itself known. Those states with equal numbers of Republicans and Democrats were virtually stalemated. If nothing changed in their delegations, they would not be able to cast a ballot, even with three tries. Most of the political pros had already figured this out, but for the millions of people looking in, this was quite a shock. *The phones and emails must be flooding the networks*, I thought. *People will want to know what happens if neither of the candidates can get 26 state's votes.* Barry continued with his comments, "The phones and emails are blitzing us here at the station."

I knew it, I exclaimed to myself.

"We are going to wait until the entire vote is done before we wade into any speculation", Barry explained to his viewers.

As the last of the states were being called, everyone was scrambling to add up the totals to see if Barnes or Anderson had the 26 votes necessary for election. After Wyoming, the last state, the television count on the screen gave everyone the news they feared, no winner. Barnes had 22 states just four short; Anderson had 17 states and 11 states had not voted because they were tied within their delegations.

USB anchorman, Barry Winston reported, "ladies and gentleman, we have witnessed history in the making. The House is deadlocked after three ballots and it looks likely, they will not be able to come to a decision. We could continue with the broadcast bringing you speculation on what lies before us. But it would be just that, speculation. Instead, we here at USB, will be bringing to you a Constitutional election expert, Dr. Lee Walters, from Washington and Lee College, known nationally for his expertise on the Constitution, at a special broadcast at 6 o'clock Eastern Standard Time. We will continue to provide you the latest in breaking news. We ask you to please join us at 6 o'clock this evening for this fascinating insight from Dr. Walters."

I quickly turned to look for any book I had in the office, which might have the Constitution in it. It suddenly dawned on me; we didn't have anything here except technical manuals. I could search the internet, but I'll bet if I found a copy I won't understand it anyway. I decided to go out and get some early dinner and let this Professor explain it to me.

I needed to kill some time until the Professor was on. I decided to go out to eat and come back to the office, rather than going home. I knew it was selfish of me, but I didn't want any distractions listening to the Professor. Driving to the restaurant I had enough hearing about politics for a while. I would be going back to it at 6 o'clock. It wasn't that I didn't have an interest but I needed a change if only to recharge my batteries. I pushed all the radio buttons until I found some music. It wasn't what I normally would listen to, but it was the only station not talking about the election. Then there was only the sound of the highway. The radio had gone dead. As I reached to try another station, a deep voice came on the radio and announced they were carrying a broadcast from President Anderson. I decided to listen.

President Anderson, "My fellow Americans we are embarking on a journey of historical proportions. While no one living today has been through the developing election process we are experiencing, our great country has seen it all before and has survived just fine. Our founding fathers have devised a document that is the envy of the world. It has sustained us in time of war and peace and will continue to provide us the guidance we need to resolve this temporary impasse. Rest assured we have a government that is continuing to work, as we speak for the good people of the United States." *That was nice*, I thought. *He needed to say something to calm the people. I'm sure a lot of people were wondering what the status of the country was concerning the Presidency.* The music returned and I mused about what I would have to eat for dinner.

I was back to the office by 6:15 pm and settled in to hear the Professor; me and 200 million others. I was mad at myself for being late. I had a good, slow dinner and it had relaxed me. It felt good at the time, but now I was worried such a big dinner might make me sleepy. I had already missed the first 15 minutes. I was fumbling with the Internet trying to find USB's broadcast. I wished I had put it in my favorites list. There it is. Looks like Barry's alone. No professor yet. Good.

"Next, we have our special guest expert we promised you. He's Dr. Lee Walters, an expert on Constitutional matters from Washington and Lee College. Professor Walters, thank you for being with us this evening. I see you have brought a copy of the Constitution with you."

Trying to put a little light humor on the subject Barry said. "I would have thought you had that memorized by now."

"Actually I have Barry, but I thought for clarity's sake it would be good to read from the actual document and try to explain what our founding fathers had in mind when they wrote it", the Professor responded.

Barry setting the stage, "Now here's where I see us at this point Professor. We have had the Electoral College meet, and that ended in a tie, 269 to 269. Then, we had the House of Representatives meet and vote by state, 26 needed to elect a President, and that ended in, well, excuse me if I use a boxing term; in a no decision. That is, no one could get the 26 states needed for a majority. Where do we go from here?"

Professor Walters took a deep breath, as to make you think his answer was going to be long and involved, "We are now at the 12th Amendment of the Constitution. I'll read what the 12th Amendment says on this matter and will break it down in language we will all be able to understand. I am reading from the 12th amendment as adopted by Congress and the states in 1804.

"I quote. *And if the House of Representatives shall not choose a President whenever the right of choice shall devolve upon them before the fourth day of March next following,*

Then the Vice-President shall act as President, as in the case of the death or other constitutional disability of the President.

The person having the greatest number of votes as Vice-President, shall be the Vice-President, if such number be a majority of the whole number of Electors appointed, and if no person have a majority, then from the two highest numbers on the list, the Senate shall choose the Vice-President.

A quorum for the purpose shall consist of two-thirds of the whole number of Senators, and a majority of the whole number shall be necessary to a choice.

But no person constitutionally ineligible to the office of President shall be eligible to that of Vice-President of the United States.

"Now remember we are talking about the Senate here. The House couldn't elect a President so now the 12th Amendment tells us as a country, to have the Senate elect a Vice President."

Barry, having no idea what the Professor had just read, asked, "Professor, can you break all this down for us a little more concisely?"

"Yes let us start with the easy statements, the last two. The last sentences simply states anyone not meeting the requirements for President cannot be elected Vice President. Remember again, the Senate is voting on who will be Vice President, the House votes on who will be President. Those requirements for being President are as follows. Number 1 you must be 35 years old. Number 2 you must be a person born in the United States. And three, you must have lived in the United States for 14 years.

The professor continued, "The next to last sentence says for the Senate to even vote on a Vice President, two thirds of the Senate must show up to proceed. In today's Senate, that means at least 67 Senators have to be there when choosing a Vice President. It then goes on to say a majority of all the Senate, is necessary to elect a vice president. That means it takes at least 67 Senators to have the meeting and vote in a Vice President, but that person would still have to get at least 51 of those votes to win. If only 67 showed up, the person would still need 51 votes to get elected."

Barry asked the Professor. "Professor, do you see the same problem I do? What if there is some political gamesmanship played where a minority party of the Senate decides not to show up to vote, then the process is stopped?"

Professor Walters replied to Barry, "Yes indeed, that's exactly what would happen."

The anchorman was puzzled. "What would happen? I mean there must be a way to get a person chosen President or is there?"

The Professor said confidently, "Well we go through the succession process. What I mean is after the Vice President; the Speaker of the House is next in line and would become President without any further discussion or voting."

The anchorman was quick to point out, "And that would be Speaker Fleming, Republican from Iowa?"

"Yes." said the Professor.

The Professor continued, "I don't think that's likely however. I think the public would demand one of the people they voted for President and Vice President should have first consideration. I believe all the Senators will show up."

"Back to the 12th Amendment Professor", Barry inquired. "The first sentence talks about a date of March 4th, does that date still hold?"

The Professor responded, "No, the 20th amendment, adopted in 1933, took care of that. The new President takes office on January 20 so all the dates back up from there."

Barry asked the Professor, "It says the House having met and not able to come up with a majority for either candidate; the Senate will probably vote for a Vice President, who will be the acting President. But does that mean the House is done? In other words, could the House continue to meet, and through, say some deal making, come up with a President? And is there a time limit for them to do this?"

Professor Walters answered, "The answer, in my opinion, is no. The 12th Amendment gives the House a deadline, originally March 4th; but amended to January 20th, and agreed upon by most constitutional scholars, to choose a President. If they are unable, it gives the job to the Senate to pick a Vice President, who will act as President, until the next election."

Barry, the anchorman, turns from the Professor and looks solemnly into the camera and states, "If the vote stays along party lines in the Senate, by my calculation that means Raymond Kline will become the 43rd President of the Unites States. Thank you for being here today, Professor, and for your very interesting and informative insights. Let's go to Tom Carter at the United States Senate building. Tom. Are you hearing anything on when the Senate plans to meet?"

"Yes, Barry the date I'm hearing is January the 17th. They really don't have many days left to choose from. They need to meet before the 20th of January."

"Tom, have you been able to talk to anyone about the plans if the Senate vote doesn't come to a conclusion? In case you didn't hear, the

Professor we had on at 6 o'clock this evening, he talked about the possibility of Senators not showing up for a quorum or not voting for their party's candidate."

"I have not heard anything like that, Barry. I've talked to a lot of Senators, and members of Senator's staffs, and they are all anxious to be part of the vote. As far as switching parties, my experience covering this Senate is that they are all pretty committed and I don't see that happening. Stranger things have happened though, look where we are today."

"Thanks Tom. If anything breaks I'm sure we can count on you to get it back to us as soon as possible. That's Tom Carter covering the Senate."

Barry Winston, the esteemed and distinguished anchorman, looked deeply into the camera and spoke to everyone watching in an obvious solemn tone, closed by saying, "When we determine the official date for the Senate to convene the vote for Vice President, actually make that the President, you'll be the first to know. Stay tuned to USB and their local stations for breaking news. This is Barry Winston reporting for USB. Goodnight."

Chapter 13 We Have a President

Senator Larson called me today. It was a call out of the blue. Except for a thought here and there of him during the House vote, I had tried to forget about him. He wanted to talk to me about the future. *The future*, I thought, *now what scheme did he want to pull me into?* I agreed to meet him, only if it was at the DOD and in the private office. This was my cocoon; I felt secure and better yet, safe there.

Diane had had a twinge of conscience, during those long hours the night of the election. She had told me about the taping device, hidden in the office. I admitted to her that Clayton had shown me the tape, but I didn't mention Larry being on the same tape. She showed me how to disconnect the taping device even though the machine no longer had a tape in it. I told her how I appreciated her concern, and was sorry for the way I acted. She looked at me and said she too was sorry, but I had to understand she was only doing her duty. I thought *there's that phase again, doing your duty.* We had parted on an amicable note and I wished her well. From then on, it became a habit upon entering the office to check that the machine was disabled.

I must admit, my curiosity was peeked with Larson coming to see me. I would have thought the Senator would be busy trying to influence his fellow Senators, instructing them on how to vote for President. Turns out, he would have some other news, news that would affect me greatly.

I was waiting for the Senator to arrive, assuming he would have no trouble getting access to our highest level. I was wrong. Seems even the Senator couldn't get to the E Level without permission. The guard had stopped the Senator at the E Level elevator and told him he wasn't on the approved list for the day. Larson explained how important it was to see me, thinking my name would get him access. The security guard ended up allowing the Senator to come up. I am not sure how that happened, but soon I heard a knock on the door of the private office.

I opened the door and was surprised to see, not only the Senator, but the person who had escorted him to the office. It was Carl Minster.

Minster, straight faced said, "I found someone wandering the halls." Minster always spoke with a solemn face, you never knew when he was joking or not.

"Hello Senator." I didn't know what else to follow that with. I had gotten the impression the Senator wanted to talk to me alone.

"Captain, how are you? I thought I would stop by and congratulate you on your work. You did a fine job." Then he whispered, "No matter how it turns out."

Minster heard all of that. I didn't know if Minster was satisfied that was all there was to the Senator's visit or not, but he took it as harmless and left us alone. We went into the office and I locked the door behind me. I walked over to the panel that hid the taping machine and verified it was still disconnected.

Larson watched and when he realized what I was doing said ashamedly, "I am sorry about that Captain." I nodded and put the panel back. I purposely gave him the distinct impression I was not forgiving when it came to what Clayton had done.

Larson said, "Captain, I thought you should know. I received word that Senator Barnes has been taken to Bethesda hospital. He's not expected to survive the night."

I was surprised. We all knew this day would come but seemed like light years ago when we first found out about his illness.

I inquired coldly, "Who all knows?"

"Well I could say just his wife, Chief of Staff, and the hospital people, but we might as well face it everybody will know shortly. You cannot hide something like this about a potential President of the United States." Larson said.

"How did you find out?" I asked Larson.

"I have a contact in his personal doctor's office. The doctor was called initially by Barnes's wife. I just hope people don't start putting two and two together. If my contact was identified it could be embarrassing, and easily traced back to me; how I knew about Barnes's illness a long time ago."

"This sort of makes the Senate vote in a few days pointless, doesn't it?" I asked.

"Well yes and no Captain. There is the possibility now some Senators may not vote for Kline, now that he would definitely become President. On the other hand, they are not going to vote for Tierney either. There may be a movement that will gather steam to get the Speaker to assume the Presidency. I have to get back to the floor and start working on this angle."

Larson continued, "However, Captain. I've got another piece of news, that's also not good." He hesitated and looked around the room, searching to see if he would be heard by anyone else. *That was strange,* I thought, we are all alone. Wait, he must be thinking of the tape machine. But he saw me turn it off.

"I turned it off.", I said.

"Oh yeah, that's right." said Larson. "Clayton seems to have eyes everywhere. Anyway, my wife was looking at the obituaries in the newspaper last night. She was shaking her head, muttering something about, so young. She looked up at me and asked if I knew someone at CIA Headquarters named Diane McKenna. I said no, because at the time I didn't know Diane's last name. I asked her for more details and she said here's a picture of her. Captain, it was our Diane and she is dead."

"Dead? How?" I said aloud. "I just saw her the other day."

"According to the obituary she died of an unexpected illness at her home."

"Illness? She looked fine to me." I said.

"I know what you're thinking. I thought the same thing. I bet Clayton's got something to do with this. First, it was your friend Larry and now Diane, too coincidental for me.
Well, I just thought you should know. I've got to get back to the Senate. Take care. Take real care Captain."

"Thanks. You take care too."

I turned to cable news on the television. Usually, I would get my news from the Internet; I would turn off the sound on the computer and position the screen so no one knew what I was watching. Now, I really didn't care anymore what anybody thought. I turned up the volume on the television and awaited any news about Senator Barnes. I needed to wrap up some documentation on the election system, for future clients, so I decided to just stay in the private office to do my work and wait for the news. *Funny*, I thought, *how things have changed over the years.* Progress I guess. Most people used to wait for the newspaper to get their news. Now it's almost instantaneous on cable news or the Internet. When a major event happens now, everyone is glued to the television, but afterwards they all run out to get that newspaper with its big bold headlines and brilliant pictures. Maybe it's a souvenir thing, something to show their grandchildren. Regular people don't stop to throw a tape into their VCR when watching breaking news.

Later that afternoon, the news broke. The screen went blank and the sound suddenly disappeared. This caught my attention as I stared at the blank screen. Then a second later, the words Breaking News, appeared on the still silent television. USB's anchorman, Barry Winston, now showed up, fumbling with some papers on his desk. Sound now could be heard. It was the noise of a busy newsroom but incoherent to the viewer. Barry Winston looked like he now got the cue; he was on.

Barry looked into the camera and announced, "We interrupt normal broadcasting to bring this breaking news. Senator Barnes has been hospitalized at Bethesda Naval Hospital with an undisclosed illness. We received word about 15 minutes ago that Senator Barnes was rushed to Bethesda earlier today. Details are still developing. Let's go to our correspondent standing by at Bethesda Hospital, Peter Schinkel. Peter, what can you tell us?"

"Barry, here's what we know as of a few minutes ago. Senator Barnes's wife, Ruth Barnes called Dr. Weingarten, he's Senator Barnes's private physician, at 9 o'clock this morning. There are no details on what the nature of the call was, but it must have been urgent because Dr. Weingarten then called 911 to send an ambulance to the Barnes's residence. We know the ambulance arrived here at 9:30 and the Senator was whisked to the emergency room, where he was received by the emergency staff and Dr. Weingarten. I'm told something rather curious then happened. The Senator spent fewer than 10 minutes in the emergency before being taken to a private hospital room."

Barry, the anchorman, then asked, "A regular hospital room? That must mean good news right?"

"That's what we are all hoping for Barry. Regular hospital rooms are not where you go if there is an emergency. So at this point lacking any more information, we are assuming it's not serious. We are currently inquiring about a press briefing. When that briefing will take place is yet to be determined. The hospital's representative is currently not returning any of our calls."

"Peter, do you know who is all there with the Senator and is the Senator conscious?" Barry asked.

"All we know for sure is that his wife, Ruth, is there, and no, we know absolutely nothing about the Senator's condition or state of consciousness. Wait a moment Barry." You could see the reporter holding his ear piece tightly against his head, trying to hear something coming through.

Peter continued, "Barry, I'm being told the Senator's two daughters are being driven from the airport to the hospital." He paused, holding the ear piece tighter, getting more information.

"Sarah Barnes, who lives in New York and works at the United Nations as an interpreter, and her sister Mrs. Allison Webber, from North Carolina has flown in on the Senator's private jet. They should be arriving any moment."

Barry said to Peter, "Should we read anything into the fact that the family is being flown in?"

Peter said, "I cannot really say Barry. Not to sound uncaring, but we are talking about a possible future President here. We do have cameras at all the entrances and if we can get a shot of them arriving, we might be able to surmise something from their demeanor."

The daughters arrived at the hospital and the cameras were there to record them. As they exited the car, you could definitely see them holding handkerchiefs to their faces. Not to hide their faces but wiping away tears.

The reporter, Peter, narrated their arrival, pointing out the obvious sadness of the daughters.

"Something more is going on Peter, more than we are being told." Barry noted.

"I agree Barry. Speculation and I repeat it's only speculation, is that the Senator might have suffered a heart attack. Barry, I'm now told the hospital administration has issued a statement. I'm getting the statement from our associate director now."

Peter grabbed a piece of paper handed to him by a person outside of camera range. "There will be a news conference at 5 o'clock today. That's only about an hour from now."

The television station now had to fill an hour. I knew what was happening and didn't need to listen to their entire dribble. Heart attack, boy they had that wrong. I figured Barnes wouldn't survive the night but, with an announcement to come at 5 o'clock I surmised Barnes had already died. I expected the news conference would confirm his death or the fact he was dying. I continued working until 5 o'clock, waiting on the news conference.

Barry Winston appeared on camera, looking very solemn. "Ladies and gentlemen we just received word that Presidential hopeful Senator Barnes has died. The official word is to come at the 5 o'clock news conference scheduled by officials at the hospital. Peter, do you have any more details for us?" The camera now returned to the reporter at the hospital.

Peter reported, "Barry, what we have been able to learn is this. Senator Barnes died at approximately 3 o'clock today. His wife and a few close campaign aides were with him; his daughters came some time later. We are being told that the cause of death is not being reported at this time, but that it was sudden."

Barry took over stating, "Well we certainly offer our heart filled condolences to the Barnes family on this sad occasion of the passing of Senator Barnes. USB news will have a special on Senator Barnes's life later tonight. It goes without saying he will be missed by his family, friends, and the country. For an insight how this tragedy will affect the race for President, let's turn to Tom Carter at the Senate office building. Tom it's probably quite a change there, from the historic mission the Senate is about to undertake to the sadness at the news of Senator Barnes's unexpected death?"

Carter, picking up his cue said, "Yes, Barry. That's certainly the case here. Suddenly the talk and speculation of what Senators would or would not do on the up coming vote has changed to a sad, grieving, and respectful remembrance of Senator Barnes."

I turned off the television. All things considered, I felt sorry for the Barnes family. They had lost a husband and father. I may not have agreed with his politics, but he did serve his country in peace and war. I was still anxious to see what the Senate would do. Now that Barnes was gone, I would have bet there were now going to be some Senators who would take a different view of their vote. How could they vote to make Ray Kline President? I could see some of the Republicans swallowing Kline as long as he was a Republican. I'm sure Senator Larson was going to push his plan to have as many Republican Senators as possible not vote at all. This would give the Speaker the Presidency. Speaker Fleming, I was told by Larson, he would make an excellent President.

Senator Barnes's funeral was a stately affair. Dignitaries from all over the world attended. After all, he might have been President and he did have an illustrious career in the Senate. His cause of death was reported as a quick acting cancer that came on suddenly. No one questioned the cause or the timeliness. Everyone's attention had now turned back to the Senate vote.

Only a few days after the funeral, the Senate met. President Anderson and Vice President Tierney had been uncharacteristically quiet throughout the past few weeks. Except for a few remarks at Barnes's funeral, they were not to be heard from. I guess they figured out that there was no possible way for either of them to assume the Presidency with Republicans clearly in charge of the Senate.

***

The United States Senate had only recently allowed television cameras into its chambers. The C-Span network, a cable station, which carried the House of Representatives live daily, had an exclusive contract to show the Senate on television. It was announced, a few days ago, that USB news would be allowed to carry the feed nationally. The entire country would now be able to view history in the making. Our children, having been put to bed, Sally and I settled in to watch the selecting of a President. The Senate had agreed to hold their session in the evening, to give as many people as possible the opportunity to view this meeting.

Barry Winston, USB news anchor opened the event,"Good evening Ladies and Gentlemen, and thank you for making USB news your source for coverage of this historical event. The Senators are still milling about the floor having conversations with their fellow colleagues and aides. With all the rumors and speculation lately we are hearing from our sources, I am assuming some of them, at least, are reconsidering their vote. If that were to occur, the drama of this Presidential first might be racketed up a notch. To get an inside opinion on these speculations we have with us, Senator Damon Larson, one of the senior Republican Senators, and possibly the next Majority Leader. First, Senator let me offer my personal condolences to you. I know Senator Barnes was not only a colleague but a close, personal friend."

Senator Larson acknowledged the sentiment, "Thank you Barry."

Barry continued, "Senator, we are hearing the Republicans are divided on Mr. Kline. Some may vote for Vice President Tierney and some may not vote at all. What can you tell me about the situation in your party?"

Larson answered, "Each Senator is free to vote their conscience. We are not a party that demands every one marches in lock step. There are some Republican Senators, to be honest, who have a hard time accepting some of Mr. Kline's rhetoric. To be fair, we also have a number of Senators who respect Mr. Kline and feel he will represent the United States well. The only thing I want to correct, Barry, is some people are reporting that Vice President Tierney cannot be elected. That is not true. If, for example, enough Republican Senators vote for Vice President Tierney, he can indeed win."

Barry asked, "Would that ultimately help or hurt your party?"

Larson replied, "I can work with either person. The party has to be big enough to do the right thing for the country. That's what we're here for, the good of the country not for the good of the party."

Barry, puzzled by Larson's statement asked, "Senator, sounds like you are asking your parties members to vote for Vice President Tierney or at least not campaigning whole heartily for Mr. Kline?"

Larson realized he was being too obvious in his own wishes replied, "Oh, no. I'm not saying that at all. I'm just trying to lay out all the possibilities that can happen. Either way it comes out, the Republicans will still maintain control of the Senate. Any legislation proposed by either Mr. Tierney or Mr. Kline, will have to get approval from our party."

"But Senator…, wait a minute, I see the Vice President now entering onto the Senate floor. We'll be taking you there shortly to hear the Vice President open the session. Senator Larson, it's been a pleasure having you here. Can you come back after you vote for a few more minutes and offer some commentary as this unfolds?"

Larson, not wanting to risk a slip of the tongue, replied, "No, I'm sorry Barry I can't commit to that, I have a number of meetings to attend already. I have to get down to the floor now, thanks for having me."

Barry said, "I understand, Senator. Thank you again Senator Larson for your time."

Vice President Tierney, as the President of the Senate, slowly made his way to the podium, where he picked up the gavel, as he was still talking to the clerk of the Senate.

Barry Winston, the anchorman, announced to the viewers, "We are fortunate to have Professor Walters, from Washington and Lee College back with us. He has been gracious enough to help us through this historic process, once again. Repeat for our viewers Professor, what you were telling me before we went on the air about the possible irony of the Vice President taking the roll call of the Senate?"

Professor Walters said, "Certainly, in most cases when the Senate votes on a bill before it if the vote is judged to be close, the Vice President is usually brought in to cast his vote if there is a tie. A lot of people don't know that the Vice President has a specific job, laid out in the Constitution; that being the President of the Senate. One of the jobs of the President of the Senate is to cast the deciding vote on matters before the Senate, when there is a tie vote. I understand the Senate will have all 100 Senators in attendance today. So if the vote is 50 – 50, Vice President Tierney could cast the tie breaking vote, and I would assume it would be for himself. Now the Republicans, currently do have 55 Senators. The Democrats have 45. So, 5 Republican Senators would have to vote for Vice President Tierney for that to occur. I don't expect that to happen, but who knows. We seem to be making history every step of the way this year."

Barry, seeing Vice President Tierney picking up the gavel says, "I have to interrupt you Professor; I see the Vice President ready to call the Senate to order. Let's listen." The Vice President gave a few opening remarks about the history they are about to make, being careful not to look too partisan. He then turned to the Clerk of the Senate and asked her to call the roll.

Here we go, I thought.

The clerk, obviously nervous by the tone of her voice, started with "Senator Albright." I had seen C-span coverage of the Senate enough to know that unless two Senators had the same last name; the clerk didn't call out the state the Senator was from, just the Senator's name.

Senator Albright, a Democrat from Rhode Island, cleared his throat and began, "Mr. President, as a Senator from the great state of Rhode Island, one of the 13 original colonies that founded this great nation, a state that has always stepped up to the responsibilities thrust upon it by history…"

I thought *you've got to be kidding. Is every Senator going to make a speech? We'll be here all night. Why can't they just get up there and say who they're voting for?*

The Senator from Rhode Island went on, "I am proud to cast my vote under authority from the Constitution of the United States, for Vice President of the United States. I cast my vote, for the next President of the United States of America, Vice President Tierney."

As the roll continued alphabetically, the eyes of most Republican Senators were on Senator Larson. His fellow Republicans were waiting to see what direction he would take with his vote. It was no secret that Larson was no fan of Ray Kline, and some Senators were teetering on whether to vote for Tierney or not vote at all. Alphabetically, Larson fell early enough to have such an influence. He would be the 8th Republican to vote with 47 more Republicans to follow. So far, there were five who voted for Kline, one who passed, and one Republican who voted for Vice President Tierney, which was Senator Collingsworth a liberal Senator from Vermont, not really a surprise.

The clerk called out, "Senator Larson." Senator Larson could not be found by the cameras. The TV people were busily scanning the floor for Senator Larson. Maybe he left? Senator Larson was picked up by one of the cameras as he slowly approached the well of the Senate.

Senator Larson stood erect in a proud manner and said, "Mr. President. I pass."

This must have sent shock waves throughout the Republican caucus. The only person who seemed oblivious to the Senator's vote was the Clerk of the Senate. She continued to do her job by repeating the Senator's vote, like she had done with all the others. Then she continued, without a beat, to call the next Senator.

At the end of the first roll call, the vote stood at 51 for Kline, 46 for Tierney and three passes. Larson's strategy of passing had failed to get enough Senators to follow his lead. A second call to the three Senators that passed was academic. All passed. Kline had 51 votes and was elected Vice President of the United States, but more importantly by this vote, he was now the President of the United States since the House had not been able to elect a President.

Senator Larson knew the next procedure was going to be a call by the clerk for vote changes. Any Senator, under this procedure would be given a chance to change their vote. Larson was trying his best to convince some of the more moderate Republicans, in the group of 51 to change their vote. His strategy was to get 2 Senators that voted for Kline to change their vote to pass, resulting in a final vote of 49 for Kline, 46 for Vice President Tierney and 5 passes. This would give Speaker Fleming the Presidency, no one having the 51 votes necessary for election.

The clerk cried out loudly, "Is there any Senator who wishes to change their vote?" I counted at least four times she asked this. You could tell there wasn't going to be any changes by not only the silence; but the fact that the Senate floor was quickly vacated.

Senator Larson was a sorrowful figure as he stood there alone on the floor, beckoning for someone, anyone, to come to his aid on the vote. The Senator was overheard to say, "My God, what have we done? We have put a mad man in charge. I tried; God knows I tried to do what was best for the country."

The anchorman, Barry Winston, after having all the reporters give us their wrap ups, gave his synopsis of the day's events. You know, all the same things that you just saw and heard for yourself, somehow had to be explained to you by the news people.

My thoughts were more matter of fact. *I guess, depending how you looked at it, one good thing was that, at least the country had a President.*

Chapter 14 Do the Right Thing

I came home early from the office today knowing I'd be alone. Sally was at a church meeting this afternoon and the kids were still in school. I just wanted some time alone at home for a change. I was now considering the private office less and less as my cocoon and my home was taking its place. I was trying to take stock of my life and where I was going. What kind of man was I?

I thought about Larry's death and how ironic it was that Kline was now President. Maybe Larry had won after all. Thinking also of Diane, had she died for a purpose? I couldn't think of one. What about me? I violated my marriage vows. I violated my oath to uphold the Constitution and that too was for what purpose? I thought how *I had destroyed the Constitution in order to save it*. Did the ends justify the means? Certainly wasn't the case here, Kline was President. As I tried to think of ways to justify my actions, my thought process was interrupted with the ringing of the phone in the background.

Normally I would walk straight to the phone and answer it with the typical anticipation of someone I knew. This time I stopped and let it ring. I couldn't help it. I was in a mood of self accusation and found myself guilty. Maybe it was paranoia or maybe it was just plain fear. The phone kept ringing and I shuttered to think that someone had found out what I did and was calling to confront me.

The telephone continued ringing. I wanted to shout out to Sally to get the phone, but realized she was not home to be my courage. I was fearful of who it might be. Suddenly, the ringing stopped. I could hear Sally saying something. She had just walked in from the garage and picked up the phone. My thoughts ran wild now. I was brave with someone else doing the actual speaking to the mysterious caller. *Who is it who is it,* I kept shouting to myself. Sally came into the family room holding her hand over the mouth piece of the kitchen portable phone.

"It's for you Gary. Some reporter, do you want to talk to him?"

I stared at her petrified with fear. I summoned up some courage and decided I might as well face whoever it was, maybe it was nothing.

"Hello," I said nervously. Not knowing what a reporter was doing calling me, I instantly went into a defensive mood.

"Hello. Is this Captain Hallstead?" said the voice on the other end.

"Yes." I replied.

"This is John Slatter. I'm a reporter with the *Washington Daily News* and I was calling about the Presidential election."

I thought, *here it comes*. "What exactly can I do for you?" I asked.

Slatter said, "I am doing a story on election reform and what changes the government has made to help the process function smoother. I thought an article on the use of computers would be a good start. I have a friend over at DOD that said you were primarily responsible for the Congressional election pilot program and the recent Presidential election use of computers."

I interrupted Slatter to ask, "Just who did you talk to at DOD?"

Slatter revealed, "My friend's name is Dale Schoolcraft. He told me he worked on the project with you. I hope he doesn't get into any trouble over giving me your name and number?"

I was a little more relieved now. "No, no trouble. Dale was a key programmer on the project. Yes, I was the project manager; just what is it you want to know?"

Slatter proceeded to explain his background and the direction he wanted to take his article, "Captain, I started out as a political beat reporter in Kansas, my hometown, where I started covering elections. I covered local elections and then statewide contests. I took a job in D.C. with the *Daily News* four years ago and was assigned as one of the reporters covering President Anderson in the 92 presidential elections. Frankly, covering politicians is rather boring; so I asked my boss if I could do more stories about how elections are actually done locally, and in the states overall. How they affect the voters, you know, paper ballots, punched cards and the old fashion machines."

Slatter was doing most of the talking and that was all right with me. *The more he talked*, I thought, *the less I'll have to*. Slatter continued to tell me about all his election experiences. I continued to find it strange that a reporter did all the talking, weren't they supposed to ask questions?

He told me about his articles in the years following the 1992 election, how close that election was and how messed up everybody thought it was.

He also covered the Senate hearings on election reform that brought about the system that I had developed. I realized later that Slatter was a man looking for a big story. He always saw himself as an investigative reporter looking to break the next Watergate. Although his editor, Dave Dorffer, thought of John more as a loose cannon, that needs watching.

I was listening to Slatter, but at the same time I was having flashes of Larry's and Diane's death, and my involvement in the election scam recently. It was constantly going through my mind. The more I listened to Slatter in his benign tone, the more I was beginning to feel at ease with him.

Suddenly I had had enough. I couldn't get those horrible images out of my mind. I felt an urgent need to confess to somebody, anybody right now.

Having a moment of conscience I said, "John would like a real story about this election? One that even you won't believe?"

John's appetite was wetted, "Of course," he said. "What kind of a story, are you talking about?"

The die was now cast. The genie was out of the bottle. It was too late to back off what I said. This was the kind of reporter who would continue to hound me until I told him the story I just teased him with.

"I don't want to talk anymore on the phone, John. We need to meet. There are people in high places that don't want this story told. It's serious enough that I'm afraid for my family."

This was enough to get John really excited. He wasn't concerned with people in high places. All he thought about was this may be the story you look for your whole life. He agreed to meet me in a place where we would be safe. He told me about a place he had used before when getting tips about politicians from informants who wished to remain anonymous. It sounded safe enough for me and I agreed to meet John there with one request.

"It will be only the two of us, right?" I asked.

John assured me, "Just the two of us; here's the directions."

I wrote down the directions and verified we would meet tonight.

Sally came back into the room. I think she had been listening because she came in just as I was hanging up the phone.

"Gary, what did that reporter want?" Sally asked.

I replied, "Oh, he's doing a story on a project I was involved in."

Sally inquired, "I thought most of your projects were rather hush, hush?"

I lied to Sally telling her, "Most of them are. Some of them I can talk about, with permission from my boss of course. I would have to get clearance first, and then they usually review the article before they can print it."

Sally still questioned me, "Is this reporter from a local paper?"

"No." I said almost bragging. "He's from the *Washington Daily News.*"

"Wow. I'm impressed", she said. "That's a big paper."

I needed an excuse to get out of the house and said, "Sally, I need to meet with my boss tonight. I have to get permission to talk to this reporter right away, something about deadlines."

"Will you be late? What about dinner?" Sally asked.

"I don't know dear. Don't wait on dinner for me. If I'm going to be real late, I'll call you."

***

I had arrived at the address Slatter had given me, wearing a high collar coat and sunglasses trying to hide my face. I even borrowed my neighbor's car, hoping not to be detected by the powerful people I suspected Fred Clayton had watching me. I would have to explain this to Sally later. I know she must be wondering why I didn't take my own car.

I walked up the three flights of stairs slowly and cautiously, my head darting around every few seconds expecting to see someone waiting to do me harm. At last, I reached Apartment 310. I was relieved I had made it this far safely. I wondered if I should knock or just burst in quickly to get out of the hallway. I decided to lightly tap on the door as to not bring any attention to myself. Nothing happened. I tapped a little louder and jumped back as the door quickly opened.

"Hello Captain," said Slatter loudly.

I became ashen faced and quickly motioned to Slatter with my hand to be quiet. Slatter looked embarrassed as he realized he was wrong to loudly announce the arrival of a man who surely was frightened by something. I looked for a place to sit where I would be comfortable. I had a long tale to tell. He closed and locked the door, came over to me, and sat directly across from where I had decided to sit. Before Slatter was to say anything, I asked him to reassure me that this place was not only safe, but was not bugged or being taped. I had some experience with that.

Slatter said. "As far as I know, only my closest informants I trust and I know anything about this place. As far as being bugged, I really can't say except that I've never had anything come back to me that was said here."

I thought, *well this is going to be as good as it gets, so I might as well begin.*

I started my almost unbelievable tale right from the beginning. I wanted to jump right to Davis's murder; this after all, was the most important thing I just couldn't get off my mind. Instead, I decided to methodically start from the beginning and move on point by point. I felt strongly; it was important for John to understand not only how the whole thing developed, but also I was hoping to get sympathy from Slatter in how I was swept up, in the "for the good of the country" line, that Sen. Larson had sold me, to get me involved. I thought *I am a patriot. I did think I was doing the right thing. I was only following orders of a sort. I mean, I didn't kill anybody. I was trying to save the country from Kline. Wasn't that a noble gesture?*

I stopped and thought about what I had just said. I felt ashamed. I sounded like some Nazi from World War II, giving an excuse on why I wasn't responsible for any atrocities. From then on I continued my story to Slatter, leaving out any more justifications of my actions.

"John, look I need to stop here and clarify something. I'm sorry I did what I did. I'm not trying to justify my involvement. I'm just trying to explain it."

"I understand. Go on." Slatter said.

I made it clear that my team at the DOD had no knowledge of the voting fraud that was perpetrated. I wanted assurance they would be cleared if any charges came of this. I continued to do a *mea culpa*, so much so that John had to interrupt.

"Captain, I said I understood about how you got caught up in this. Get on with the rest of the story." Slatter pleaded.

I finished what seemed like a marathon of talking, but felt relief as anyone one does when confessing a transgression. Slatter stared at me with a glaze over his eyes. The silence was unbearable. Slatter got back his composure and went into reporter mode.

"Well, that's quite a story Gary." He felt easier now calling me Gary instead of Captain feeling like he had now established a bond with me. We did seem to hit it off. Almost like a male bonding type of relationship was going on.

"This is serious." John continued, "Is there any proof, I mean besides just your word?"

"The only proof I have, besides my word," I said with a sarcastic tone, "Is that I did keep a copy of the software fix we used to insert votes into the network, however, the whole transaction is not traceable. I think we did too good of a job covering it up."

Slatter knew it was his turn to come up with something to say. He just sat there staring at me. I was hoping he was thinking of something profound to say, or better yet a plan of action I could deal with.

He let out a sigh and said, "I'm going to have to talk to my editor, Dave Dorffer. Now don't worry. I won't say too much. I know how to protect my sources. I even went to jail one time because I wouldn't give up a source. Dave's the kind of guy you can talk to. He's old school."

"What does old school mean?"

"Well, you know. He's the kind of guy that will follow through on a story. He wouldn't just shrug it off. He's been real good about letting me stay on a story until it proves out one way or another."

"That's sounds good to me, John. But, do you really think you have enough to do a story?"

Slatter looked at me and said, "I'll be honest Gary. We need to come up with a way to prove all this. You're talking about some very connected people here and I mean connected in a bad way. You're saying Sen. Larson, CIA director Clayton, this boss of yours Carl Minster, and Sampson at the RNC; anybody else?"

I thought a moment. "No outside of Diane, I didn't meet or talk to anybody else."

"None of these guys are going to talk and Diane obviously was an agent working for Clayton. Even if she wasn't dead, I doubt if she would have been willing to talk. The problem I have now is how are we going to keep you and your family safe?"

I felt relieved that John was concerned about the well being of my family, "So you do believe me." I said to Slatter.

"To be honest I did check you out, at the minimum you're no kook. Has anybody called or have you been in contact with any of these people lately?"

"No. The last time I talked to anybody was just before the Senate vote. Senator Larson came to me to tell me about Barnes and Diane. That was it."

John concluded, "I'll bet they are still keeping some kind surveillance on you and maybe even your family. I wish I had known what you were going to tell me ahead of time. I wouldn't have called you and setup this meeting over your home phone. You've got to believe their tapping your phone. The only thing is for you to go home and sit tight until I talk to Dorffer. Try to protect yourself and your family. Oh, I forgot to ask you. How much of this have you told your wife?"

"I have told her nothing, nothing at all. I haven't told her anything mainly because I was too ashamed of everything, especially that tape Clayton has of me and Diane. I guess it's about time to tell her."

"I understand, but I agree it's about time to fill her in. It's more than just an affair now." Slatter consulted.

Slatter got up and was ready to go and talk to Dorffer. I knew what I had to do and didn't look forward to it. I had to tell Sally. I kept trying to figure out a way to tell her everything except the affair part. That will just devastate her. I realized that everything would eventually come out, now that I talked to John. The only thing to do right now is to tell her the whole story. God, I didn't want to do that. I'm the one who screws up, and it ends up my whole family suffers. *Just do the right thing* I kept telling myself all the way home.

I pulled into my driveway and noticed Sally was at the front door peeking out. I thought to myself, *oh no I hoped nobody has called her. She does look worried.*

As I walked up to the front door Sally greeted me, "Hello dear. You didn't call. I was worried".

"Why, is something up?" I asked.

Sally said, "No, I was just worried, you were so late. You said you would call if you were going to be late."

I asked Sally if anyone had called or visited the house.

Sally said, "No, we didn't have any calls and no one came, why?"

I told her, "We need to talk about something important."

Sally got that look about her that all women get when their husband says he's got something to talk over with them. Women seem to have a sixth sense that alerts them when their husband talks in a tone of voice that reminds you of a little boy who has done something wrong and needs to confess it. Women also seem to know the subject will be something to do with their husband's fidelity.

I stepped right into it. I was feeling so guilty I could not even wait to enter the house, right at the front door of the house, I said, "Sally, what I need you to know first of all is that I still love you. What I'm about to tell you might shatter your faith in me, but you and the kids mean the world to me." I realized the front entrance of the house was no place to have a serious conversation and stopped talking and went into the house, Sally following.

Sally had this terrible, worried look on her face that most women do when a husband wants to talk to his wife this way. She must be thinking I was having an affair. Maybe this project didn't take all the long nights that I said it was taking.

We proceeded to the family room. I poured myself a drink and asked Sally if she wanted one and, of course, that was strange to Sally. I knew she didn't drink at all. She must have been thinking why is Gary acting so strange? We sat down together in the family room knowing we would have some privacy as the kids were in bed and fast asleep.

"Sally," I said. "I just got through talking to a reporter. That's where I was this evening."

"Yes, but I thought you had to clear it with your boss first? Did you do that?" Sally asked.

"No. I went to meet the reporter first. His name is John Slatter and he really is from the *Washington Daily News*. He's the same one you talked to earlier. I set up a meeting with him to tell him the whole story of what I've been up to the last few months."

I then proceeded to tell Sally, in detail, the whole story. Once again, I felt I was in a talking marathon. I didn't leave out any of the details, but when I came to my tryst with Diane I stopped, lowered my head, and had a look of ashamed about me. My voiced lowered and I confessed I had a sexual encounter with Diane, but it was just the one night. I tried to justify it really quickly by saying it was only a one night stand.

"I don't know what happened, we were all tired, working so hard, and she was coming on to me. I guess I just lost it."

Tears started to well up in Sally's eyes, I knew she felt betrayed. I could sense her thoughts. She must have been thinking how could I ever trust him again? I moved to put my arm around her, but she shrugged it off. *I deserve that*, I thought. I had to bring the story back to the danger we were in quickly. I continued to tell her about the tape that Clayton had which only served to make matters worse for Sally. I grabbed her by the shoulders and shook her lightly.

"Sally, wait, you must understand something about this guy Clayton. I was wrong to get mixed up in this, I know that, but this Clayton is a powerful man who has had people murdered."

"Murdered?" Sally exclaimed.

"I can't be absolutely sure, but I am convinced Clayton has had two people murdered over this. You remember Larry? I think he was murdered by Clayton's people to shut him up. Then, he had Diane killed to keep her quiet."

Sally said, "My God Gary, what is going on? What are you involved in?"

Sally had suddenly come to her senses realizing there was more to this than just an affair. There was murder. There was defrauding the Presidential election of the United States. Her husband was involved in more than just an affair. Not thinking about herself now, she realized her children might be in danger. When a mother thinks her children are in danger, she becomes as ferocious as a mother tiger protecting her cubs. Her emotion changed from tearing up and feeling betrayed, to one of how can I secure my children's safety.

"Are the kids in any danger?" she asked.

"I don't know for sure. I haven't talked to anybody involved for sometime now, but Clayton's the kind of man who is not beyond doing anything he needs to do to save himself. With the deaths of Larry, then Diane, I felt I had to tell someone what was going on. I just couldn't continue to live with this any longer. Now that I've told you about the affair, which was one of the things they were blackmailing me about, I feel I need to do something to make these people accountable. That's why I agreed to talk to John at the newspaper. Can you ever forgive me?"

"You know I will always love you Gary no matter what, but Gary, what about the children?" We both realized now was not the time to dwell on my shameful affair, but to find a way to protect ourselves and our children.

I told Sally that John Slatter was talking to his boss at the *Daily News*, not only about my story, but what the best way was to protect our family. I tried to calm Sally by telling her Slatter had said not to worry, his boss would find a way to help protect us. Now that's not exactly what Slatter said, but I needed something to help Sally feel a little more secure about our children. I knew Slatter or his boss, wouldn't be able to do anything immediately, and while I told Sally some white lies to calm her down, I felt a little panicked myself. As the man of the house, I had to show some initiative.

"Sally." I said. "I don't want you to take the kids to school tomorrow."

"Where will you be?" Sally said.

"I'm staying here with you and the kids. I'm going to see what I can do to secure the house. One thing I want is a caller ID machine. You know something that shows you the phone number of anyone calling before you answer the phone, so when Slatter calls me I'll know it's him. I didn't realize at the moment that I would have to call the telephone company to activate that device.

We were scrambling to protect our children. We were doing some irrational things without thinking, but I felt better, at least I was doing something. I did the right thing, telling Sally. I did the right thing telling John Slatter. At least I thought I did.

Chapter 15 Someone Believes Me

John Slatter came into the *Washington Daily News* office anxious to talk to Dave Dorffer, the chief editor. He had done enough research on me to be comfortable going ahead with my story. Fact was, I did wonder how much of John's commitment was to me or to the story? I would find out sooner or later. A lot depended on his editor and how he viewed John's credibility.

It was very busy as the evening edition was getting ready to be published. Slatter walked straight past his desk and right in to Dave's office hoping to sit down immediately and tell him the fantastic story he had just heard. Slatter's concern over Gary and his family was fast fleeting from his mind, as all he could think about what a story this could be. It might even win him a Pulitzer Prize, he mused.

Dorffer was busy trying to get the evening edition out when Slatter walked in without knocking. Dorffer looked up from a pile of press clippings and yelled, "Get out of here Slatter, I'm busy." Slatter wasn't about to leave without talking to Dorffer.

"But Dave, this is really important. It's the next Watergate, and I got the whole story." John started. He now had Dave's attention. Dave was a veteran from the Watergate days and the invoking of that name always got Dave's attention.

"OK," said Dave, "You've got five minutes."

"When you hear what I have got to say, you'll give me five days."

Slatter took a deep breath. He heard Dorffer give him five minutes, but he wasn't going to rush. He knew once Dorffer started to hear the details of his story; he would have all the time he needed. "Dave. What would you say if I told you the Presidential election was fixed?"

"Fixed? How so? What are you talking about?" Now Dave wanted to know more.

Slatter smiled and said, "Hold on. I told you you'd give me more than five minutes, right?"

"Wait a minute John. Frank." Dave called out for his Administrative Assistant Frank. Dorffer had a voice that carried right through the glass partition in his wall. Frank jumped up from his desk and came running into Dave's office.

"Yes Dave. What do you need?" asked Frank.

Dave instructed him, "Frank, I want you to take these clippings for the evening edition and give them to Mike. Tell him I want him to handle the evening edition for me, and Frank."

"Yes sir?" Frank inquired.

Dave said with a grin, "I don't want to be disturbed for five days."

"Five days?" Frank was puzzled.

"I'm just kidding Frank, but I don't want to be interrupted as long as Slatter is in here. Understand?" Dave commanded.

"Yes sir." Frank carried out a big pile of news galleys for the evening edition. Dorffer was a hands on editor and always had to give his final approval for the front page. Slatter now was really convinced he had Dorffer's attention.

As soon as Frank closed the door behind him, Dorffer was leaning over his desk towards Slatter, and said, "Ok John. Now what exactly do you mean the Presidential election was fixed? The Senate chose the President; I mean the Vice President or whatever. Are you saying the Senate vote was fixed? What exactly are you saying?"

"Hold on Dave. Let me start from the beginning. You need to hear the whole story to put it all together."

Dave sat back in his chair and said, "Alright John, tell it your way, but it better be good. You're interrupting the evening edition editing. You know that's one of the things I don't normally let anybody else do."

"Dave, you may want to take some notes to help you follow the story."

"Just get on with it John." Dave was getting frustrated at John's stalling. John was having a little fun at Dave's expense. He knew how excited Dave could get waiting for someone to get to the point.

John started his story, "I was doing that story on the new computer system used in this last election. You know the one the government approved a couple years ago. They wanted a way to ensure a more fair election after that debacle four years ago. They first used it on the

Congressional election in I think, five states. Well I found out, from one of my sources over at the Department of Defense, who the chief designer was. His name is Captain Gary Hallstead. He also works out of the Department of Defense. That's where they developed the system. Well we had the strangest conversation last night."

Dorffer interrupted John; he had to know more details about people as Slatter named names. It was his experience as an old beat reporter coming out. "This Captain Hallstead, what do you know about him?"

"I think Hallstead's an alright guy, I mean I think he's credible. He's been at DOD for a lot of years doing computer work. Some regular things, but he's done a number of top secret stuff too. He's married with two kids. From everything I can gather, a pillar of the community type."

"Ok. Go on." Dave said.

"Here's where it gets interesting. The Captain tells me he was approached by some high officials in the government to fix the election in favor of President Anderson. Actually it was more like a way to defeat Barnes and keep Kline out of the White House."

"High officials, then they must be Democrats if he was fixing it for Anderson." Dave said assuredly.

John corrected Dave, "That's where you're wrong Dave. They were Republicans."

Dave was surprised and intrigued at the same time, "Republicans? But why would they want to screw their own people?"

"The Captain told me they knew a while ago about Barnes's terminal illness. They knew he wouldn't survive the next six months. They were scared to death of the prospects of Kline becoming President." John told Dave.

Dave said, "I know what you mean about Kline, but to go so far as to fix an election. That's unbelievable."

"It gets better Dave. Seems they convinced the Captain to fix the computer system to deliver Texas to Anderson. Hallstead agreed and tried to accomplish the task without any of the rest of his staff knowing about it, but he couldn't quite do it. So he had one of his best people, a Larry Davis, help out. This Davis ended up dead."

Dave was shocked, "Dead? Who are these people? I mean these high government officials you're talking about?"

"Hold onto to your hat Dave. There are four of them. The first one is the Captain's boss, Carl Minster. He's a real mystery. I mean I couldn't find a thing out about him at first. I had to cash in a lot of favors over at the DOD to find any information about Mr. Minster, and came up empty. So I talked to a informant I have, who knows some people at Langley."

Dave asked, "Langley? You're talking CIA."

"Right on Dave, my source couldn't confirm it but he said there has always been a question about this guy, Minster. He thinks he has seen the name Carl Minster on some documents. He believes he is some kind of CIA liaison over at the Department of Defense. The only other thing I know is that he is in charge of special projects at the computer center there. But who he answers to? I don't know. He's got an office on E-Level, which is top secret. Nobody gets on E-Level unless they want you to; which the Captain confirmed."

Dave pointed out, "That's not much of an indictment. Your source *thinks* he connected to the CIA, but he's not sure. Your source *thinks* he's seen his name on documents. So far, John, I'm not impressed, who else are you talking about?"

John felt his story beginning to sound shaky at best to Dave. "We have Ralph Sampson, the Chairman of the Republican National Committee. The Captain said he was the second man at the meeting. The Captain didn't really know how he was involved; Sampson didn't say much at the meeting. My own judgment was that he was there for the election mechanics, handling things within the Party. He's from Texas and has a lot of local contacts there. Maybe that was his role. Like I said, the Captain didn't really know Sampson's role."

Dave was getting a little annoyed at John, "Okay, have I got it right so far, you got this mystery man at DOD, who might have connections at the CIA; and you have Sampson over at the RNC, who you don't really know what his involvement was. There better be more to this story than that?"

"Definitely, I was saving the best until last, Dave. The one who the Captain said seemed to be in charge was none other than Senator Damon Larson."

Dave became interested, "Damon Larson. Wow. Are you sure? Damon was Barnes's right hand man in the Senate. He's in line to become the Majority leader with Barnes gone. You better be sure about him."

"Now it gets even more serious Dave. The last guy, according to the Captain, is Fred Clayton, Director of the CIA. He's the guy who setup Hallstead with this girl..."

"Girl? What girl?" Dave asked.

John explained, "I forgot to tell you that part Dave. Clayton had a woman put on the Captain's staff, Diane McKenna was her name."

"Was?" queried Dave.

"Yeah, was. She's also dead, probably at the orders from Clayton. Anyway Clayton wanted some insurance that Hallstead would follow through on the election fix. So he had this Diane put on Hallstead's staff through Minster, Hallstead thinks it was Minster that got her the job. Her real job was to get the Captain on tape making love to her. She succeeded and they used it as blackmail, however that wasn't all. They got Davis on tape threatening to spill the beans about the whole election fix. This Davis had figured out what was going on, and the next thing you know, he was dead. I think these deaths were the last straw for the Captain. I think his conscience got to him, along with the meeting with Clayton, where the Director threatened him and his family."

Dorffer's eyes grew wider and wider as the details unfolded. He kept his composure however as he continued to jot down notes. John couldn't help but grin at Dave's sudden interest in note taking.

John continued, "When Michigan, I think it was Michigan, yes it was Michigan, upset everything by going to Barnes, the whole election fix was basically for nothing. Hallstead said the process to fix Texas for Anderson went as planned, but Michigan and I think one other state made the whole fix pointless. Ultimately, the House and Senate involvement was just the normal procedure for electing a President in case of an Electoral College tie."

Dorffer looked up from his note taking and asked. "What kind of proof do you have? Or do you have any proof at all?"

John's excitement waned a little. He knew he didn't have much in the way of solid evidence. He believed in Capt. Hallstead so much; he hadn't let little things like proof get in the way. John confessed, "Not a lot. I've got the Captain's word and he's got a copy of the code they used to fix the Texas results."

"That's it?" yelled Dorffer. "You expect me to authorize investigating some of the most powerful people in Washington with that kind of proof?"

"I know it's not much, but Dave, I do believe this guy. He's genuinely scared. If you would talk to him, I know you'd believe him too."

"That doesn't matter John. We've got to have more to hang our hat on than his word. Slatter, do you realize what kind of accusations you're making? These guys are nationally respected people."

"How about this, Dave, I think our weakest links might be Sampson and then Larson. I don't know if I want to tackle Clayton now. Frankly, these guys at CIA can make people disappear. Not that I wouldn't ever take them on, but for now let's see what Sampson will give us. We'll start slow. I'll call for an interview with Sampson. Can you pull some strings and get me an appointment?"

Dorffer was quiet. He was thinking about Slatter's plan. The best part of which was the going slow part. "I agree. That's a good place to start. I'll set up an interview with this Sampson. The Chairman is in a powerful position in the party. They just don't give that slot to anybody. Hold on a minute John. I'm thinking out loud. If I call it a piece on the role of the party chairman in this historic election, he might go for it. Let me make a few calls and I'll let you know. In the meantime, figure out how you want to approach the interview. You don't want to walk in and ask him if he's part of an election conspiracy."

"Sounds good to me." John replied.

Dorffer continued to think out loud. "I do know Nancy Caldwell pretty good. She's the Director of the FBI you know. We worked together on a lot of cases years ago. I don't want to brag, but she does owe me big time. I spiked a lot of stories for her, helped her to solve some big cases. I wouldn't think she'd be involved in anything like this. What do you think about talking to her?"

"I'm glad you brought up someone like her; we still have this protection issue with the Hallsteads. I promised to help them with that."

Dave answered, "Yeah that was still on my mind. If there is something to this, then they will need some help. Let's try and meet with Nancy and see if she can't help with some security ideas. Hang on, John. I'll call her now."

Dorffer was hoping to get through to Caldwell right away. He knew lives might hang in the balance. Dorffer was not a religious man, but he said a little prayer as he waited for someone to answer the phone at Caldwell's office. *At least give me a person and not a voice mail,* he thought.

"Director Caldwell's office, how may I help you?"

Great, thought Dorffer. *I made it to first base, actually got a real person.*

"This Dave Dorffer, editor of the *Washington Daily News*. It's important I speak to the Director."

"Please hold. I'll see if the Director is available to take your call." the voice replied.

Dorffer put his hand over the phone and whispered to John. "Second base."

"The Director can speak to you in a few minutes. Can you hold?"

"Yes. Thank you." He whispered again to John, "Third Base."

A click was heard by Dorffer and then a smile came over him. A familiar voice said, "Dave. It's good to hear from you."

Dorffer mouthed to John. "Home run."

"Hello Nancy. How are you? Long time no talk."

"Yes Dave. Is this business or pleasure?"

"Well I afraid its business Nancy, nasty business."

"You sound serious Dave. What's up?"

"Nancy. Is this a secure line? What I have to talk to you about is better done privately." Dave inquired.

"If that's the case, maybe we should meet for dinner. You free tonight?" Nancy asked.

Dave said, "That would be perfect. Then later, I need to introduce you to a reporter of mine, if that's ok?"

"That's fine Dave. Let's meet at the Italian place on 5th Avenue, you remember, we've eaten there before. How about eight o'clock?"

"Yes, I remember the place, sounds good. After dinner we can meet with John at a more secure place. See you there at eight."

Nancy paused on the other end of the line. A minute passed before she said anything. She then agreed to meet Dave for dinner that night; however she would not agree to meet with John at John's secret apartment where John had met with Captain Hallstead. Even at Dave's insistence.

Nancy knew Dave just wanted a place a little more secure than a public restaurant. Although she knew Dave well, she felt a little uncomfortable meeting with two men at a secret apartment. She would rather the meeting take place at the restaurant. It seemed a bit strange to Nancy for Dave to suggest this private apartment meeting. She knew Dave well and was anxious to find out what he was up to. For Dave to suggest a clandestine place to meet, it must be important.

Nancy thought the restaurant, which was a bit out of the way, about 15 miles outside the city, should satisfy him.

Nancy ended the conversation with "If you want your reporter to meet with me, it will have to be at the restaurant.

Dorffer decided he had to bring John to dinner if Nancy wouldn't meet with him at John's private apartment. He didn't feel comfortable talking about this at a public restaurant, especially how quiet this had to be kept. He thought if he wanted John to meet with Nancy also, he would have to bring John.

Dave and John arrived at the restaurant first, hoping to get a table in a secluded corner where it would be hard for anyone to see them. Dave stood every minute or so, stretching his neck from behind a wall, hoping Nancy would spot him when she arrived. Finally, there she was, at the door, looking for Dave. Dave motioned her over to their table.

Dave had told John not to worry about Nancy. He knew Nancy Caldwell, the Director of the FBI, as a fair and honest person. He said she had rose from the rank of agent to Director over a period of 38 years in the Bureau. She was promoted, not through any affirmative action plan, but through hard work. Nancy had gained a reputation of someone who would investigate a case where the facts took her and was not easily intimidated. As an agent some years ago, she followed a case all the way to the Governor's mansion in New Jersey.

Dave and John brought Nancy up to date on John's story about Captain Hallstead and the election fraud. Dave, skipping over any talk of proof, asked Nancy for her ideas on protection for the family. Nancy, being the intelligent agent she was, was having none of this and asked, "What kind of evidence do you have?"

John explained the little they had, almost ashamedly, knowing he had nothing that would satisfy a professional like Caldwell. Nancy now understood the importance of Dave's request to meet, in Dave's phone call to her.

"It's very difficult crossing over into CIA territory. They can hide people; even put them overseas where we can't go. How credible is this Captain?" Nancy asked.

Dave looked to John.

John answered, "I find him extremely truthful. He has told me, he would take a lie detector test or anything else it takes to get someone to believe him."

Nancy said, "You know, you're asking me to take on some pretty important people, with basically no evidence, all on the word of a Captain in the Army."

Dave nodded his head in agreement with Nancy.

John pleaded his case, "But he's not just any Captain. He was the leader on the election program team. He has that copy of the code they used to fix the election. You know for Texas. He's willing to take a lie detector test. And besides, why would he go through all this if there was nothing to it? If it's true, he and his family really need protection. Isn't there anything you can do?"

Dave had known Nancy as a tough agent. She had come through the ranks where a woman had to be tough just to survive. All these years she had fought back her maternal instincts to not look soft, but now a family was possibly in danger and felt she would do something.

Nancy decided she couldn't take the chance this was some crack pot Army Captain. Dorffer, whom she respected, seemed to believe this reporter. The Captain was willing to take a lie detector test. But a million reasons ran through her mind, telling her not to get involved.

John must have sensed a weakness in Nancy. He started talking more and more about the Captain's wife and two children. He reminded Nancy of the Captain and his family's service to the country and especially the fact that two people were already dead.

Nancy looked at Dorffer. She seemed to ignore John and his pleadings. She had to feel comfortable on her own to make any decision. She asked, "Can you have the Captain at my office tomorrow? I'll set up a lie detector test. We'll do it under the pretense of his being appointed to a sensitive position in the Pentagon. We do this sort of thing all the time."

Dorffer had to defer this to John, "John, can you handle this? You're closer to the Captain than I am."

"No problem. He'll be there." John realized he had made progress with Nancy. He wanted to hear something about protecting Hallstead's family, but decided to wait and hear more from Nancy before bringing it up.

Nancy continued to John's relief, "I have no choice but to error on cautions side, especially when it comes to the family." Nancy now turned to John. "When you talk to the Captain, and I suggest you go to his house, don't use the phone. Tell him to have his family ready to move to a new location. I can order a witness protection program for them. I'll think of some reason. They won't need to bring anything just their clothes and personal items. I will have a car for them at 10 o'clock tomorrow morning."

John was happy as he listened to Nancy. She was impressive as she walked through her plan. It satisfied all of John and Dorffer's requests. Getting protection for Hallstead's family and a chance for the Captain to get a lie detector test and prove his case. John and Dorffer were almost ready to second guess one point however. How could Nancy be sure of the agents she was talking about doing this? John thought, *not to be paranoid, but we are talking about the CIA here.*

Nancy continued and alleviated John's fears. "I have two special agents on my staff that I know I can trust implicitly. I also have a safe house available only at the Director's discretion I can use." she bragged.

John then related to Nancy his and Dave's plan to interview Sampson and then Larson. He wanted to get her approval to go ahead. Nancy was receptive to the idea with one suggestion. She asked John to consider wearing a wire. John was, at first, nervous about doing it. He explained he had never worn a wire before. Nancy insisted making the point they needed all the evidence they could get. John finally agreed.

Dorffer said, "I'll call for that appointment tomorrow, John."

They were all satisfied with the plan, finished their dinner, and agreed Nancy would be in touch with Dorffer. She confirmed it wasn't at all unusual for the Director of the FBI to be in touch with major newspaper editors.

***

It was early in the morning when I heard someone knocking on my door. Then, whoever it was, they started ringing the door bell also. I looked at my clock and to my surprise; it said 5:00 am. Who in the world could that be? *It wouldn't be any of Clayton's people,* I thought. *They wouldn't knock or ring the bell. They would just find a way to enter.* I decided I couldn't hide in my bed any longer and went downstairs to the front door. Looking through the peep hole, I could see it was John Slatter.

I greeted him like a long lost relative. When John told me of the plan to protect my family, I broke down in tears. Composing myself, I thanked him and whoever else was involved. I looked forward to the lie detector test and the chance to prove to anybody who would listen, that I was telling the truth. I started to tell John I wanted to get my wife up to meet him. He said not this time. He had something he needed to do.

As he moved toward the door to leave, I said. "You don't know how good it feels to have someone believe you."

Chapter 16 Apply the Pressure

Slatter arrived at FBI headquarters to get wired for his interview with Ralph Sampson. He told the receptionist who he was and who he was there to see. The receptionist checked a list then made a phone call. As she hung up the phone she motioned to a security guard standing beside her desk to come over.

"Please take Mr. Slatter to room 323. Have a nice day Mr. Slatter."

"Thank you, you too." said Slatter.

John Slatter was a typical investigative reporter. He had no fear interviewing people of importance. With a probing, almost confrontational manner, he would get straight to the heart of the matter. John could walk that fine line between just doing his job and being darn right nasty to the people he was quizzing, but not this time. As he tried on the wire that would hopefully get the evidence he needed, he was nervous. In fact, he was sweating so profusely, the agent fitting him was getting frustrated.

"Mr. Slatter, you've got to calm down or we'll never get these patches to stick. Your perspiration will also cause a bad signal back to the recorder." the agent said.

"I can't help it. I sweat a lot normally. Do you have anything like a stay dry powder or something?"

"We can try that. We have a powder we sometimes have to use on guys like you. I'll have to pull off these patches and start over. Hold on this will hurt a little."

The agent pulled off the transmission patches. He took out a container that looked like a baby talcum powder holder and started to shake it over John's chest. The dust from the powder created a cloud over the both of them.

"This is why I don't like to use this powder. Not because of the mess it makes now, but the chance it might give off a smell or worse yet start to puff out as you walk, but we don't have any choice."

"I see what you mean." said John, as the cloud of powder settled over his dark pants.

The agent wiped off the excess powder and proceeded to attach the wires to the transmitter, hidden on John's back near his belt line. Slatter was feeling foolish having to wear a wire. He thought how he was now the informer. He was used to dealing with informers, which is how he was able to become a successful investigative reporter. But he always carried a tape recorder in his pocket to record his informers' information. He would tell them he was recording their statement right from the beginning. Once that was announced, Slatter could concentrate on the informer's information and not worry about his recording people. Slatter wondered if he would be so concerned about not having his recording device discovered that he would sound like a blithering idiot in his questioning with Sampson.

"There. You're ready to go. Now don't think about the device at all. It will only make you self-conscience and your body language will give you away, not the device." the agent said.

John laughed, "Easy for you to say. You're not the one wearing it."

The agent replied, "Mr. Slatter, I've worn many a wire in my day. If there's one thing I've learned, it's that all you have to do is forget about it. If you can convince yourself you're not wearing the thing, so will the person you're talking to."

John sighed, "Ok, you're the expert."

Slatter still had second thoughts, but told himself he had a job to do. A lot of people, and even the nation, were counting on him. Slatter was a brash, cocky, even annoying type of reporter, but he always delivered on his stories and that's why Dorffer liked him. Slatter was losing that edge now that he realized he was not just uncovering a news story. The fact that this story would shake the very foundations of the country, and that lives were at stake, made Slatter realize he was not just reporting a story. He was saving the future integrity of the United States.

Dorffer had arranged for Slatter to interview Ralph Sampson at his office over at the Republican National Committee Headquarters. Sampson agreed to the interview only if it was what Dorffer had said it was going to be, being an interview about the Republican Party's thoughts on the historic events concerning the Presidential election.

Dorffer told Slatter that he got the impression Sampson seemed a little more concerned about something other than the interview. Sampson was very adamant that the interview stick to the script they agreed to. Dorffer related to Slatter that he should be very careful in his questions or Sampson might just shut the whole meeting down quickly. This only served to heighten Slatter's worries.

***

Ralph Sampson was pacing the floor in his office, waiting for Slatter to arrive. He worried about whether he should have agreed to this interview in the first place. He thought about calling Senator Larson and asking permission to do it, but he thought, *I'm a big boy. I can handle this reporter. After all, it's just a story about the election. But what if he knows something? What do I do then, Sampson thought? I still have time to call it off. I could reschedule, and then I'd have time to talk it over with Larson. Better yet, I could talk to Clayton. He could give me a heads up on this Slatter guy. I know Dorffer, over at the Daily News. I trust him. He's always given us a fair shake in his editorials. I've always thought, he's more of a Republican than he can admit to. If they knew something, I'd bet on Dorffer calling me directly. He wouldn't send some reporter. I'm getting upset over nothing. Let's just see what this guy asks me. Besides if they had anything, they would go to some authority, not a newspaper.*

The buzzer went off on Sampson's intercom. His secretary's voice came on and announced that John Slatter, from the *Washington Daily News*, was here for his appointment.

"Send him in." Ralph said.

Slatter, still worried about the wire he was wearing, entered Sampson's office.

"Good morning Mr. Slatter. How are you today?" Ralph said.

"I'm fine, Mr. Sampson. Please call me John. Thanks for doing this. I'm looking forward to your party's thoughts on the election."

"Have a seat John. I'm a down to earth guy also. Please feel free to call me Ralph. Is this going to be a question and answer type of interview or more of a conversation? The only reason I ask is if you don't mind, I prefer to just have a normal conversation about the past events. It's just more relaxing to me."

John picked up on Ralph's obvious request to stay away from a direct questioning method of interview. In John's experience, this was almost always the sign of a guy who didn't want to be asked tough questions. It was a way to filibuster an interview and eat up all the time the reporter was allocated.

John responded to Sampson's request, "Well, I only have an hour Ralph and I do have some specific questions I want to ask. I need to try to keep the interview moving. So if you don't mind, I may have to interrupt you from time to time to get all my questions asked. I'm saying this up front, so don't think me rude if I interrupt you. I just need to get enough material to do the story justice."

"Ok John. Where do you want to start? Oh can I get you anything to drink, coffee?"

"No. I'm fine, thank you. Ralph, looking back to the night of the election, were you surprised at the results from Michigan and Texas? Wasn't your campaign strategy to carry Texas and not Michigan?"

"Well you know the saying John, the best laid plans of mice and men. We had a strategy in Texas that we thought would continue to give that state to us. It was close. Michigan, that's another story. We had hoped to eat into the President's normally solid support among blue collar workers, due to the unemployment rate, and it looks like that's just what we did."

"But Ralph, how do you explain the fact that the party spent five times the money and time in Texas than in Michigan? I mean Barnes hardly ever visited Michigan and those visits were early on in the race."

Ralph said, "Don't forget it wasn't only Michigan. We carried New Mexico and that put us over the top. We had a plan that..."

John interrupted, "Was Kline your secret weapon? He went to Michigan, New Mexico, and seemed to excite the people there. And if that was the case then why..."

Sampson felt compelled to jump in. "No, yes, Ray Kline was used. Wait, let me rephrase that. Kline was an asset in Michigan because of the conservative Democrats, but he helped us a lot in the Southwest as well. In New Mexico he was very effective."

John asked, "Along those lines I was going to ask if Kline was that effective in the Southwest, why wasn't he sent into Texas? I mean it sounds like you had a strategy working here that would fit Kline's style. Texas has been a solid Republican state for years and I would have thought if Kline was used there, he could have helped deliver that state easily, couldn't he?"

Ralph was starting to fidget with his coffee cup. He looked a bit flustered. There was silence as Slatter waited for a response from Ralph. The two men were at an impasse. Ralph was thinking how to answer the question about Texas without the party looking like they were either stupid in their strategy, or the fact that he didn't want them to win Texas in the first place. Slatter was worrying he had pushed too hard and fast in asking questions about Texas. Ralph broke the silence first.

Ralph responded, "I guess we should have spent more time in Texas." Ralph decided to take the tact of party strategy stupidity.

"But look John aren't we spending too much time on campaigning? I thought this was an interview about the House and Senate historic events. It's not that I mind discussing the mechanics of the campaign, it's just that I was more prepared to talk about the things I agreed to with Dorffer. You know more along the line of how or why Senators voted the way they did on the Vice President."

"Oh, I was going to get to that Ralph. I'm kind of a Monday morning quarterback when it comes to elections, campaign strategy's, and stuff like that. I was just curious about some of the moves your party made, but let me ask you one last question about Texas."

Ralph, visually upset said, "No, I'm not going to talk anymore about Texas. If that's all you are going to talk about, this interview is going to end. I told Dorffer when he set this up, I was only prepared to talk about events after the Electoral College vote. Now John, I'm really very busy and we only have about twenty minutes left anyway. So if you don't have any other questions, I need to get back to work."

John knew he had gotten under Ralph's skin with all the questions about Texas. *What to do now*? He thought. *Should I ask some questions Ralph would feel comfortable with? Or should I just accommodate him by leaving? Oh, what the heck. Here it goes.*

John pursued his line of questioning, "Ralph, why don't you want to talk about Texas? Is there something more than meets the eye here?"

There, now it's out, I did it, John thought. *Ralph's got to smell something now.*

Ralph stood up abruptly. "Mr. Slatter, this interview is over. Thank you for coming and have a good day."

With that Ralph walked to his private office door, disappeared behind it leaving John sitting there.

John hoped he had gotten all this on the wire. He worried, however, if what he got was going to be enough. John also was concerned he may have pushed too hard on Texas. He knew something else; this would be the last interview he could ever expect to get to talk to Sampson. He got up and walked to the front door. It dawned on him that Sampson would probably contact Senator Larson about their meeting. Senator Larson certainly couldn't be interviewed now.

***

I had the tough job of sitting my family down and telling them they would be whisked away to a strange place to live for an unknown length of time. Sally wouldn't be much of a problem. She was all about protecting our kids.

Sally and I woke up early; we were too excited to sleep. I'm sure Sally's fears had been somewhat relieved when I had told her about the protection they were going to be receiving from the FBI. Sally was never worried about her own safety; it was always the kids that mattered. For me, it was more anticipation than excitement of my family being taken away to an unknown place to live. I had the tough job of sitting my children down and telling them they would be whisked to a strange place to live for an unknown length of time. I could leave it up to Sally, but I felt I owed them this much, having caused their dilemma in the first place. The kids were going to take it hard. Not at the beginning, though, it would seem like an adventure to them to start. After a few days it would get old, not going to school and seeing their friends. The only truly happy one was me. I was going to take that lie detector test to prove my veracity. It was important for me to regain a sense of well being. Not to excuse what I did, but to at least put me back on the right side of things.

I struggled to explain what was going on to the kids. How much could I tell them? They were old enough to know their father had done something wrong. They were also old enough to realize their father was trying to do something right. I certainly was not going to talk about my affair. They were not old enough to understand, and I didn't want to scare them about the deaths involved. What could I say to them? Their father was a crook?

Sally was sensing my difficultly and bless her soul took over. Her voice was calm and reassuring as only a mother's voice could be. While I was a logical, fact driven person, Sally approached things from the more humane and sensitive way. Making it sound like an adventure, with exciting details, Sally had the kids actually looking forward to going. I am blessed to have her.

I had asked Slatter to rearrange my test so I could see my family off. I needed to be there not only to show some stability, but for my own satisfaction that they would be safe. The car arrived at precisely 10 o'clock. Two men in dark suits got out. You couldn't mistake them for anything but some type of government agents. One walked to the door, while the other stood by the car looking around the neighborhood. I let the agent into the house even before he showed me his credentials.

I hugged and kissed my kids and told them to be their mother's helpers. I looked at Sally and felt ashamed. I was putting my family through this and they were the innocent bystanders.

Sally, always the healer, put her arms around me and whispered, "I love you."

I felt good now, ready to take on the world. The agent told me my car had just arrived and I should wait for the agents to walk me to the car. The agent assigned to my family radioed his partner they were ready and he came up to the house. They walked my family down the sidewalk to the car, protecting them on both sides. I watched out the window, waving to my family, as the agents confirmed the car that just arrived was credentialed. As my family drove away, my agents approached the house. It was my turn now. I was ready.

I was taken by the agents to the FBI Headquarters building. To a room that had only a table, three chairs and a menacing looking machine sitting on the table. The room had no windows. I was sitting there alone. It wasn't long before two people entered.

I had to break my tension. So I remarked to the two men, "Did you guys know you all dress alike?" They just smiled politely and set about their business of hooking me up to the machine.

The agent instructed me, "Don't worry Captain. This won't hurt. Just relax and answer my questions with a simple yes or no. When I start asking questions, I'm going to ask you to lie on purpose. We need to do this to establish a level for the machine, any questions?"

I replied, "No, I'm actually looking forward to this."

The test was completed in a little over an hour. They told me someone would be in to see me shortly. I was to remain here in the room. I asked them if they knew any results from the test. If they could at least give me a hint on how I did. They just said I would have to get that information from someone else. They only administered the test, others did the evaluation. No sooner had they left, the door opened again. It was another agent who asked me to accompany him. We walked through a lot of long hallways that all looked the same to me. Looked like the Pentagon I thought, long hallways all painted the same color. Unless you were familiar with the place you would surely get lost fast. It was surprisingly quiet for such a large office building.

We entered a door with no marking on it. I found myself in a rather plush looking room. Complete with sofa, chairs, dining table, and a large ornate desk, this looked more like someone's living room than an office. The agent told me to have a seat and wait here as he left. I noticed what must be lunch sitting on the dining table. Looked like lunch for two. I hoped I was one of the two; I was hungry. A woman entered the office from another door in the room.

"Captain Hallstead, I'm Nancy Caldwell, Director of the FBI."

"Hello. How's my family doing?"

Nancy said, "They are fine. They are getting settled in their new accommodations."

"Thank you so much for doing that for my family. I was really worried about them."

"You're very welcome Captain. I have some more news here." she said holding up a hand full of papers. "It's your test. Looks like you've been telling the truth. Please, come over and sit at the table and have some lunch, you must be starved."

"Thank you. I could use something to eat. Is my family in a room, a house, or an apartment? I mean, are they comfortable?"

Nancy replied, "Oh yes. They are fine. They have all the amenities of home. Don't worry, they are being well cared for. What we need to do now is to figure out what we are going to do with you while we continue our investigation."

"Then you are going to investigate this?" I asked.

Nancy's tone turned more serious and she said, "To be honest Captain, I need more proof before making this an official investigation. So we are going to have to proceed cautiously. What I've decided to do with you is to keep you here. Not here in my office, but here in the building. You're not under arrest; we are doing it only as a precaution."

I interrupted the Director, "Can't I be with my family?"

"No, that would not be wise." She said firmly. "We will probably need access to you frequently and I don't want anybody seeing us coming and going to the safe house where your family is. I have a place down the hall from my office that we'll use. We will be able to protect you much easier there. The room has a sleep sofa and small bathroom. Not exactly the Ritz, but it will do for now."

I thanked the Director over and over, not only for my family's protection, but for continuing with the investigation, official or not. I thought things were looking up. If only we could apply a little pressure on these guys, they might make a mistake.

With the Director telling me she was waiting for John Slatter to report back on his interview with Sampson, I was hopeful it would provide more evidence for her to continue the investigation. I also wondered now how Slatter's interview with Sampson had gone. They must be done by now.

Slatter was undecided if he should return to the FBI building with his wire, or go and see Dorffer to report his interview. Dorffer was his boss, he thought, but the FBI was nobody to ignore. He decided to call Dorffer and see if he would meet Slatter at the FBI and kill two birds with one stone.

Dorffer took the call from Slatter and rearranged his schedule to be able to meet Slatter at FBI Headquarters. Dorffer was pretty excited. Slatter briefly told him what had transpired at the Sampson interview.

Dorffer didn't know if what he had heard was enough evidence to be optimistic or not. He decided to call Nancy Caldwell and see if she could meet with them while they were there. Dorffer was surprised to get through to her so quickly.

"Nancy, I was surprised to be able to get to you so easily."

Nancy told Dave, "I left word to put your calls directly through to me. I was going to call you anyway to update you on the Captain and his family. The family is safe. Captain Hallstead came through with flying colors on his test. There is no doubt in my mind he's telling the truth. Did your reporter, what's his name, John, get done with his interview with Ralph Sampson?"

"That's why I was calling, Nancy." said Dave. "He talked to Sampson and got him pretty upset. John thinks he's got something on the wire and is heading back to your place now. He wanted to know if I would meet him there. I agreed, but first I thought I had better talk to you."

Nancy replied, "Yes, thanks Dave. I'm going to leave word that Slatter is to be brought up to my office along with our wire agent. I'll be interested in what he's got also. We'll wait for you. See you then. Bye."

They all met in the Director's office. John felt a little embarrassed as a female agent opened John's shirt to remove the taping device. *FBI agent or not she's a woman*; John thought, removing his shirt completely. The agent was taking a long time removing the device. She was trying to be careful not to hurt Slatter when she pulled off the tape. John was feeling uncomfortable just sitting there with no shirt on.

The agent removed the recording media that was carried in with her in a case, and was directed by the Director to insert it into the machine on her desk. Nancy then instructed the agent to explain to her how to run the machine to play back the conversation Slatter had with Sampson. After confirming she knew how to run the machine, the Director politely ordered the agent to leave the room. Nancy rationalized the fewer the people who knew anything at all about this, the better. She wasn't thinking of the recording itself, she knew the agent had heard it while it was happening. Nancy didn't want any other people privy to the discussion that would take place after hearing the recording.

The three of them listened to the tape. Then, they listened to it again. They played the tape four times. John didn't interrupt yet. He decided to keep his silence until he was asked to say something.

Nancy spoke first, "It's not a smoking gun, however, you could tell he was rattled John."

John quickly said, "Oh he was, definitely. I actually think he was a little scared I knew something, and that I was probing for more." John offered, "If he really was rattled, as you put it, I think he'll go to Senator Larson or maybe even this Clayton at CIA. Can you tap any of their phones?"

Nancy grinned and said, "It's not unheard of to get a tap on a Senators phone, but the CIA? That's another matter. No, I don't think we should move on Clayton yet. There's just not enough there. There are enough judges I know who would like to get something on the CIA; they just hate that group over there. I'm afraid though; their people are too savvy even for us to get a tap on their phones without them knowing it. Now as for the Senator, that's a whole different can of worms. It's more political than technical. I'll have to give that some more thought."

Dorffer, listening to all their options seemed to be looking up for guidance, to validate his idea before speaking, said, "How about we run a story about John's interview with Sampson? But instead of the piece we promised Sampson, we do something that might shake up all of them?"

That peaked Nancy's interest. "What did you have in mind Dave?"

Dave continued, "Well, I was thinking of something that would apply some pressure on them. You know, we'll talk about Texas. We can ask the question, why did the Republicans ignore Texas so much? We can then come up with a couple of suggestions, such as it was bad campaign strategy, things like that. Then, we can offer another suggestion and say; could it have been that the campaign had known they were sure to lose Texas? And if so, how did they know? Especially when all the polls, and I mean all, even the Democrats top pollsters, had them winning Texas. You know, after the first time I talked to John about this, I called Brad at the Democrat National Committee. He told me, yes, the Anderson people had some kind of Hispanic strategy going, but they were overwhelmed with the backlash on Anderson's immigration policy there and knew Texas was a lost cause. They were very surprised at the outcome.

Nancy agreed to Dorffer's plan. "I think applying pressure at this point might just be the key. It sounds to me like Sampson is the weakest link here. We can keep up surveillance on him and see if he reacts to the story. In the meantime, I'll continue to work on a way to get some wire taps."

The next day, the *Washington Daily News* had a small but strategically placed article by reporter, John Slatter, covering all of Dorffer's points about Texas and the Republicans mysterious lost there.

Chapter 17 The Easy Way Out

Ralph Sampson settled into his desk at the Republican National Headquarters. The interview he did with that reporter from the *Washington Daily News* was far from his mind this morning. His main concern centered on how he would keep his job as Chairman. Now that Ray Kline was President Kline, Sampson knew his days could be numbered as the leader of the party's campaign machine. Sampson thought about past practice, where the new President usually changes the Chairman of the Republican National Committee to someone in tune with their own principles. Sampson knew his moderate tag wouldn't stand up to Kline's conservative requirements. Besides that, Sampson was smart enough to know history wasn't on his side. His position, even if he were a conservative, normally went to a political friend of the President's. Sampson laughed to himself. He was pondering how Kline must be licking his chops at the prospect of controlling the party. A party who not only did little to help Kline, but a case could be made, they sabotaged him. Even though Kline was now President, Sampson knew Kline wouldn't see the victory as one of Sampson's doing.

Bad news for Sampson, about his job, but this was nothing compared to the news he was about to discover.

Sampson's secretary tapped lightly at his door and entered. It was her normal task at that time to deliver mail, papers, and the daily newspaper. Sampson pushed aside the papers; he would look at them later. Right now was his time for mail and reading the newspaper with his coffee. He proceeded with his routine of looking through the mail, tossing the bulk mail and advertising into the waste can. The mail of importance he separated into an A, B, and C system. The A mail was important and needed reading and response that day. He would go through that just before lunch. The B mail was tackled at the end of the current day. The C mail could wait until he got to it, usually a day or two. His routine now directed him to the reading of the daily newspaper. It was an important task for any Chairman of a political party to be abreast of not only the current news, but also the gossip columns.

Sampson scanned the front page for anything he needed to read in more detail. After reading a couple interesting articles on the election, which was still big news, he turned to page two. A byline caught his attention immediately. It was fate that took him to that small type where he saw a name that was familiar. By John Slatter it said. Sampson's eyes quickly looked up at the story headline. It said, *How Could GOP Lose Texas?* Sampson's hands were shaking as he started to read the whole story. As he read the article, his emotions dramatically changed. At first, he was mad at Slatter. *How could he print something like this?* He thought *I had an agreement with that editor; this article was to be about the party only or there was to be no article at all.*

Then a different emotion poured over him, like a chill or shiver down one's back. Sampson spoke to himself, *they know something. My God, I bet they know. I've got to get a hold of Larson right away.* Sampson tried to calm himself first. *Let's see,* he thought, *Should I use the phone from here? No. Who knows, Clayton might have my office wired. How about my cell phone? That can't be wired, can it? I can't just get in my car and run around looking for Larson. God knows where he might be. There's a good chance he's at the Senate, but can I interrupt him? He might be on the floor. I'm going to just call his office from my cell phone.*

"Senator Larson's office, Alice Cannon speaking, how may I help you?"

"This is Ralph Sampson, Chairman of the RNC. I need to speak to the Senator as soon as possible. It's very important."

"Just a moment Mr. Sampson, I'll see if he's in."

Sampson knew that was code for he's there, but I'll see if he wants to talk to you. If not, they'll tell you he's unavailable to take your call, do you wish to leave a message?

"Mr. Sampson, the Senator will take your call. I'll connect you."

"Ralph. What's so important?"

"Did you read today's *Daily News*? Page two."

"No, I haven't got to it yet. Hold on, I see it on the coffee table. There I got it. Page two you said?"

"Page two. At the top, about half way down. You can't miss it."

"I see it. *How Could GOP Lose Texas*?"

"That's the one. See the byline? John Slatter?"

"Yes. What about him?"

"That's the guy I had the interview with yesterday."

"Interview, are you crazy? What possessed you to talk about Texas? Why..."

"Wait a minute Damon. I didn't talk about Texas, it was this reporter. Hold on, let me explain what happened. I got this call from their editor. He asked if he could send a reporter over for an interview. They were going to do a story from both parties' perspective about the election. I told him I would agree if the story was only about how we felt about the election process. You know, how it was so historic and such. Then this reporter, Slatter shows up and begins to ask questions about Texas. I tried to change the subject, but it was useless. He kept probing and probing me on why we didn't do anything there. Damon, I'm telling you they know something."

"Calm down Ralph. If they knew anything they would have said so by now. Could be just an honest curiosity on why we didn't do more campaigning in Texas. I'm sure if we..."

"Damon, there's one more thing. Now you know I'm not prone to conspiracies, but I am convinced I'm being watched. This morning, from my house to the office, I was followed. I am sure of it. I'm looking out my window now, and I'm telling you the same car is sitting out there. Damon they know."

Senator Larson was thinking to himself, *if Ralph is right how did they find out? Must have been the Captain, I told Clayton he pushed him too far. That tape of him and Diane, threatening his family, murdering people. I was afraid he might break. If it's anybody, it's the Captain, certainly wouldn't be one of us.*

"You still there Damon?" Ralph asked.

"Yes, Ralph. I was just thinking about something. The only person it could be is the Captain. My guess is he has contacted the newspaper and they are just trying to sniff out a story. If there were more to it than that, we would know about it by now."

"How would we know about it?" asked Ralph.

"Clayton. Ralph, that guy knows everything, sometimes even before it happens. If anything else is happening, I mean with authorities, Clayton will know. I'm going to see him right now and find out. I'll get back to you."

Ralph sounded very worried as he said to the Senator, "Damon if this comes out, I can not imagine how my boys will take it. Their both in college you know. James's a senior and Danny just started. This would devastate them. I can't go to jail over this. I just can't. My family would have this over their heads all their life."

"Don't do anything stupid Ralph. Wait until I talk to Clayton. It may be a lot to do about nothing."

"Damon, you know it won't be long until I'm out of here anyway. Kline's going to put his man in over here. Without my work, and my family shamed, and me in jail..."

"Ralph, I told you, hang in there until I talk to Clayton. Goodbye."

***

Senator Larson went directly to CIA Headquarters at Langley. Not surprisingly, he was able to meet with Clayton without delay. Fact was Clayton was about to call the Senator concerning the article written by Slatter. Larson didn't even stop at Clayton's receptionist. Instead he walked briskly right into his office.

Larson was greeted by Clayton with a simple, calm command to "have a seat Damon."

Clayton got right to the point, without letting Larson say a word. "Damon, first, let me say, yes, I read the article. That's probably what got you excited, right?"

"Well, yes Fred. That and the call I got from Ralph. He was all shook up about the article. But more so about being watched and followed. What's really going on?"

"I don't think that article means anything. I did decide to have you and Sampson watched to see if any one was watching you. This just started a few hours ago. We can't find the Captain or his family anywhere."

"So that means it was your people Sampson saw. He'll be relieved."

"I didn't finish Damon. Those weren't my people. I had their plates run and found out they are FBI. Hold on, I'm still not done. We've got nothing interesting on this reporter, Slatter, but that editor Dorffer is a very close friend of the FBI Director, Caldwell. This is the way I see it. The Captain must have talked to the newspaper. Dorffer probably called the FBI and they took an interest. My guess is the FBI has the Captain and his family tucked away. Minster, at DOD, is going to be hard for them to get to, I've warned him already. That leaves you, Sampson and me that know anything. How did Sampson sound?"

"Frankly Fred, he sounded scared. I'm not sure what to make of a few of his comments. To tell you the truth, I'm really scared myself that Sampson might crack."

"Yea, I agree. Sampson would talk if pressured. Before we have to deal with Sampson, I'm thinking we might have a talk with that editor, Dorffer."

"What do you mean a talk?"

"No, it's not what you're thinking Damon. If we can get Dorffer to back out of this story and convince Caldwell there's nothing to it, the FBI will be out of it and we'll be home free. Caldwell must have been dragged in on her friend's word to begin with. I'm sure they gave the Captain a lie detector test and that convinced them even more to look into it, but they know that test can be deceiving. Yeah, the more I think about it the more I'm sure that's the way to go. Find a way to get Dorffer scared enough to get the FBI convinced to drop it. They may wonder, but without any evidence they'll drop it, believe me. I have just the right person to talk to Dorffer, but first we need to do some checking on him. We'll look at his family, friends, and any skeletons in his closet, standard stuff."

Senator Larson made his way over to the Republican National Headquarters. He was anxious to fill in Sampson on what Clayton's plan was. He knew Sampson would be happy to hear this whole thing could go away. Larson was still a little concerned over something Clayton had said though. He couldn't help, but wonder at Clayton's comment that only he, Sampson, and Clayton knew the whole story. Larson wondered why Clayton was so quick to exclude Carl Minster. *Sure*, he thought. *Minster is one of them. CIA buddies and all that. Clayton's safe, being CIA, they never get those guys. He will always find a way out, even if he has to knock off everybody else. The Captain and his family have the FBI,*

Minster and Clayton are safe, which leaves Sampson and me. Clayton did say Sampson might talk. I even said that to Clayton. I better check on Sampson and warn him.

Senator Larson now had more to worry about than an election scandal. He and Sampson might have to be worried about staying alive.

Larson pulled into the driveway leading to the RNC Headquarters. His driver said they couldn't get to the front door, because the police and an ambulance were parked there with lights flashing. "Get as close as you can." Larson ordered his driver.

"This is as close as I can get. There's a policeman telling me to stop here. He's coming over to the car Senator."

As the policeman approached the Senator's car, Larson pressed the power down window button.

"I'm sorry Senator I just recognized your car. I'm afraid I have to ask you to back up out of the way. We have a serious injury coming down to the ambulance."

"That's fine officer."

Larson put his window up and told his driver, "Joe, I'll walk from here. You better back up and find a place to park."

As the Senator walked up to the front door, he was met by the D.C. police. They were putting yellow tape across the sidewalk, not allowing anyone in or out. Larson was pulling out his identification, hoping that would get him into the building to see Sampson. He was just about to speak to the policeman standing there, when paramedics came out of the front doors pulling a stretcher. The Senator was close enough to make out who was laying on the stretcher. It was Ralph Sampson. The paramedics stopped just before the ambulance doors and pulled a sheet over Sampson's face. He was dead. Larson just stood there in stunned silence.

The Senator was still standing there, looking shocked, when a woman approached him crying her eyes out.

"Oh Senator, it's horrible, just horrible."

Larson came out of his trance and recognized Sampson's secretary standing in front of him.

"What happened?"

"It's Mr. Sampson Senator. Mr. Sampson, he killed himself."

"Killed himself? How?"

"I found him. I came in with his afternoon schedule of meetings and there he was, hanging from the ceiling. It's horrible."

"From the ceiling? How is that possible?" Larson questioned.

"I don't know. All I know is that when I came in, there he was." The secretary was more composed now and offered a few more details. "The ceiling tiles were gone over his desk. He had his belt tied to the sprinkler pipes and you know..."

Larson now was thinking, *Clayton. I'll bet he did this. That just leaves me*. The Senator turned to leave, looking for his driver. He saw his car, parked over by the visitor's spaces. Larson took off toward his car quickly, without another word to Sampson's secretary.

The Senator's driver saw Larson hurrying across the parking lot toward the car and stepped out to open the door for Larson. He asked the Senator, "Do you know that person they took out?"

"No." Larson said abruptly and jumped into the car. "Let's go," he commanded. Larson's driver knew the Senator was upset and that something wasn't quite right, but his job was to drive and said nothing more to the Senator except "Where to Senator?"

"Back to the Senate." Larson told him.

He figured that would be the safest place to be right now. Clayton couldn't do anything to him there, too many other people around.

***

The *Washington Daily News* was a bee hive of activity. The news that Republican National Committee Chairman, Ralph Sampson, had committed suicide was going to be the lead story for the evening edition. Dorffer and Slatter were together in Dorffer's office pondering how to cover the story.

"What do you make of the Sampson suicide? Think it was a suicide, or do you think someone might have helped him commit suicide?" Dorffer asked Slatter.

John pondered the question a moment and said, "I think it was legit. I think if Clayton wanted Sampson dead, he would have found a better way to do it and avoid any questions. It's been my experience; people who kill themselves out of guilt or embarrassment don't usually leave notes.

That's the whole point. They don't want people to find out something. Or if they do, they don't what to be around when it happens."

"I guess you're right John. It's the easy way out for them. You know that only leaves three people, the Senator, Minster and Clayton. In a sick sort of way, if Clayton takes care of Senator Larson, we may not be able to get enough on Clayton to continue this thing."

"I'm afraid you're right Dave. I was thinking the same thing, but you're leaving out a few people."

"Who are you talking about John?"

"There's you and me, Dave. I don't mind telling you that makes me a bit nervous."

They were interrupted by Dorffer's secretary buzzing into his office. She informed Dave he had a strange call waiting. She explained how she would have normally just taken a message, but the caller insisted it was extremely important. She went on to say there was something eerie about his voice that made her interrupt Dorffer.

"Okay, put him through. Hello, this is Dave Dorffer, editor's office."

The unknown caller said, "Mr. Dorffer, listen carefully. I'm only going to say this once. You will stop all further inquiry into the story you are working on. Next, you will tell the FBI Director that you have discovered holes in the Captain's story, that has lead you to believe it has no credibility. If not, your son will suffer the consequences."

"Who is this? How do you know about...you know who?

"Never mind who I am. I know John Slatter is your son. The one you walked out on years ago. If you have any feelings for him at all, you will do what I told you. His life is in your hands." Click. The phone went dead.

Slatter could tell by Dorffer's face this call had upset him. He waited for Dorffer to say something. Dorffer just slowly hung up the phone and sat back starring at the ceiling.

"Anything wrong, Dave?" John asked.

Dorffer said nothing. Then as a person suddenly awaken from a deep sleep, Dorffer shook his head, blinked his eyes and looked at Slatter. He was struggling with what to do. Should he just tell Slatter he was his father? Should he comply with the orders from the man on the phone and drop the whole thing? *I could take the easy way out too*, he thought *no, not suicide. I could just stop this whole investigation.* Like the caller said, *I could tell Nancy it was just a big misunderstanding. No, it's about time I tell John.*

"John, I have something to tell you."

"Does it have to do with that call you just got?" John asked.

"Well sort of. John, a long time ago I met this woman. She and I were, you know, just friends. One night we both drank too much and one thing leads to another and, well you know how that goes." Dorffer was struggling to tell Slatter the bottom line.

"She ended up pregnant. I was married at the time and didn't want to leave my wife."

"Why are you telling me this?"

"It's because John, well, you were that child."

John was stunned. He gathers his composure and asked, "Then you are my father? I was always told my father had died."

"Yes John. It's what your mother and I agreed to. I continued to support you both over the years, but I just couldn't have any contact, what with my wife and all. I hope you understand?"

"I don't know what to think, Dave."

"I know this comes as a shock to you John, but the reason I had to tell you now was that phone call. That person somehow knew you were my son. He wants me to drop the whole election fraud story or they said they will kill you. I can't let that happen John. I've caused you enough pain over the years. I must drop this story, don't you see?"

"No, Dave, not at all. I'm not afraid. Listen, we must be getting somewhere or they wouldn't be resorting to this. I don't care what they do; I'm staying with the story. If you drop it, I'll just keep going with it."

"If that's the way you feel, then I'm with you John. I always knew you'd make a fine newsman. We've got to get with Nancy and fill her in. Let's go."

Chapter 18 Out of the Darkness

Slatter and Dorffer arrived at the FBI Headquarters hoping Nancy would have some answers on Sampson's death. They were both convinced his death was anything, but a suicide. Clayton must be involved they thought. Dorffer had another concern he did not want John to think about. He was worried about the threat he received on his son's life. His relationship with Slatter was now totally different. You will help a friend or co-worker, but when it comes to your child, you will do anything to protect them. Slatter did not have those same feelings, at least not yet. He had been without a father so long that he had become independent of any parental relationship.

Nancy received Dorffer and Slatter into her office, just as anxious to talk to them as they were to her. Dorffer started the exchange with, "You must have heard about Sampson?"

"Yes, I immediately sent a team over to his office. We didn't find anything unusual. Look's like a suicide to my people." Nancy explained.

"But don't you think it's awful coincidental?" Slatter chimed in.

"You may see it that way. I trust my team; they have been doing this type of crime scene analysis for a lot of years. Believe me, they are good at it. What I think happened was that your interview and story pushed him over the edge. I'm not saying it's your fault. Sampson was the kind of person that could not take a scandal. Whether it was his ego, or embarrassment of his family, he just could not take it. Therefore, he saw the only way out was not to be here, when it comes out."

Dorffer was satisfied, even if Slatter was not. Dorffer had a more pressing problem now. "Nancy I got a call this morning. The caller found out that John is my son. He threatened John's life if I did not drop the whole story. Also, I was to convince you somehow, that the story was some kind of a fabrication from the beginning."

"John's your son? I didn't know you had any children? What else did they say?" Nancy wanted to know more.

"Yes, John's my son. In fact, I just told him this morning after I got the call. I told you everything he said. It's got to be from Clayton's people. What can we do? John's decided he is not going to drop the story and wants to go forward."

"You're right Dave; we have to take it serious. With Sampson gone, we only have Larson left, assuming we can't get at Minster. I'm tired of waiting the Senator out. I think we should have a chat with the Senator. Since Sampson's death, I've been thinking of a way to get at the Senator. Clayton's too insulated to get at. He can hide behind national security or some nonsense like that, and he would probably protect Minster just to cover himself. Frankly, I don't know how we would get to talk to him without a subpoena. We can't get a subpoena without more evidence. Besides, I got a feeling Senator Larson is more like Sampson."

"Which way is that?" Dorffer asked.

"I think the Senator just might respond to our own threat. He knows the Bureau has some pretty wide ranging powers when it comes to investigating Congress. Congress has their own people to look into certain allegations, but they also know the FBI can and has started investigations independent of them. If we can get some information from the Senator, we can get a committee to look into this also, and they have subpoena power, especially when it comes to one of their own. I know just the guy to help us when the time comes. Senator Sam Hustings. He's a fair and honest man even when it comes to investigating someone in his own party. I'll leave him out of it for now."

"Nancy, what kind of a plan do you have for Senator Larson?" Dorffer inquired of Nancy.

"I'm going to handle the Senator myself. I'll arrange a meeting here in my office. That will put him on my territory and make him a little uncomfortable to begin with. I'm then going to bring the Captain in and we'll have a little confrontation. That should really make him sweat. Then...well I'll save that until the meeting."

Dorffer and Slatter agreed. This sounded like a good plan and they couldn't wait until that meeting, hoping it would provide the evidence they needed to expose the whole mess. Dorffer then had to remind Nancy of the threat on his son. "Nancy, what about John?"

"Oh yes. I'm sorry Dave. I think if you and John do not mind, we'll just keep John here with the Captain. He'll be safe here, don't worry dad,

I'll take good care of him." Nancy said with a grin that let Dave know she understood how he must feel now, discovering a new son.

John stood up and objected, "Now just hold on a minute everyone. I have something to say. Son or not, I'm a journalist first and should be reporting on the story, not being a part of it. I agree to stay here only for the purpose of getting the story. Then I'm off to write it. I appreciate what all of you are trying to do, but that's the way it's going to be."

"I like the spunk son; what do you think Nancy?"

"I'm the Director of the FBI and my job is to protect and defend. If you leave John, I wouldn't be able to guarantee your safety. You'll be on your own."

"Then that's the way it's going to have to be." said John.

When John turned to walk back to his chair, Nancy gave Dave a wink, indicating she would have an agent watch out for John. Dave smiled back; he understood Nancy wouldn't just let John go without any protection.

***

When Senator Larson received a call from the Director of the Federal Bureau of Investigation, he waited a moment to take the call wondering what Director Caldwell was calling him for. He shrugged off the notion it was anything to do with the election fraud, or even anything to do with Sampson. After all he thought *I've been called before by Ms. Caldwell for other reasons.*

Senator Larson was extremely busy, working on a piece of legislation for the upcoming transportation bill. His time was being eaten up from all the Senators trying to hang their own special pork barrel amendments to it. He thought about ignoring the Director's call and telling his secretary to put Ms. Caldwell off, saying he was unavailable and he would call her back. The Senator had this inner voice telling him he had better take the call or risk looking like he was trying to avoid the Director, so he took the call.

"Hello Nancy. How are you? What can I do for you?"

"Hello Senator. I'm good and hope my call finds you well. I called to invite you to a meeting at my office. We need to talk about some things."

"Oh, and what are these things we need to talk about?"

"I think that's best left to when we meet." Nancy said coyly.

"You're sounding awful cryptic Nancy. To tell you the truth, I'm really busy with this transportation bill. If it can wait..."

"No it can't wait Senator. It happens to be very important. The sooner we meet the better, how about tomorrow morning?" Nancy had decided to purposely give Larson overnight to think about what was up.

Larson was getting irritated at Nancy's word games. He came to the conclusion Nancy was not about to reveal anything more over the phone. Larson decided to give in and agree to the meeting without anymore details.

"Alright Nancy, what time?"

"How about 9 o'clock?"

"Nine is fine. I look forward to see you then." Larson ended the call thinking, *don't get sarcastic with her, and be polite*. He knew he had to keep the appointment or it would look very suspicious. Larson now pondered his next move. He began to think about what role Clayton might be able to play in this. Larson was all about getting consensus on everything he was facing before he committed to it. He wondered if he should call Clayton and have Clayton wire him for this meeting. He changed his mind after realizing Clayton wasn't about to look out for him; Clayton was all about protecting himself. *No*, Larson decided, *he wouldn't even tell Clayton about the meeting at the FBI. If Clayton knew about it,* Larson thought, *Clayton would find a way to make sure he didn't appear. Didn't appear anywhere!*

Next morning at the Director's office, found Senator Larson waiting in the reception area. Nancy had again, purposely been late, giving the Senator even more time to worry. She was already in her office, but had told her secretary to tell the Senator she was not in yet. Nine o'clock came and went. Nine fifteen arrived and Nancy decided it was time. Nancy asked her secretary to show the Senator in.

The Senator was escorted into Nancy's office where he found her behind her desk writing something. Nancy looked up and asked the Senator, to "please have a seat". She would be with him in a moment. Senator Larson was now even more agitated. He left a busy office to come to an important meeting and not only was the Director late, but now she had to finish some work. Larson was not only agitated, but he was thinking this cannot be all that important or the Director would have been here on time and ready to confront him. He started to relax. Negative thoughts about this meeting were beginning to fade from the Senators mind.

"Senator, I'll get right to the point. When you hear what I have to say, you will understand why I might have seemed somewhat, well, somewhat mysterious on the phone about this meeting. It has come to my attention that there was a problem with the Presidential election. A problem that might lead one to believe there was corruption of the election itself."

"Really, what kind of corruption?"

"There is strong evidence that the election was rigged through a computer system to add votes to one particular candidate. This is a very serious matter" Nancy added.

"Oh my God, I agree. What kind of evidence do you have? Is your information good? Did you need me to start some kind of inquiry?" said the Senator.

"There's more Senator. There might be at least two murders and a suicide also involved. In addition, there are ongoing threats to innocent people."

Larson, pretending to be shocked said, "Murders? My God. We're going to have to get to the bottom of this. Election fraud is one thing, but murder. We definitely have to look into these murders." Larson was hoping to turn the inquiry away from the election and toward the murders. He thought if he could put the light on the murders, Clayton might be the focus of any investigation. The election, he was praying, would be put aside, leaving him out of it.

"I'm glad you want to get to the bottom of this, Senator. I want you to meet someone." Nancy turned to her private office door and opened it. In I walked, much to the Senator's surprise.

"Senator, I think you know Captain Gary Hallstead." Nancy said.

"I, uh, uh… no, I don't know this man."

Nancy decided to push the Senator further. "Senator, you and I both know that's not true. The Captain has told us the whole story, every detail he was aware of. He passed our lie detector test, twice." Nancy was now walking about the room gesturing in a manner like a prosecuting attorney giving a final summation.

Nancy continued, "Sampson did not leave a suicide note. He left something better. Just before hanging himself, he called the *Washington Daily News* and spoke to the editor, who just happens to be a friend of mine. The confession was taped. Just like the Captain and Larry Davis were taped. You see Sampson was a man who had a conscience. He could take being involved in an election scandal, although that pressed heavily on his mind. But murder? No way. Sampson was not going to have his family think of him as a murderer."

Nancy was bluffing; Sampson didn't call the Washington Daily News or anyone else. Nancy hoped the Senator would believe her, see the handwriting on the wall and confess.

Larson jumped in at this point in an effort to clear himself of any murder accusations. "Sampson was no murderer and neither am I."

It worked. Nancy's prosecuting style, twisting of the facts, and a little white lie here and there had brought the Senator's involvement out into the open.

Senator Larson, realizing he had admitted his involvement, only wanted to plead his case now. "All I wanted to do was to save my country. My God, who wouldn't want to do something to keep the White House from that mad man? He's going to get us in a war with China, you mark my words. And, and, the border problems, why Kline's going to start a war down there too. Before he builds that wall, you're going to have millions streaming across. Nancy, don't you see I had to do something. I was the only one with the guts to save this country. The murders? That was all Clayton. I told him not to do anything stupid. But oh no, he was the great CIA Director who knew how to handle these things."

I honestly could not help, but feel a little sorry for the Senator. Instead of the proud, sophisticated man I originally knew, he had become a blabbering simpleton. But when I came to my senses, I could not help but think of the murders that happened. Like it or not Larson had been involved to the extent that the whole election scheme he developed, helped lead to the murders.

Nancy knew it was all over for everyone involved. She had the Senator's confession on tape. She had enough to go to Senator Hustings and blow the story wide open.

Nancy and I stood there a moment starring at Senator Larson. He sat there with his head down still muttering something. We could not make out what he was saying, it all sounded like mumbling. I don't know what Nancy was thinking about the Senator, but I do know what my thoughts were. *The Senator has made patriotism a dirty word. That's a shame. Patriotism, as I knew it, had been shown by the men fighting in our wars over the years. These men had bled and died protecting the country from those who attacked us from without. I was angry that the Senator had made a mockery of what true patriotism was all about. I was ashamed also. Like the Senator, I could not escape the fact that I was part of it all. I was just as guilty for going along with it in the first place.*

Nancy broke the silence. "I need to get Senator Hustings on the phone and fill him in on what's been going on. Senator, you can leave now."

Nancy was one tough lady. I thought, *here she reduced a prominent Senator to a common criminal and babbling idiot, and then promptly dismisses him. Leaving to go who knows where and do who knows what. It did enter my mind he might just go the way of Sampson.*

The Senator snapped out of whatever state of mind he was in and slowly got up and left. I guess Nancy would know where to find him when she needed to.

Nancy expected to see me relieved and happy it was all coming to an end. "I guess that takes care of the Senator, doesn't it?" she asked.

"What do you mean?" I said. "What's to stop him from denying everything he said here?"

Nancy got that coy look on her face and said "I have the whole thing on tape. We also know a thing or two about capturing people on tape."

"I just worry about the country madam Director.

Nancy replied to me, "The country's going to be just fine. We have survived other scandals and tragedies. It's a good thing we're a resilient people, other countries would have a revolution over less. I'm confident when the story is told; Americans will rally around their government. At least, I pray they do."

I asked Nancy, "What about Kline? What do you think will happen to the Presidency? I mean even with the fraud, a case could be made that Kline won the Presidency fair and square. It may have taken the U.S. Senate to do it, but he won. And, oh yeah, what about your job as

Director. I'm sure Kline will be appointing a new Attorney General. You worried?"

Nancy carefully considered her answer. She did report directly to the Attorney General, and it was definitely the tradition, a new one would be coming. She thought about the fights she had with the current one, especially over her pursuit of terrorists and illegal immigrants. She mused to herself, Kline might be just the guy we need to clean up some of the messes. Nancy kept her politics to herself as any good civil servant had to, but she had viewed Kline's ascendancy to the Presidency with some joy. "I never worry about things I have no control over. I'm still the Director and until I'm replaced, and I will continue to do my job. All I'm focused on now is getting the investigation going with Senator Hustings."

Nancy now ordered me to return to my quarters.

***

Nancy was confident her old friend, Senator Hustings, would want to see justice done. He and she were a lot alike when it came to the law. They were able to put personal opinions aside and move forward with investigations, no matter where they led. Hustings had another admirable quality like Caldwell. When it came to the law, he was blind to his party affiliation. A quality that was rare in Washington. Nancy was on her way to meet at Senator Hustings's office. Nancy felt since she would be asking Hustings for something; it would be smart to go to him on his turf.

Senator Hustings was curious why the Director of the FBI had requested the meeting. She was a friend of his going all the way back to his early days as a Representative. They met during the late '80's when he asked for FBI support to help investigate a banking scandal occurring in his district. Since that time, they had become good friends and followed each other's careers. Hustings knew Nancy would never be caught crying wolf over a matter. He knew when Nancy moved on an investigation, it always proved to have merit.

Nancy came into the Senator's office carrying her large briefcase she had become famous for. It was a large, bulky, old fashioned style of luggage which most professionals had long since discarded. Nancy had become comfortable with it. It gave her the ability to have her notes, legal documents, and other important papers at her side at all times. This had served her well over the years of giving testimony on Capitol Hill. She had all the evidence she needed for Senator Hustings right there in that briefcase.

After pleasantries were exchanged, Senator Hustings joked, "I see your bag is unusually full today Nancy." Nancy was in no mood for jokes, given the gravity of the situation.

"Yes Sam, sadly so. The reason for the large file I carry is precisely why I am here today. It contains evidence I'm afraid will shock even you, Senator. Evidence that affects the very foundations of our Republic. It will be a sad day for you, me, and the country when I tell you the whole story."

Senator Hustings was now more serious and moved forward, rather than ready to sit back and receive news about a possible minor investigation. He had heard many of these requests from the Director of the FBI over the years. Some more disturbing than others, but he had never heard a Director so impassioned before.

"Nancy, are you telling me you have a possible investigation of a high official in the government?"

"Sam, I do. It concerns Senator Larson."

Hustings couldn't believe his ears at Nancy's request that Senator Larson to be investigated. "Damon Larson? What in the world are you talking about?"

"I'm afraid so. Sam, let me give you the whole story. I'll try to be brief. I know you will have questions as I go on. Please feel free to interrupt me if you need further detail or clarification."

Nancy pulled out a large note pad from her briefcase and readied herself to begin.

"Senator Larson was the Chief Architect of a plot to effect the election of the President of the United States. He gathered a team of people that included the following: Captain Gary Hallstead at the DOD, Ralph Sampson, the Chairman of the RNC, and there was also a woman named Diane McKenna, involved."

Senator Hustings had to interrupt at this point. "Are you sure? My God, if that is true, it will have an effect on all our basic institutions. Please tell me you are only requesting an inquiry here Nancy."

"I am sorry Senator. This is more than an inquiry. I have enough evidence here that I am asking for a full Committee investigation. It gets worse. There is even multiple murders involved to silence people. I know how much this must be affecting you Sam, but let me continue so you can get the whole story. I think, then, you will be able to see I have the evidence you asked about."

Nancy continued by pulling out a tape recorder from her bag and set it on the Senator's desk. She would play the tape of her talk with Senator Larson later. She thought, *just showing Hustings that she had some physical evidence, should send Senator Hustings a message that she did indeed have some hard evidence.*

Nancy took the Senator through the whole, horrible story, delivering as much detail as she could without slowing down the process. Her goal was get the Senator enough facts that the meeting wouldn't be delayed with too many questions left unanswered. Her goal was to get to a plan of action only she knew the real purpose of. After almost an hour of divulging all the disgusting details she had, Nancy stopped and looked at the Senator, "Sam, you see how sick this whole thing is."

"Yes, Nancy I do. I just can't get Damon Larson out of my mind. My God, what was he thinking? And poor Ralph. I thought I knew him better. He was like a son to me, you know. This Captain, sounds like Damon was able to convince him to go along. It's a shame about his friend. It looks like this Larry Davis was quite a hero, in a way. But murder? Damon? I just can't see Damon involved in any murder. Are you positive about this?"

Nancy was sensing Hustings was feeling a little sorry for some of the conspirators and snapped back at the Senator. "I'm glad to hear you acknowledge the murder of Davis. You know whether Larson or Sampson was directly involved in the murders or not, they would not have happened except for these people launching this plot to begin with. As far as I'm concerned, they are all responsible. Granted, punishment can vary from person to person, but as far as I am concerned they are all guilty of these terrible crimes. These are crimes against, not only people, but crimes against the United States of America."

Nancy continued "We know Senator Larson didn't actually murder Davis and the girl, he had someone else do the killings. My agents are busy as we speak, trying to track down his hired assassin."

"I do have the Captain's confession, and a lie detector test here, as well as Senator's Larson's confession to me personally." Nancy was reaching into her briefcase again.

Senator Hustings remarked, "The dark bag again, Nancy. I am beginning to look at your briefcase as the epitome of darkness."

"Senator I look at it a little differently. I see it as the light coming out of the darkness".

They both agreed a plan of action was needed. Senator Hustings asked Nancy if she would help lead his Senate investigating team with the procedures. Senator Hustings would now set up a plan to call the Congressional hearings necessary to bring this to a conclusion. He knew criminal action was to be a separate matter for the appropriate authorities, and left that to Nancy. He stated his goal would now be to, as Nancy put it, "to bring light out of the darkness."

Nancy was to proceed with getting an indictment and an arrest warrant for Senator Larson. Senator Hustings provided the name of a Federal Judge she could use. Nancy was to have Senator Larson arrested by the U.S. Marshall Service.

Nancy sat quietly as Senator Hustings laid out his plan, waiting for the right moment to offer hers. When it looked like Hustings was finished, Nancy was ready to give the Senator something to think about.

"Senator Hustings," Nancy became very formal in your tone as she addressed the Hustings, I have a different idea on how to handle this."

The Senator was surprised. "Oh, and what is that?"

"Do you think it's really necessary to drag the whole country through this scandal? Let's look at the situation again. We have Senator Larson confessing to setting up the conspiracy to begin with. We also have Captain Hallstead admitting his involvement in the election fraud. We know Ralph Sampson helped them. I really came to you, because of your influence on Senator Larson. I was hoping, for the country's sake, that you could talk Larson into retiring from the Senate, say for health reasons. We still would have his confession to hold over him to keep quiet. Sampson's dead and what good would it do for his family to learn of his disgrace? Captain Hallstead, I can definitely tell you, is truly sorry about it all. And the murders, there will be justice, I can promise you that. We will find the assassin and deal with him, in our own way. So who is really hurt? I'll tell you, it's the country, that's who. Do you see what I mean?"

"Well. That's quite a plan, certainly different from mine. I do see your point, Nancy. Your right about dragging the whole country into this, it wouldn't serve any purpose. There would be nothing good to come out of it. You do know we will be guilty of a cover up, don't you?"

"I know Sam, but I think it's for the good of the country and…"

"Where have I heard that before? Watergate I think." Hustings said feeling very depressed about the choice he faced.

Nancy leaned over to Hustings and said pleadingly "We don't have a choice Sam, we must do what's best for the nation."

"Alright Nancy, I'll talk to Damon about resigning. Let's hope this just goes away."

***

On the way back to FBI headquarters, Nancy had her driver pull into a restaurant. She told her driver she had to use the restroom. Nancy went into the ladies restroom, looked around the room, and under all the stalls to make sure she was alone. She then pulled out her cell phone and entered a phone number.

"Fred?" she asked when someone answered.

Assured it was Fred Clayton who answered, she continued.

"Fred, I just talked to Sam Hustings and he's going to get Larson to resign, we agreed health problems would be a good reason. I'll talk to the Captain today he'll agree to keep quiet as long as there's a threat over his family. I'm sure he wants to be done with this. I think we're going to be okay."

"Nancy you're forgetting some people. What about those newspaper guys?"

"I'll handle them. They have no evidence, I have all the tapes. If they try and print a story, I have a way to stop them."

"Good. We'll get through this Nancy, just stay in there. Is that all?"

"One question Fred. Have you talked to Anderson yet, you know about the Attorney General appointment?"

"That's all taken care of Nancy. Don't worry, it's in the bag for you."

“I wasn’t worried, just curious, what if Kline actually being the President…”

“Nancy, I said don’t worry. Anderson’s got Kline right where he wants him. You’ll see, just be patient.

Nancy called her office on the drive back from the restaurant. “This is Director Caldwell; put me through to Agent Pointer. Agent Pointer, how’s Captain Hallstead getting along? Good. Make sure he stays put.”

Chapter 19 Truth and Power at Odds

Dave Dorffer appeared at the FBI Headquarters, anxious to hear how Nancy's investigation was going. He had other items on his agenda though. The more personal one was checking on his son, John. Deep down he knew he was safe, Nancy had an agent shadowing him, but there is nothing like a parent making sure. Dorffer's other agenda item was to talk Nancy into letting him break the story John was writing. He was at heart still a newspaper man and this was the biggest story he had ever been privy to.

Nancy not only decided to meet with Dorffer, but had sent word to have Slatter join them. She also had me brought in from the safe room. When we all saw each other there, we knew Nancy was going to give us an update on all her meetings and we were all anxious to know what had been decided.

"First, let me thank all of you for your steadfast support during these trying times. Dave, John, and especially you Captain, are all to be commended for your bravery and your work to get the truth out. Now for my meeting with Senator Hustings, let me say first how appalled the Senator was at hearing this story. I have known Sam personally for a lot of years. I knew he would take this very seriously, especially with the evidence we were able to provide. The Senator and I have come to an agreement on how to proceed. The way we have agreed to handle this situation may be somewhat upsetting to you, but when you think about it, I hope you agree it's what best for the country."

I thought, *what's best for the country? Where have I heard that before?* What in the world is she saying?

Nancy continued "Senator Hustings and I have decided to spare the country this nightmare, especially with the way the Presidential elections have turned out. He is going to ask Senator Larson to resign from the Senate immediately, due to health reasons…"

Dorffer interrupted at this point, "Nancy, what am I hearing? Are you saying you're going to let Larson get away with it?"

"Dave, what good would it do for the country to be dragged through another Watergate style hearing? The election ended up as though nothing happened out of the ordinary. It is really what's best."

"What about Clayton, I mean my God the man has committed murder. What about him?" Dave asked.

Nancy revealed "Don't worry Dave, Senator Hustings and I have a plan to force him and his accomplices to resign also. With Larson's confession, we met with the President that day, and he has agreed to clean out that mess over at the CIA."

Dave responded "I want to propose something that I think will help keep Clayton and his people from doing anymore harm. How about giving John and me permission to print this story right away? This will put such a spotlight on Clayton and he will not have time to get away with doing something to one of us. Look, Larson is our only witness that will have some credibility, retired or not, against Clayton. No offense to you Captain."

I gave Dorffer an indication by nodding that I took no offense.

Nancy looked like she was considering Dave's request, but said, "You can't print anything, Dave. Senator Hustings and I have agreed that our way is the best way to save our nation from this horrible story. I don't like to say it this way, but you give me no choice. Larson will be allowed to retire, Clayton and his people will be handled by the President, and you will not print anything about this story, understand?"

Dave said nothing, the room was silent.

I looked at Dave and John and saw a look of shock on their faces. I too was stunned, as I then turned to look at Nancy. Her face did not have that same look, she looked firm and resolute.

John was not happy with what he had just heard and broke the silence. He protested saying, "With all due respect Ms. Caldwell, I was the one who brought this story to you in the first place. I'm a reporter, and you're asking me to sit here and watch the most important story of the century being spiked?"

Nancy said to John. "I'm sorry John, it's for your own well being. Actually it's the best for all of us and the country that we put this behind us and move on. Again I hate to say this to you both, but I hold all the evidence there is; Larson's confession, your tape with Sampson, John, and the Captain's lie detector test and computer code. You have no story without them."

Nancy then got up from her chair, walked around her desk and stood before the group. She said sternly "It has also been decided that should you try and go public with this story, it will not only be denied, but you will open yourselves up for slander and libel charges. We, I mean they, will have the networks and major newspapers, other than yours, tell the people of this country your story is untrue. Look I know how upsetting this is to you, but believe me; you will see it as the best way to go, like the rest of us."

I pondered what Nancy was saying, but couldn't help but think how this was going to affect me.

"What about me and my family, Nancy?" I asked.

Nancy replied "I see no reason that you and your family can't return to your home. Like I said the President will take care of Clayton and Minster. You will be able to return to the Department of Defense and continue in your work there. Now that's all I have to say, good luck to you all."

Dorffer and his son, John, returned to the *Washington Daily News*. They were still thinking about whether to publish the most important story in their lifetime. They discussed the fact that if they hurried they could still make the morning edition. The morning edition had always had the greatest readership.

Dorffer and John were about to commit to writing the story when the Associated Press teletype started up. The clatter of the story that was being transmitted over the wire was so annoying, John walked over to shut it down. He reached for the off switch, but hesitated as something caught his eye on the paper being printed.

"Dave!" John yelled. Look at this."

Dave walked over to the teletype and saw the headlines, being printed in bold type, which had got John all excited.

SENATOR LARSON KILLED IN CAR CRASH. Dave and John continued to read the details.

Senator Damon Larson, the Majority Leader of the United States Senate, was killed early this evening when he apparently lost control of his car and crashed in the hills of the Lake Higgins area. According to a spokesman for his wife, Irene Larson, the Senator was driving alone up to their mountain retreat for a few days of rest.

"What do you make of this John?" Dave asked.

"Too coincidental for my tastes. With that story Nancy told us I don't know whether to believe it was an accident or suicide."

Dave said "I can't help it John, I smell Clayton again."

"Your right Dave, I smell Clayton as well. President or not I think Clayton is still running around eliminating everyone involved. That leaves you, me, and the Captain. I never thought I'd say this Dave, but I'm scared. If you agree, I think we should just lead with this story, and forget the other one for now at least. That may prove to Clayton we're not going to say anything."

"Okay John, I'll go along. I wonder if Nancy was scared too. You know she might have been scared all along and that was the reason she came up with her plan. I wouldn't blame her, what with dealing with the CIA and all. Then again, it could be just an accident."

"Let's play it safe and go with the accident story. We'll just have to live with it." John said.

The morning edition hit the streets with the headline, *SENATOR KILLED IN CAR ACCIDENT.* Under those headlines was the whole life story of Senator Damon Larson. It covered the equivalent of a whole page, providing every detail of his life and all his accomplishments. It wasn't the story Dave and John wanted to write. It was the story they were forced to write.

***

At CIA Headquarters Fred Clayton, Carl Minster and Nancy Caldwell were meeting in Clayton's office.

Clayton had called the group together to view a speech by President Kline. Kline was to address the nation, finally on major issues of the day, and to announce his choice for his Vice President.

Clayton had every one take a seat, and turned on his television. On the screen was the Presidential seal with no audio. A flicker of the screen and there was President Kline, sitting behind his desk at the oval office looking down at the papers he held in his hands. He obviously was cued; he was now live, looked up and began.

"My fellow Americans, this is my first time addressing you as President of the United States. I have three major topics to talk to you about.

The first will be our relationship with China and the situation concerning the Immigration policy of the United States.

The second will be concerning the recent, historical election results which you are familiar with by now. A scandal of national implications, has been brought to my attention. I am going to be a President that tells you the truth, no matter the consequences.

The third topic will be my desire to bring hope and confidence back to our great country.

I am sure those of you who have listened to past President's speeches, are noticing a change in style in speaking to you. When I campaigned for this office, one of the promises I made to you, was that I would always speak to you, in a manner that was straight forward. My goal is that no one will wonder, what I said afterwards. In other words, I will always speak in a clear, straight from the heart manner.

I know many of you are concerned about our relationship with the country of China. Many of you have expressed concerns over my strategy dealing with China. Let me make it clear. While I have not backed off of my campaign promise to correct the trade imbalances going on now, I have sent the Premier an invitation for us to meet as soon as possible and work out an equitable agreement. Don't worry. I am still going to protect American jobs, as promised. I believe we will both see the value of cooperative behavior, working in the best interests of all.

There is no question America has a problem with immigration, legal and illegal. While our country has always welcomed immigrants, we must have some control over the process and, yes, the numbers. We can only handle so much assimilation at one time.

I will be asking Congress to look into establishing a fair, but manageable numbers of immigrants. As far as the illegal situation goes, I will make every effort to work with the President of Mexico, to help us put a stop to this. I single out Mexico because; let's face it that is where we are experiencing the most problems.

Finally, my fellow citizens, all these problems cannot defeat the undying spirit of the American people. My trust is in you, the hard working men and women of this country. You are the ones who pay the taxes, fight the wars, and support the charities, all while raising your families in your moral and loving homes.

The scandal I referred to in my opening is going to test the very fabric of our Republic. There was an attempt to influence the election, by way of a fraudulent computer system. As horrific as that plot was, a case can be made that the actual outcome was not really affected at all. The details of the plot indicate that the goal was to defeat Senator Barnes and myself. While the election took a historical twist, the end result was that we were not defeated and their plot failed. I am prepared to take whatever action; I can legally take, to insure that the person responsible is brought to justice.

I am making a move to bring our country back together again, after the trials and tribulations of the last election. I have asked, and he has accepted, and with the approval of Congress, President Anderson will become the next Vice President of the United States.

Nothing will bring down this great country. No scandal can prevail. No problem cannot be solved. Why? Because we are Americans. God bless you, and God bless the Unites States of America. Goodnight."

Nancy jumped to her feet "What the hells going on. Clayton did you know about this? I thought we were going to keep this quiet?"

Clayton smiled "Sit down Nancy. Let me explain. Yes, at first we thought keeping quiet was the way to handle it. But after talking to Carl here, he reminded me of the history of cover-ups. What always happens when government problems occur, and no one wants to take the fall? I'll tell you what happens; they try and cover it up. And then what happens? The cover-up ends up worse than the problem. All the people involved are not only caught, but many innocent people are destroyed in the cover-up. Let's take stock of where we're at. Sampson, Diane, and Larson are gone. We have destroyed all the tapes and confession evidence. That leaves the editor and reporter without a story they can prove. Senator Hustings only knows about Senator Larson and the Captain. With Larson out of the picture, and the President's announcement tonight, Hustings will be happy to see the truth exposed, instead of leaving the whole story drop."

Nancy said "So you're going to let Captain Hallstead take the whole fall?"

Clayton responded "It's not like he didn't do anything, Nancy. If someone has to take the heat, better him than any of us. Look, we all got involved in this for the same reason, to stop Kline from being President. And in a strange way, it's going to work out after all. Like war, sometimes one has to sacrifice for the good of the many, and I'm talking about the whole country, not just us. Yes, Kline is President, but he will have people in his administration that will, well let's say will guide him along."

Nancy asked "You mean me."

Clayton smiled and said "Oh, not only you at the Attorney Generals office, but we will have Minster at the White House as an administrative assistant, and of course Anderson as Vice President. I must admit, it was brilliant when we had Kline believing the election fix was to defeat Anderson, and help him win Texas. You should have seen his face when we told him he was the man to lead the nation against China, and the immigrants, and how he was our man at the CIA and FBI. He bought into it hook, line and sinker. He was even more convinced after we told him about Barnes's illness."

Clayton couldn't help but continue bragging about his cleverness in carrying out his plan. "Now that I have told Kline about where a great deal of his campaign contributions came from, he has come around and done the right thing."

Minster wanted some credit also and said "Like the big donations from Chinese Army officials, wealthy Mexican businessmen, and especially those from radical right wing groups, we planted."

Clayton asked Minster "You did take care of that didn't you?"

Minster replied "Oh, yes. We have all the documentation and witnesses ready to go, if we need them."

"Kline will play ball. If he didn't chose Anderson as VP and appoint you guys, he knows Anderson's people would have exposed those contributions to the press and moved for a Congressional investigation, leading to impeachment proceedings." Clayton added.

Nancy said "So, all that's needed now is to blame the whole thing on Hallstead. What's Kline going to do to him?"

Clayton replied "Kline's going to have him arrested by the military, and tried in an Army court martial."

Nancy said "It's a shame; he's the only one who wanted the truth to come out, even if it hurt him. Looks like he'll get his wish, the part about hurting him."

Clayton said "The truth has nothing to do with power, and power has nothing to do with the truth. He did his duty, as he saw it, and now he's a casualty of that duty."

***

As I sat watching President Kline's speech my mouth hung open.

I was shocked. Who was that man? That was not the Ray Kline of the last campaign. Was he fooling everybody about what he really believed, just to get elected? Maybe he was a smarter politician, than all of us. Like Larry always told me, *Remember, they are all politicians at heart, not statesmen, never ever forget that.*

I kept thinking *Nancy said it was all done. The whole story would be kept quiet, for the good of all of us, and the nation. Now the President has told everyone what had happened. But wait, he said,* ***the person*** *will be brought to justice. He didn't say they, the group, or all involved, he said* ***the person****.*

Sampson, Diane, and Larson were all dead. Did Kline mean Clayton or Minster or did he mean me?

Sally turned to me and asked the same question "Gary what did Kline mean when he said the person? Wasn't there more than one person involved? Gary, I'm scared."

I didn't know what to say to Sally.

The door bell rang. I moved like a zombie towards the front door, not concerned who might be there. I opened the door to find two Military Policemen standing there.

"Captain Gary Hallstead?" they asked.

Still stunned, I nodded in the affirmative.

They asked me to turnaround and place my hands behind my back. They proceeded to put handcuffs on me.

I do remember one of them saying "Captain Hallstead, we are placing you under arrest, pending a General Court Martial."

Sally came running to the door and saw me being handcuffed. With tears in her eyes, she frantically asked "What's happening Gary? Where are they taking you?"

One of the MP's replied "Your husbands being placed under arrest and taken to Fort Still. You can find out more details there."

***

It was now my turn to be in the spotlight of this saga. I was sitting here in court in a daze, drifting in and out. I was not trying to recall details for my testimony; I simply had no control over my thoughts. My mind was taking me back to the beginning, as it continued to replay the whole story over and over. It was like a song set to play in a continuous loop.

I suddenly realized I was really here, the defendant in a General Court Martial. I had relived it all over again. It was like a person dying, when they say their whole life flashes in front of their eyes, not only once like they say. It flashed continuously. *It must be part of my punishment*, I thought.

I told the court my story knowing no one would believe me. This time there was no John Slatter to come to my rescue. No Dave Dorffer to publish the true. I never did understand why they wouldn't tell the truth, maybe they were just scared, or maybe they were a part of whatever was happening, on a higher level of the whole plot. No Nancy Caldwell, she's now the Attorney General, that must have been her thirty pieces of silver.

I have to forgive Dale. He only testified what we talked about on the smoking patio. I wished now, I hadn't been so vocal about my support for Ray Kline, which was so taken out of context.

That computer code, where did they get it? It must have been Caldwell or Minster. They only said it was provided to the prosecutor by someone in high authority, and they had signed an affidavit swearing I had done it. My only evidence of the truth, turns out was used against me.

I heard the noise of the court room start to come down to a whisper. I looked toward the front to see General Caulkins taking his chair. The banging of the gavel this time was bringing the trial to order, my sentencing was about to be announced.

There was a silence that hung over the room, which had everyone waiting and staring at the General and his five jurors. When would he say something? The paper he was holding was shaking slightly, as he leaned over to one of his fellow generals, and whispered something. He looked unsure of what to do next.

General Wayne Caulkins turned on his microphone and began, "The accused will stand. The General Court Martial of Captain Gary Hallstead has concluded its deliberations and has come to the following verdicts. For the charge of conspiracy, the defendant is found to have acted alone, and therefore under the definition by the Military Justice Code, a vote not meeting the two thirds, required for a guilty verdict, the defendant is found not guilty.

For the charge of the act of treason against the United States of America, which under the Military Justice Code can carry a sentence of death, three quarters of the votes of the jury required having not been met, finds the defendant not guilty.

For the charge of sedition against the United States of America, which under the Military Justice Code requires two thirds of the votes of the jury, having been met, finds the defendant guilty. Before passing sentence let me say, I hope we will be judged by what we do here, and not by the actions of a renegade in ours ranks. We sought the truth no matter how painful. Our desire is to bring light to a very dark situation, and ensure that justice be done. May God help us to restore the faith in our Republic, and may God save the United States of America.

Captain Gary Hallstead having been found guilty of the crime of sedition against the United States of America you are hereby sentenced, accordingly.

One, you are to be dishonorably discharged from the United States Army, forfeiting any claim to rights or benefits.

Second, you are to be confined to the Federal prison at Leavenworth, Kansas for a period not to exceed 10 years and for a period not less than7 years, to be served at hard labor. May God forgive you."

I thought about my family, of how they would survive without me, my country, would it ever forgive me.

As I stood there, waiting to be taken away, Sally raced to me, put her arms around me and said "I will always love you. I know what really happened, and I won't stop until the truth comes out."

In the end, one thought prevailed over all the rest, "*Larry, I am so sorry.*"

Printed in the United States
45540LVS00007B/18

9 781905 363773